MURDER WITH CLOTTED CREAM

When she reached the butler's pantry, the paneled door was closed.

Was Margaret inside on the phone?

Daisy put her ear to the heavy wood door but could hear nothing.

She rapped but there was no answer.

Daisy slowly turned the knob and the door creaked open.

She froze.

Cold chills raced up and down her spine.

Margaret Vaughn lay on the floor.

Daisy's gaze shifted to the brushed nickel knife holder on the counter. The middle knife—which Daisy suspected was the largest in the set—was missing . . .

Books by Karen Rose Smith

Caprice DeLuca Mysteries

STAGED TO DEATH
DEADLY DÉCOR
GILT BY ASSOCIATION
DRAPE EXPECTATIONS
SILENCE OF THE LAMPS
SHADES OF WRATH
SLAY BELLS RING
CUT TO THE CHAISE

Daisy's Tea Garden Mysteries

MURDER WITH LEMON TEA CAKES
MURDER WITH CINNAMON SCONES
MURDER WITH CUCUMBER SANDWICHES
MURDER WITH CHERRY TARTS
MURDER WITH CLOTTED CREAM

Published by Kensington Publishing Corporation

Murder with Clotted Cream

KAREN ROSE SMITH

KENSINGTON BOOKS
www.kensingtonbooks.com

KENSINGTON BOOKS are published by

Kensington Publishing Corp.
119 West 40th Street
New York, NY 10018

All Kensington titles, imprints, and distributed lines are available at special quantity discounts for bulk purchases for sales promotion, premiums, fund-raising, and educational or institutional use.

Special book excerpts or customized printings can also be created to fit specific needs. For details, write or phone the office of the Kensington Sales Manager: Kensington Publishing Corp., 119 West 40th Street, New York, NY 10018. Attn. Sales Department. Phone: 1-800-221-2647.

Kensington and the K logo Reg. U.S. Pat. & TM Off.

First Kensington Books Mass Market Paperback Printing: June 2020

ISBN-13: 978-1-4967-2394-9
ISBN-10: 1-4967-2394-5

ISBN-13: 978-1-4967-2395-6 (ebook)
ISBN-10: 1-4967-2395-3 (ebook)

10 9 8 7 6 5 4 3 2 1

Printed in the United States of America

For moms who try their hardest to do their best

Acknowledgments

Thanks to Officer Greg Berry. I take his advice and use the law enforcement info he gives me to maintain accuracy. He's a valuable asset and I always appreciate his input.

Chapter One

"But what if Margaret doesn't like the apple ginger-bread with clotted cream?" Aunt Iris asked Daisy as they stood at the sales counter of Daisy's Tea Garden.

Daisy Swanson was co-owner of Daisy's Tea Garden with her aunt Iris. Willow Creek, in Lancaster County, Pennsylvania, experienced a thriving tourist trade even into November and December if the weather held. However, business was sporadic in November and Daisy was glad to accept catering events in order to keep up their revenue around the holidays. She knew her aunt Iris was worried about one such cater-ing event coming up in a few days. They were con-cerned about all of their events being as perfect as they could make them, but the woman who had hired them to present afternoon tea in her historic farm-house had a reputation. Margaret Vaughn, former New York City actress, was particular.

There were only a few customers in the tea garden at nine a.m. on a Monday morning. Still, Iris lowered her voice. "Since Margaret's husband built her that

theater, and she made herself director of their productions, she's even more persnickety. What if she
doesn't like what we serve? We worked on that clotted cream for three days!" Iris's ash-blond short curls
bounced with vehemence.

Daisy's friend Vanna Huffnagle, Willow Creek
Community Church's secretary, had recommended
Daisy to her sister, Margaret.

Margaret had insisted on genuine clotted cream
for the catered tea. Daisy had assured her that they
would oblige. Her aunt Iris was correct. The clotted
cream was a lot of work to make. To buy it would be
terrifically expensive. Daisy had wanted to give Margaret a competitive quote so she wouldn't choose
someone else to cater her event. She didn't intend to
disappoint either Vanna or the very exacting Margaret.

Daisy took the elastic tie from her shoulder-length
blond hair and refastened it into a low ponytail.
"Vanna told me that she and Margaret don't always
get along. I know too well sisters can be like oil mixing with water. I got the impression that they hadn't
had much contact at all during Margaret's acting
years in New York. It's only since Margaret married
Rowan Vaughn and they moved to Willow Creek that
she and Vanna see each other frequently."

Iris swept around the counter and counted the
scones that were inside the case. Then her hazel eyes
met Daisy's blue ones. "Even though Vanna left her
Mennonite faith behind when she married her husband, she adhered to its values. Margaret didn't."

"Just because she wanted an acting career didn't
mean she left her values behind," Daisy offered, slip-
ping her hands into the pockets of her yellow apron
with its large daisy logo.

"Maybe not," Iris agreed. "But Vanna believes big-city life changed Margaret." Iris thought about their conversation for a few moments. "Since Vanna's husband died, I think she's been lonely. She was glad when Margaret moved back here. But I also know she believes Rowan building his wife that Little Theater and setting up an endowment for future expenses was really over the top of anything a husband should do."

Most residents of Willow Creek knew Rowan Vaughn, a land developer in Lancaster, Pennsylvania, was worth millions. At least that's what the Willow Creek gossip mill indicated. Vanna had shared with Daisy that Margaret had run away to New York City when she was fifteen. An actress was all she'd ever wanted to be. To escape the life and faith restrictions she didn't want?

Emerging from the kitchen, Daisy's kitchen manager, Tessa Miller, came over to where she was standing. Tessa was a colorful addition to the tea garden with her flowing orange and green smock and her braided caramel-toned hair interspersed with orange ribbons. "Do you have the menu worked out yet for the tea at Margaret Vaughn's house? If I have time today, I thought I'd run through the food and make sure everything is tip-top. The apple gingerbread recipe has turned out delicious every time I've baked it. Do you want me to serve it in ramekins or do you want to serve slices on dessert plates?"

"Which do you think would look better with the clotted cream?" Daisy asked.

"I think the slices would look best," Tessa answered. "The gingerbread cuts well, and our tea guests can see that spicy goodness and apples along the outside edge of the slice."

Iris nodded. "I think Tessa's right. Not only that, but we won't have as much difficulty transporting the cake pans. Ramekins can slide all over the place. Besides that, you'd have to make sure when you dump the gingerbread out of the ramekins that it's a perfect shape. Slices make sense."

"Slices it is," Daisy said with a smile, then motioned Tessa to her office. "I have the menu on my desk. I was going to have Jazzi print off enough for Margaret's guests when she comes in after school."

Jazzi, Daisy's sixteen-year-old daughter, earned money by helping at the tea garden after school and on weekends.

Her voice gentle, Tessa leaned close to Daisy to say, "I'll bet Jazzi is looking forward to spending a weekend with Portia and her family."

Tessa's words caused a twinge in Daisy's heart. Adopted, Jazzi had gone on a search for her birth mother a year ago and found her. Since then, there had been emotional ups and downs for all of them. Portia Smith Harding hadn't known if she wanted to disrupt her life by telling her husband she'd put a baby up for adoption before she'd met him. She'd finally revealed her secret, which had caused marital issues. But now Portia and her husband seemed to be on stable ground and Jazzi was going to spend a weekend with the family. All were hoping Jazzi and Colton, Portia's husband, could connect. Daisy didn't want her daughter getting hurt.

Responding to Tessa's comment, Daisy said, "Jazzi's looking forward to it, but she's nervous, too. She won't admit it, but I think she's afraid she'll do or say something wrong. She doesn't want to cause any more problems for the couple."

"Jazzi would be a wonderful addition to any family," Tessa said.

"I tell her the same thing," Daisy agreed with a wide grin.

When Daisy had lost her husband to pancreatic cancer four years ago, she'd taken a year to try to balance her emotions and her life. Finally she decided moving back to Willow Creek from Florida with her two daughters would be the best decision for all of them. Violet, who was three years older than Jazzi, had been more vocal about her feelings. Jazzi had kept a lot of hers inside.

Iris peeked around the corner of Daisy's office. "Vanna's here and she's upset. I think you should talk to her."

Daisy checked her watch. Nine thirty. Vanna's hours at the church were flexible. Daisy bet that more than a scone and a cup of tea had brought the church secretary into the tea garden this morning.

Daisy hurried from her office to the main tearoom, which had been painted a soft, welcoming green when she and her aunt Iris had renovated the Victorian. Her customers seemed comfortable with the glass-topped tables and mismatched antique oak hand-carved chairs. At the beginning of November, before the Thanksgiving season, a rustic bud vase with dried herbs, lavender, and a white mum decorated each table.

As Vanna moved forward to meet Daisy, Daisy could see that her friend was upset. Her hair was steel gray in a no-nonsense short cut. She was wearing a chocolate-colored pantsuit with no coat. She'd probably driven from church or from home. It was too chilly a day to be running around without outerwear. Vanna's sturdy tan tie shoes clicked on the floor as she approached Daisy. Her hazel eyes brimmed with something akin to . . . frustration? Disappointment?

There was no point in guessing. Daisy motioned her into the adjoining spillover tearoom, which was painted the palest yellow. Its white tables and chairs always looked fresh. The seat cushions in blue, yellow, and green pinstripes added a whimsical look. This room, where they took reservations for and served afternoon tea on specified days, reflected the finest aspects of a Victorian with its bay window, window seat, diamond-cut glass, and crown molding.

Vanna followed Daisy into the room. As Daisy motioned to a table for two, she asked, "How about a cup of Earl Grey and a blueberry scone?"

Vanna let out a huge sigh. "The tea sounds nice, but I don't have an appetite."

Although Daisy wanted to know what was going on, she said, "I'll be right back. Relax for a few moments."

Daisy's Tea Garden was all about relaxing, chatting, and appreciating different blends of tea as well as baked goods, salads, and soups. Daisy said to her aunt, "Two cups of Earl Grey. I'll try to find out what's going on."

Returning to Vanna's table, Daisy sat across from the church secretary. "You look upset."

"I *am* upset. I recommended you to Margaret. I knew she could be difficult, but I didn't want *you* to suffer for it. And now she's thinking about canceling the tea."

That was a surprise to Daisy. "*Why* is she thinking about canceling?" Daisy emphasized the first word, knowing the reason for Margaret's state of mind could mean everything to Daisy figuring out what to do next.

Vanna waved her hand at the green room. "Her decision has nothing to do with you or your tea or your food. It's about *her*, really, and it's her own fault."

"What's her fault?"

Cora Sue, one of Daisy's servers who worked full time and was as bubbly as the bottle-red hair curling in her topknot, brought a tray with two Royal Doulton teacups as well as a matching four-cup teapot. After she greeted Vanna, she unloaded the tray onto the table quickly as if Iris had given her specific orders to serve and leave. Along with the tea service, she left a petite dish of sparkling sugar, a stone-craft cup with wildflower honey, and a crystal dessert plate with slices of lemon and a small fork.

Vanna looked it all over as if she couldn't decide whether to answer Daisy's question or fix her cup of tea. As if she decided she needed the bracing liquid, she used a spoonful of honey and squeezed in a lemon slice, setting the rind on her saucer and wiping her fingers on her napkin. "You do know how to serve tea," she murmured.

Daisy smiled at the grudging compliment, thinking she'd take good vibes when she could get them. Vanna didn't give her time to give thanks.

"You know, don't you, that Margaret imported a lighting expert and a stage manager from New York City."

"No, I didn't know that. She didn't want to use local talent?"

"Her attitude was that she couldn't *find* local talent." Lines around Vanna's mouth became more evident as she frowned. "I don't think she looked very

hard. Glenda Nurmi, who wrote the play, believes *she*
should be the director, not Margaret. After all, she *is*
the playwright. But Margaret doesn't agree with
that."

Daisy had heard the name of the play was *Christmas in the North Woods*. Now she repeated to Vanna
something else she'd heard. "Heidi Korn, from the
Rainbow Flamingo, is in the play as well as Arden
Botterill, right?" Arden owned a shop called Vinegar
and Spice.

Vanna let out a big sigh. "Since Heidi owns the
dress shop, she wants to give Margaret advice on the
fashions for the play. But Margaret, of course, won't
take it. Even when she was five she was right about
everything."

Daisy suppressed the urge to chuckle. Margaret
definitely was an opinionated, take-charge woman.

"You know Daniel Copeland's in the play too,"
Vanna offered.

Daisy hadn't heard that. Daniel was the assistant
manager of the Willow Creek Bank. He had an attitude similar to Margaret's. As soon as she thought it,
Daisy chastised herself for judging the man. She didn't
know Daniel all that well.

"There are a few others from town," Vanna went
on. "As you know, Jonas is helping with the set design, not that he has any say in it. But he is helping to
construct it."

"He seems to be enjoying that." Daisy had been
dating Jonas Groft since last New Year's Eve. Their relationship had experienced bumps, but some highs
too. He was a former detective from Philadelphia
who had seen enough of the seedy side of life. He
now owned Woods, a furniture store down the street
from Daisy's Tea Garden. He crafted furniture to sell

along with the other pieces he took in on consignment.

Daisy thought about everything Vanna had told her while Vanna seemed to relax a bit as she took a few sips of tea. When the secretary closed her eyes, Daisy put together the pieces and figured out what was probably going on.

After adding a half teaspoon of honey to her own tea, Daisy stirred it in. Vanna opened her eyes again.

Daisy guessed, "So what you're telling me is that Margaret is upset because there are problems between her cast and the production staff?"

"That's exactly what I'm telling you. The cast seems to resent the people from New York telling them what to do, especially since Glenda doesn't seem to have much input and she should. The New York duo, even though this is what they do—go on the road to help developing theaters—seem to resent the fact that the cast thinks their opinion should count. I stopped in at the theater yesterday, and to me it all seemed like a muddled mess. Margaret's not sure everyone will pull together and that's why she's thinking about canceling the tea. Why should she go to the expense of a full-course tea service for everyone when they can't seem to get along?"

"Why did Margaret wait so long to think about having the tea?"

"I don't know. She's not used to organizing. She's used to acting. I was the organized sister. She was the flutterbug, though a determined one who followed the wind."

Daisy imagined that that was resentment she heard in Vanna's tone. Firsthand, she knew about sisters and resentment, but she definitely didn't want to go there right now. She took a sip and then another of her tea, letting the warm brew calm and settle her. She'd opened the tea garden with her aunt because she wanted the residents of Willow Creek to have a place to come that was safe, calming, and a respite where friendships were formed and made stronger.

"Thank you for coming to me today," Daisy said. "I think I should talk to Margaret myself. I'm going to need a final decision if my staff and I need to prepare for her tea. I need to know now. I'll give her a call and see if I can meet with her."

"There's a rehearsal tonight, but I think she said she'd be at home most of the day. Maybe you can catch her."

"I'll do that. In the meantime, before you go back to your job, wouldn't you like a muffin or a scone or a brownie?"

Vanna, gazing around the restful room, rethought her previous decision. "A brownie before noon. That sounds decadent, doesn't it?" She had a twinkle in her eye. "I think I'll have one since that's as decadent as I get."

Daisy took a few more sips of tea then rose from her chair. "Enjoy another cup of tea. Cora Sue will bring you a brownie."

As Daisy was about to turn away, Vanna called her back. "I wish Margaret was more like you. I'd have a real confidante then."

Daisy felt herself blush. "You can talk to me anytime, Vanna. You know that, don't you?"

Vanna's eyes seemed to mist over and she simply nodded.

Daisy was going to tell Cora Sue to serve Vanna an extra-large brownie.

*   *   *

A few minutes later Daisy was headed to her office to call Margaret when her son-in-law opened the tea garden door. Foster Cranshaw let Violet precede him inside. His russet brown hair was mussed from the wind and his rimless glasses fell low on his nose.

Daisy felt empathy and sympathy for her daughter, who was counting days at the end of her pregnancy. Daisy remembered those last few weeks of her pregnancy well. She hadn't been able to see her feet, and fatigue interspersed with moments of high energy prodded her to do everything she had to do before the baby was born.

Daisy didn't waste any time in showing the couple to the spillover tearoom. Foster wasn't slated to work until tomorrow. He had classes this morning. Her daughter was supposed to be at home resting.

As soon as Foster pulled out Vi's chair and helped her remove her black-and-white color-blocked wool cape, Violet said, "I wish I hadn't stopped working so soon. I'm so bored I don't know what to do." Vi's honey blond hair had grown a ways down her back. Its natural wave was wind-tossed this morning. Her cheeks were fuller than they'd been before her pregnancy.

Foster looked frustrated as he sat at the table with his wife. "Otis misses her at Pirated Treasures. Even though she's kept his inventory list and his bookwork up-to-date, as well as Arden Botterill's bookkeeping, she doesn't know what to do with herself."

Vi ticked off tasks with her fingers one at a time. "I have the baby's area ready. I have receiving blankets and clothes all washed. Clean sheets are on the crib mattress, and I dusted our whole apartment until I can't dust anymore. I wanted to take a walk farther than from our apartment to your house, but Foster won't let me."

"Not when she's alone," Foster confirmed to Daisy. "I'm not taking any chances."

"When do you see the midwife again?" Daisy ventured.

Vi shifted, trying to arrange herself more comfortably in the chair. "Tonight. You're welcome to be there. Willa knows you're worried."

Daisy thought she'd hidden her concern about Violet having a midwife deliver her baby in their apartment. Apparently, one woman to another, Willa knew how Daisy felt. She was a Mennonite woman who was a nurse practitioner as well as a midwife and well-qualified for her profession.

"Yes, I'd like to be there," Daisy assured her daughter.

"Vi asked me to bring her here so she'd have a change of scene," Foster explained. "I need to meet with my professor at the college this afternoon."

"Anything wrong?" Daisy asked, then thought maybe she shouldn't have. She really tried to let her daughters make their own choices, and let Foster guide where he wanted his family to go.

Foster pushed his glasses higher on the bridge of his nose and answered easily. "No problem. Actually, we're talking about independent study after the baby's born. It would make my hours more flexible."

"Rooibos iced tea with a scone?" Under Daisy's direction, Vi had learned what teas were safe for her to drink during pregnancy. The herbal tea with ginger and mint had helped her morning sickness. There were teas that were unsafe during pregnancy like cleansing and detoxification teas as well as those with certain herbs such as black cohosh. Daisy had also counseled Vi that she should limit her tea intake to one cup a day. Two or three cups were supposed to be safe, but as with everything else, since a pregnancy scare back in August, Vi wanted to go in the direction of caution. She stayed away from any drink with caffeine.

Violet looked almost like the little girl Daisy remembered when she asked, "Can I come back to the kitchen and visit with Tessa? It will give me something to do. Then I just want to sit here and watch your customers. Can I do that, Mom?"

Daisy would do anything to help the last few days of Vi's pregnancy go smoothly. Her older daughter was welcome to watch passersby and tea drinkers if that would help her occupy herself. "I'm sure everybody in the kitchen would be glad to see you."

Foster raised a brow. "You'll watch over her?"

"Of course. If I don't, Iris will, or Cora Sue, or Eva."

Looking relieved, Foster stood and he helped Vi to stand too.

Vi sighed. "I don't think I ever realized that pregnancy would be like carrying around four bags of sugar or flour. I've gained twenty pounds," she bemoaned.

"And you look beautiful," Daisy reminded her. "You're healthy and strong, and according to your OB/GYN, the baby is too." Willa had a gynecologist backing her up just in case she needed one. Fortunately, Vi's doctor was on board with everything they were doing.

"You have to say that," Vi murmured. "You're my mother."

Daisy could tell Foster was suppressing a smile.

"She doesn't believe it when I tell her she's beautiful either," he said. Then he kissed Violet and left the tea garden.

Daisy walked with Vi to the kitchen, where everyone welcomed her. Before Vi had had a scare with her pregnancy, she'd worked at the tea garden beside everyone who was working there now.

The aromas that wafted from the kitchen were cinnamon and chocolate, vanilla and sugar. There was a yeasty smell too, which meant Tessa was baking cinnamon rolls.

Vi caught the scent right away. She said to Tessa, "If any of those cinnamon rolls are baked, I'll have one."

"They're almost baked." Tessa looked Vi over. "You're glowing. Pregnancy becomes you."

Vi just shook her head. "You all made a pact to make me feel good, didn't you?"

As Tessa laughed, and she and Vi began talking, Daisy said, "I have a call to make. I'll be back in five minutes."

She hoped it would be five minutes.

In her office, Daisy called Margaret from the handset on her desk.

"Vaughn residence," someone answered on the other end of the line.

"This is Daisy Swanson from Daisy's Tea Garden," Daisy explained. "Is Mrs. Vaughn in?"

"This is Tamlyn Pittenger, Mrs. Swanson. Mrs. Vaughn is in a meeting right now in her study."

"I was wondering if it would be convenient for me to visit her later this afternoon. Could you check for me?"

Tamlyn hesitated. "I . . . uh . . . I can try."

That sounded a little odd to Daisy.

About a minute later, Tamlyn was back on the line. "Mrs. Swanson, I don't know who's with Mrs. Vaughn but the door to her study is closed. There's an argument going on inside. I don't think I should disturb her right now."

"I see. I really need to talk with her today, and I'd like to do it face-to-face."

"All right. Let me check her calendar. She usually writes all of her social engagements on it. She still doesn't like using a phone app for that. The calendar is in the kitchen."

While Daisy waited, Tamlyn reached the kitchen quickly and related, "Mrs. Vaughn doesn't have anyone listed on her schedule for right now, even though she's in a meeting. It's also empty for this afternoon. She usually has lunch at one. Why don't you give me a call around two? If she's free, I'll let you know."

"I'll do that," Daisy agreed. "Thank you, Tamlyn." She ended the call. However, as she did, she thought about everything Vanna had told her this morning. Just who was Margaret arguing with?

Chapter Two

Daisy drove up the lane that led to a circular drive-way. She knew two acres surrounded the historic house that Margaret Vaughn now lived in with her husband. Once the area had been densely wooded with Norwegian spruce trees along one side and maples and oaks on the other, continuing to the rear of the property. The front entrance had been mostly hidden by arborvitae that had grown out of control as well as mop bushes that, for the most part, kept their round shape and almost covered the porch railings.

After Rowan Vaughn had bought the place, he'd had many of the trees and their trunks uprooted and the shrubs around the house torn away. There had been plenty of space for a circular stamped drive, and he'd had one of those created. A decorative wheelbarrow sat in the center. It was filled with mums and marigolds that had seen their last glory days.

The house itself was a sturdy-looking edifice. The

porch ran across the front, and set-back side wings extended about twelve feet from each side. The edifice stood two and a half stories with dormers positioned on each side of a triple window in the center of the roof point. Five windows with shutters allowed light into the second floor. The middle one sat directly above the double door entrance into the main floor. She suspected the house was about fifty-five hundred square feet, which included a bedroom on the third floor. She'd only been in the house once, when she'd originally discussed the tea with Margaret.

After Daisy parked, she climbed the steps to the main door. The doorbell sound seemed to reverberate through the house. About a minute after she pushed the button, Tamlyn opened the door. Margaret's housekeeper was young, probably in her early twenties. She wore her long brown hair in a knot on the back of her head. Her uniform, if you could call it that, was navy slacks and a pale blue oxford shirt. Daisy knew that when Tamlyn was working in the kitchen or the butler's pantry, she wore a white apron. The young woman's cheeks were full, her lips wide, and her bangs practically covered her brows.

She looked a bit nervous now as she said in a small voice, "I told Mrs. Vaughn that you'd be stopping by. She's still in a grumpy mood from her meeting. Maybe you can change that."

As the young housekeeper guided Daisy through the foyer and living room down a hall, Daisy couldn't help but admire the rich woodwork that trimmed the door frames and windows with wide windowsills. Speaking to its historic past, the plank flooring was a bit uneven and creaked. The newel post was fashioned of the same aged oak as the mantel above the stone fireplace.

At one of the heavy paneled doors, Tamlyn stopped. She rapped and when Margaret answered, "Come in," Tamlyn opened the door.

Daisy entered the office as aware of the antique mahogany desk as of the woman sitting behind it. The computer on the old-fashioned credenza to the side of the desk together with the ergonomic office chair looked out of place. Margaret, on the other hand, didn't. Although her steel-gray hair was expensively cut in a short do, her clothes reminded Daisy more of her Mennonite upbringing. She wore a midilength gray wool skirt as well as a white silky blouse and gray wool vest. It was a severe yet stylish outfit. Her makeup was expertly applied, from a perfectly formed brow to the almost nude coloring on her lips. Her appearance almost looked like a reconciliation between the past and the present. Had her life become that too?

As Tamlyn quietly exited the room, Margaret rose and extended her hand to Daisy with a smile that seemed genuine. "I know why you're here. You want to convince me to go ahead with the tea. I imagine your business can slow down this time of year."

Margaret was apparently going to be blunt. In that case, Daisy could be blunt too.

As Margaret took her seat in her office chair, Daisy perched on the practical suede leather chair positioned in front of Margaret's desk. Before she spoke, Daisy decided she could be blunt, but she also knew how to be tactful too.

Many photos were propped on Margaret's desk—Vanna and her family including her deceased husband, one of Glenda and Margaret together, a photo of the cast, and the largest, a wedding portrait of Margaret and Rowan.

Daisy motioned to the photo of Vanna and her family. "Your sister is concerned about you. She knows how much *Christmas in the North Woods* means to you, and having the production go well."

"I don't see what that has to do with the tea." Margaret's mouth formed a petulant frown.

"You mentioned our business slacking off. That's true of the tourist trade to a certain extent. But I arrange special events at the tea garden to pick up the slack. We're having a gingerbread house–making contest with children. An author is coming to share her latest release along with tea and discussion. And, of course, we'll have special Christmas celebration teas. So your tea, here in the farmhouse, won't dent my revenue too much if you cancel it."

"Then why did you take your time to come here?" Margaret asked, sincerely curious.

"I know you have doubts about the tea because of disputes with your cast."

"Vanna talks too much," Margaret grumbled. "She's always been jealous of me and my acting career, places I've been, the sights I've seen."

Daisy had never gotten that impression from Vanna. Vanna had once told her that as a little girl her dream had been of meeting a man who would love her forever. She'd dreamed of having children and creating a good home. That's what she'd done. Although her husband was gone now, Daisy knew Vanna reveled in her children and grandchildren, and loved having them around her. But she wasn't going to go into that with Margaret.

"I just believe—" Daisy began.

Margaret's cell phone, which was sitting on the edge of her desk, played the theme from *Phantom of the Opera*. Margaret didn't even glance at the screen. She picked up the phone. "I have to take this. It's my husband."

"Would you like me to step out?" Daisy asked.

Margaret shook her head and waved to Daisy to stay seated. She answered, "Rowan? Will you be home tonight?"

As she listened, Daisy could see that whatever Rowan Vaughn had said to Margaret affected her. She frowned and looked older than she had a few minutes before. Although Daisy was sitting there, ready to leave if Margaret said the word, Margaret simply wheeled her office chair around until her back faced Daisy and lowered her voice.

However, Daisy could still hear her as she said, "If you don't clean up the mess quickly it could affect everything, including the play and ticket sales. Your endowment won't last long if the theater can't bring in money on its own."

Daisy heard a catch in Margaret's voice.

"Life in Willow Creek is difficult enough," she murmured.

After listening again for a minute or two, Margaret said, "I'll see you when you get home."

Daisy wasn't about to comment on the call. She simply sat there until Margaret wheeled her chair around, looked down at her desk, then back up at Daisy. The stiff guard she'd had in place seemed to disintegrate before Daisy's eyes. She placed her hands on her desk and intertwined her fingers. "Rowan has lived in Lancaster all his life."

Since Margaret seemed to want to talk, Daisy went along with it. "Has he?"

"Yes. His father had made a name in commercial development in the area. Actually, in the state. I think Rowan always wanted to outshine his father. Men and competition." Margaret shook her head. "Of course, I suppose women can be the same way, or maybe competitive in a different way." Margaret appeared to be lost in her thoughts for a few seconds, then she returned her attention to Daisy. "I was from Willow Creek, as you know. Did Vanna tell you about our upbringing?"

"I know you were brought up in the Mennonite religion."

"We were, and I hated it. I hated the restrictions. I hated the rules. I hated dressing like someone from the eighteenth century. Vanna didn't mind it as much, maybe never minded at all. I left to escape. She left, reaching for a dream. She found hers until her husband, Howard, died."

"Did you find yours?"

Margaret stared down at the leather insert on her desk. "It took me a lot longer. I was a struggling actress for years. But then I fell in love with Rowan and coming back to Willow Creek had seemed right. Now, however, I don't know. Maybe I simply don't like to do the same thing for any length of time. I spent my childhood wanting to escape my life and now I find I want to escape again, at least away from Willow Creek. Don't you find small-town values and gossip restrictive?"

"Maybe I like to live within some restrictions," Daisy offered with a smile. "Willow Creek has always felt like home. I was away for years. I always thought of Willow Creek fondly. When I met my husband, we moved away and he was my home. After he died, I decided moving back here with my daughters was our best decision, and it was. I believe we're happy here."

"Your daughters might want to flee small-town living."

"They might, and I won't dissuade them if that's what they want to do. I'm still hoping that Willow Creek will always feel like home to them."

Both women seemed to consider what they had said, then Daisy asked, "Do you really want to cancel the tea? An afternoon that the cast spends together, not in dispute over the production but simply getting to know each other deeper during a relaxing time, could help them form better bonds."

Margaret peered out the window over the grounds of the property, seeming to study the trees that had lost most of their leaves. Finally, she said to Daisy, "You might be right. Maybe one of the reasons the cast is having problems is because everyone's busy. When they're not working, they're rehearsing. They aren't socializing. We're on a schedule at the theater too. It could be that we all merely need time to take a breath, and maybe breathe the same air. But I don't think I'll invite Keisha and Ward, my production team from New York. Their presence can lead to discord." She stopped. "All right, I'll go ahead with the tea."

Heaving a sigh of relief, Daisy couldn't help but be thankful that the work that had already been put into planning the tea wouldn't go to waste. "I'll e-mail you the time that we'll arrive to set up."

Margaret stood, effectively dismissing Daisy. She stood also.

"I check my e-mails at least every half hour. Would you like Tamlyn to help serve?"

"If she's willing. We'd be glad to have her."

Margaret said, "I'll relay that message to her. She's probably working in the kitchen now. I'll see you out."

As Margaret walked Daisy to the door, Daisy couldn't help but wonder how long the actress would reside in Willow Creek. If the theater was a success, would it keep her here? Or would her need to escape be more powerful than keeping her hand in the acting community in Willow Creek?

As Daisy walked from the rear parking lot of the tea garden to Woods, Jonas Groft's store, an Amish buggy with a beautiful bay horse, sturdy and strong, clattered down the street. It was a closed buggy, so she couldn't see who was inside. Her friend Rachel and her family used a horse and buggy, and Daisy had ridden in the Fishers' buggy often. As a child she'd ridden in Rachel's parents' buggy, which hadn't had the bells and whistles some of the new models sported today—like a gas heater inside or battery-run lanterns on the outside.

November had added an edge of iciness to the air that had been missing in October. Daisy raised the hood of her fleecy cat-patterned jacket and hurried along the sidewalk. At Woods, she stood outside for a minute glancing over the window display. The store had a distinctive look. In the main window an office arrangement with an oak desk, an oak captain's chair, and a rolltop desk gleamed in the sunlight. She opened the door and stepped inside. As she always did, she glanced at the giant cubicle shelves built along one side of the store from floor to ceiling. Ladder-back chairs stood in each of the cubicles, ranging in colors from distressed blue to teal to cherrywood and a dark walnut.

As she walked down the main aisle, her glance swerved from side to side to the islands built with re-claimed wood and a granite-topped sideboard to an armoire hand carved along its arched door and a cedar chest that many young women used as hope chests. Every piece of furniture was handcrafted by local craftsmen including Jonas. Expecting to see Jonas or his manager at the sales desk to the rear of the store, she stopped short when she realized who Jonas was talking to—Detective Morris Rappaport.

The two men, both detectives aware of every sound, sight, and sensation in their immediate sur-roundings, glanced sideways at her and ended their conversation. Daisy wasn't sure whether to slow down or pretend to be looking at some of the furniture.

But Jonas beckoned to her even though the detec-tive was frowning. She wondered why. The two men had a rapport that had aided them both in solving murders. At first when Daisy had become involved in solving those murders too, Detective Rappaport had been antagonistic. Now, after four cases, they'd es-tablished a friendly rapport.

The detective's frown eased away as he nodded to Daisy and a half smile quivered on his lips. "How are you doing, Daisy?"

"Having trouble keeping warm today. It's nippy out there."

Detective Rappaport seemed glad she was dis-cussing the weather. He gave a shrug. "That's why I'm glad I drive a car and not a horse and buggy. I don't know how those Amish do it."

The detective had experienced culture shock when he'd moved from Pittsburgh to Willow Creek.

She still didn't have the story behind that. By now, he'd even developed a liking for snickerdoodles and whoopie pies. He still wouldn't sample her teas except in the iced version, but she was hopeful. "You know, don't you, a bracing cup of hot tea could warm you up."

He shook his finger at her. "You keep trying, don't you?"

"One of these days I'll come across a tea you'll like, or else you'll be so cold you won't have any choice but to try one."

"What this town needs is a coffee bar," he grumbled.

"Detective, your big-city roots are showing. Sarah Jane's Diner serves a good cup of coffee, and there's always McDonald's."

The fifty-year-old detective gave a harrumph. "Well, I've got to get going. There's a tower of paperwork on my desk. It never ends. I had to separate two football fans at Bases last night. They did some damage, and there's always paperwork involved in that."

"Doesn't a patrol officer usually take care of that?" Jonas asked.

"Yeah, well, I just happened to be there watching a game too. Even when I'm not on call, I'm on call. Around Christmas, I'm taking time off."

"What will you do with your time off?" Daisy asked.

"Going north to Raystown. I have a sort of a time share at a hunting lodge. I never use my time, though. This year I'm going to." He gave Jonas a look. "Remember what I said." Then he nodded to Daisy and strode out of Woods.

Jonas approached Daisy and wrapped his arms around her. After he kissed her, she smiled. "That's what I needed. Now I'm not chilled anymore."

"Are you taking a break from the tea garden?" he asked with a grin.

"No, I'm heading back there. I visited Margaret Vaughn to try and convince her not to cancel her tea." Daisy briefly explained the reasons why Margaret was thinking about canceling.

"I'm enjoying working on the production set," Jonas told her. "It certainly is different from building furniture."

"Artistic in a different way," Daisy offered.

"Exactly. I try to stay out of and close my ears to the squabbling I've heard. It doesn't seem to be anything serious. Personally, I think that playwright, Glenda Nurmi, should have the final say. After all, she wrote the play. But Margaret Vaughn's word seems to be law."

Daisy nodded. "That's what Vanna told me. We're going ahead with the tea. Maybe sharing a beverage and food will help."

"You want everybody to get along," Jonas suggested fondly.

"I do. And speaking of getting along, why was Detective Rappaport here?"

Jonas took a step away from her and hesitated. She recognized that stone face of his. It didn't mean he wasn't feeling anything. It meant he was probably feeling too much. The question was—would he share his feelings with *her*? They'd been seriously dating about nine months now. They'd come to a general understanding that they liked being together, and they were taking their relationship wherever it would go. But they both knew Violet's baby could change that relationship. Jonas had insisted he'd support Daisy any way he could, and he'd stick around. But she wasn't so sure.

Jonas began with, "The good detective wants me and Zeke to mend fences."

Zeke Willet was also a detective who'd come to Willow Creek from Philadelphia. He was now Rappaport's partner. But Zeke and Jonas had a history.

"You want that too, don't you? You were best friends once."

"We were. But Brenda's death changed all that."

Jonas's significant other had been his partner in the Philadelphia police department. Brenda had been a friend of Zeke Willet's too. The bottom line— Zeke blamed Jonas for her death.

Jonas and Brenda had been ambushed and Jonas had been hurt. Brenda had died. As far as Daisy was concerned, she didn't think Zeke Willet was looking at it rationally. However, when you lost someone you cared about, could you look at their death rationally? She knew it had taken a good long time for her to move past her husband Ryan's death. It wasn't as if she ever forgot about him. It wasn't as if a wave didn't overtake her now and then and bring tears to her eyes. She understood loss. But she couldn't quite understand the bad blood between Zeke and Jonas, and Jonas couldn't either.

"Why is he pushing for you and Zeke to get past your history?"

"He believes the tension between us affected Zeke's performance in their last murder investigation, and he might be right. Zeke missed more than one piece of evidence."

Daisy knew for a fact that was true because she'd been involved. "So what are you going to do?"

"I'm not sure. Maybe I'll ask Zeke to go to Bases to watch a game with me and have a beer."

"The same place fights broke out last night?" she asked with a bit of sarcasm.

Jonas shrugged. "I don't think that ever happened before there. Besides, I don't intend to let Zeke rile me enough to make me want to fight him. I understand why he blames me for Brenda's death. Sometimes I wonder if I could have done something different. I know if we hadn't had that argument before we left for our shift, everything might have been different. Maybe I would have been more alert. Maybe thoughts of her being pregnant or having her IUD removed without telling me wouldn't have been clouding my mind."

"You couldn't know that the suspect you wanted to interview was going to ambush you. That was *his* doing, not yours."

Jonas studied her for a few seconds, then took her hand in his. "You're good for a man's ego."

"Nonsense. I'm just speaking the truth."

Looking a bit embarrassed and as if he wanted to change the subject, Jonas did. "The last time I spoke to Jazzi, she told me she's going to spend a weekend soon with Portia and her husband."

"It's all planned. I don't know how it's going to go. She's excited about it, but also afraid that Colton will just shut her out and not want her to be involved in the family."

Colton, Portia's husband, had separated from Portia for a little while when he'd learned her secret—that she'd had Jazzi and given her up for adoption—because he hadn't wanted his life to be disrupted. But Portia was Jazzi's birth mother, and the two of them got along. Colton could complicate their relationship.

"I have a meeting with Vi and her midwife tonight. Willa thinks the baby could come at any time. Jazzi desperately wants to go to Portia's, but she's afraid Vi will have her baby while she's there and she'll miss it."

"Even if Jazzi goes to Portia's," Jonas said, "we can let her know as soon as Vi goes into labor. I can be on standby to go get her if Portia or her husband doesn't want to drive her back home."

"Really?" Daisy was still surprised when Jonas wanted to go out of his way for her. Maybe *she* was the one who couldn't trust.

"Really," he said. "Allentown's a three-hour drive. Hopefully, I could have her back before Vi delivers. First labors are supposed to be long ones, right?"

"They can be. I know Jazzi would be grateful if she knew you were her backup."

"Then assure her that I am," he said. "Tell her when she gets a chance to stop in and we'll talk about it."

Since Jonas was instrumental in finding Portia to begin with, Jazzi trusted him. Maybe Daisy should take a lesson from her daughter.

Chapter Three

"Do you like your mother?" Iris asked with a most serious expression the following day as she and Daisy waited for Rose to arrive for a late lunch.

Daisy's breath hitched as she glanced toward the front door of Sarah Jane's Diner before she even thought about answering her aunt's question. Sarah Jane was hostessing and stood at the front desk talking to one of her waitresses. Her strawberry blond curls fell over her forehead. She was a bit overweight but had twice as much energy as a woman half her age. She was pushing hard for a meals-on-wheels service for Willow Creek, but for now the town council and the Chamber of Commerce were set on building a homeless shelter for the community instead.

Daisy focused on that tangent of thoughts, as well as Sarah Jane's blue gingham apron and her fuchsia and green sneakers. That way she could avoid answering the question her aunt had posed. Daisy knew she couldn't postpone answering for very long. Her aunt wouldn't let her, and it would probably only be a few minutes until her mother arrived.

"Do you like her?" Iris pressed. As Rose Gallagher's sister, Iris Albright obviously thought she had family rights to ask awkward questions. Daisy knew she could answer flippantly or truthfully. By the look in her aunt's eyes, she knew her aunt wanted the truth.

"I don't know my mother very well. That's horrible to say. But I don't."

Now Iris was the one who looked awkward, maybe thinking she shouldn't have pressed. How was it that Daisy didn't know her mother very well? She'd lived with her, her dad, and her sister until she'd gone to college. She'd always communicated with her father. Why hadn't she been able to communicate with her mom?

Before her aunt could respond, Rose Gallagher came in the front door of the diner. She spotted them sitting in a booth and waved.

"It's not your fault," Iris said seriously in a low voice. "Remember that."

Daisy's aunt Iris had been leading up to something for weeks now. She wished Iris would just tell her mother's secret, or Iris's secret, or whoever had a secret. Twenty questions just made Daisy even more uneasy.

As Rose approached the booth, Daisy patted the red vinyl cushion beside her. "You can sit on my side," she said with an easy smile. At least she hoped it was easy.

Rose gave a nod of her head as if she appreciated the gesture, slipped off her coat, and hung it on the hook that rose from the back of the booth. Then she set her purse on the seat next to Daisy and slid in. "Have you two ordered yet?"

Iris suddenly looked down at her menu. "No, we didn't. We were talking."

Daisy glanced from her mother to her aunt Iris, wondering all over again what was between them. Why had there always seemed to be an uneasiness or tension?

"What were you talking about?" Rose asked, innocently enough.

A bit nervously, Daisy stepped into the silent breach. The idea of these luncheons was to get to know her mother better. Maybe she could do that without bringing up anything controversial.

"Little things," Daisy answered. A memory had come back to her while she and Iris were talking, so she used that as a conversation starter. "Do you remember the vacation we took to Ocean City when I was about six and Cammie was eight?"

Her mother's brow creased with a serious line as she thought about it. Not even attempting to look at her menu, she nodded. "I do remember that. It was a terrifically hot summer. The air-conditioning unit at the garden center gave up the ghost. It was early September, the week before school began. Sales had diminished for the season, so your father and I decided to close up the nursery for a long weekend and take you and Cammie to the shore."

"You were so relaxed on that trip. Do you remember why?" Daisy's mom had seemed like a different person . . . away from the nursery and away from home.

Her mother gave a soft laugh. "I didn't have any responsibilities. I couldn't worry about the nursery because it was closed. I guess I could have worried that a tornado would blow through, but that seemed far-fetched. I also didn't have any housework chores. We went to restaurants and bought takeout. The maids took care of the motel room. It was an enjoyable vacation."

"Yes, it was. I remember the day Daddy took Cammie sailing. Neither of us wanted to go out on the water, so you and I played miniature golf and then visited the tourist shops. We bought Christmas presents."

"I'm surprised you remember all that in such detail," Rose said.

"I loved that time. We all got along so well."

"You and Cammie didn't even argue on that trip," her mom mused. "I considered that totally amazing. It's a shame we never repeated it."

Other vacations had been sightseeing vacations or cabin vacations to cut the cost of going away. On sightseeing vacations, they'd rented a room with a kitchenette so they could make their own food and clean up after themselves. The same had been true of cabins. And when they camped, the chores were just chores. Daisy enjoyed the camping, her dad showing her the constellations as they lay in sleeping bags under the stars. Daisy had slept in a tent with Cammie, being a little afraid of what was outside in the dark . . . bonding in a way they didn't at home. But her mother— On *those* vacations, there had always been something to worry about or plan or do. That one vacation had just been different.

"What made you think of Ocean City?" Rose asked.

"I was thinking of times we were all happy when we were together, other than holidays."

"I see," Rose said softly. "Weren't you happy at

other times, like when you won an award at school or helped plant flowers in the garden?"

"I was happy then too." Daisy thought out loud as she added, "And when I helped Dad deliver trees or bushes to clients." She stopped before she said too much. Whenever she'd helped her mom at the nursery, she'd felt as if Rose had been looking over her shoulder, just waiting to point out something if she did it wrong. When she'd helped her dad, they were . . . chums.

"What's *your* favorite childhood memory?" Daisy asked her mother.

"My favorite memory was selling penny candy at the school carnival. I had a wonderful teacher that year. She picked me to manage the stand."

Daisy thought it odd that one of her mom's favorite memories didn't include her parents or Iris.

Rose glanced at Iris. "What's *your* favorite childhood memory?" Since Iris hadn't contributed to the conversation, it was as if Rose was trying to draw her in. They were all trying.

"That's an easy one. Remember when we found that beagle pup and we took care of him for a week?" Aunt Iris's eyes lit up with the memory.

"We both loved that pup. We wanted to keep him. I think Mom would have let us, but Dad found someone who wanted him. He was going to use him for hunting." Rose's voice had turned cooler. As if Iris knew Daisy was going to ask more questions, she gave a little shake of her head giving her the signal not to. The words *Why not?* rang in Daisy's mind.

Iris suggested, "We'd better order." She picked up her menu. "If we don't soon signal our waitress, Sarah Jane will just think we're here to gab."

That *was* why they were here, Daisy thought, wasn't it?

After they ordered lunch—baked chicken pot pie all around, with sides of applesauce and coleslaw—Daisy, Iris, and her mom discussed Thanksgiving.

"Cammie's not sure what time she'll arrive," Rose told them. "Unless she takes off work the day before. I don't know if she'll do that. She's working extra hard on her company's business promotion."

"Do you want me to push the time from five to six on Thanksgiving?" Daisy asked.

"That might be a good idea. Make sure you notify everyone. We wouldn't want to have guests coming early."

As far as Daisy was concerned, their guests could arrive whenever they wanted. They could join her in the kitchen, chat, or just relax. But she didn't contradict her mother.

Daisy had just dipped her fork into the creamy coleslaw when her mother asked, "Have you convinced Vi to go to the hospital to have her baby instead of having a midwife?"

"She's determined, Mom. She wanted Willa to be her midwife and she wants me to be her doula."

"Doula," her mom scoffed. "The nurses at the hospital are paid to gather up bloody sheets and do housekeeping."

Daisy had volunteered for the job of doula. Midwives in the area often had women work with them, women who took care of the mom while the midwife took care of the baby. Daisy had volunteered to do it. Vi was her daughter. She'd taken care of her during any and every illness she'd ever had. Not that this was an illness. But she knew Vi would need a caring hand

and she could provide it, along with good nourishment and a sympathetic ear.

Her mom went on, "Maybe you haven't tried hard enough to change her mind."

Iris's back straightened and she pushed her dishes slightly away from her. "Daisy has raised Vi and Jazzi to make their own life choices. She stands back and lets them work through them. It seems to me that's the better way to handle children."

Rose's lips pursed. She clasped her hands in front of her tightly, and she looked hurt.

Daisy realized the three of them hadn't progressed at all.

After Daisy and her aunt closed the tea garden for the day, Daisy drove straight home. Foster had a late class, and she'd asked Vi to come over and join her and Jazzi for a good wholesome meal. She knew Vi certainly didn't feel like cooking these days.

After Daisy parked in the detached garage that housed two vehicles under Vi's and Foster's apartment, she walked up the path to the house. She stared up at the multi-paned window that had once been a hay hatch, and her gaze rose higher to a smaller window that let light into the attic space.

A shadow passed the hayloft window. That was Jazzi's room. The second floor had been divided into two bedrooms with a bath that had been perfect for her daughters.

The barn home with its red siding, repointed stone base, and white-trimmed windows and dormers was a comfortable home. The door was unlocked and the alarm system off. Daisy walked into her living room and heard Vi and Jazzi upstairs. Vi had moved from her old room to her new apartment over the garage, but she'd left a few belongings here. Daisy could picture a banner from Lehigh that hung over her sleek walnut desk. The drapes and spread were hues of green which were perfect for a guest room if Daisy needed it for that.

As Daisy laid her coat over the deacon's bench under one of the living room windows, she heard a meow come from the open stairway to the rear of the living room. She flipped on the wagon-wheel chandelier and she could see Pepper scampering down the stairs. Pepper, a black and white tuxedo cat, ran to her, sat before her, and meowed. It was the best kind of hello.

Daisy picked her up and nuzzled her nose in the ruff around Pepper's neck. "Have you been helping Jazzi and Vi with whatever they're doing?" she asked conversationally. She always talked to her cats as if they were humans.

Pepper rubbed her nose against Daisy's cheek and meowed again.

"I'm so glad you were. Do you want to go back upstairs and join them again?" Since Pepper didn't wiggle in her arms, she took that as a *yes*. Pepper was the cuddlier of the two cats that Daisy and her girls had adopted. Marjoram, a dark tortie with a split-colored face, couldn't abide being held for long.

Daisy glanced toward the floor-to-ceiling stone fireplace, a focal point on the east wall. The dining table and chairs, which she'd refinished herself, stood nearby. There was no light on in the kitchen. She passed through the living room, where the furniture was upholstered in green, blue, and cream. The braided blue and rust rugs, crafted by a local Amish woman, were soft under her feet.

Flipping off her shoes, she left them at the foot of the stairs. As she looked toward the upstairs, Marjoram also came to say hello and stood on one of the upper steps. One side of her face was mottled like a tortoise shell in tan, brown, and black. But the other side was completely dark brown. Colors from orange to cream spotted her back and flanks, and her chest was a creamy tan and rust, the colors also split down the center.

Again she heard Jazzi's and Violet's voices. Vi's was lower than Jazzi's.

"What are they doing?" Daisy asked Marjoram, but the cat just turned and headed back to Jazzi's bedroom.

Still carrying Pepper in her arms, Daisy walked into Jazzi's room, where her eyes grew a bit wider. Clothes were strewn all over the whitewashed bed and its powder blue spread trimmed in white.

"What's this all about?" Daisy set Pepper on the side chair where a jacket lay. Every surface seemed to be covered with clothes, including the dresser that was strewn with scarves.

Vi sat on the bench at the small white vanity, holding up a dress for Jazzi's inspection. "Jazzi's trying to decide what she'll pack next weekend for her visit with Portia, but she's second-guessing everything I propose."

Jazzi had donned one of her favorite dresses in raspberry and teal swirly patterns. It had three-quarter-length sleeves and a swingy skirt. "I'd like to take this along in case Portia and her family go to church, but I'm afraid it's too short. What do you think, Mom?"

"You'd wear it to church here, wouldn't you?"

"I have," Jazzi admitted. "But maybe people in Allentown are more conservative."

"Maybe. Do you have another choice?"

"I don't have that many dresses. I just don't wear them. And my slacks, well, they aren't the kind you'd wear to church. Some have slits at the knees, others are skinny jeans. I'm just afraid Colton will disapprove."

Ah-ha. There was the rub—Portia's husband.

Vi threw her mom a concerned look that easily said what Daisy was thinking. Jazzi had to relax about her visit or it would go south quickly. "Honey, what do you think Colton would approve of?"

"I don't know. That's the problem."

"What would Portia approve of?" Daisy inquired.

"Totally anything I wear."

"Are you asking me if you can buy a new outfit?"

"I guess I am. I don't want to use my savings."

Jazzi was saving for a car with no idea how long it would take to do it. But she was determined. She had saved tips and babysitting money and everything she made at the tea garden. So Daisy had no problem saying, "If you want a new outfit, you can buy one. Just be reasonable about it."

"I'll ask Stacy if she's free to go shopping this weekend, unless you need my help desperately at the tea garden."

"We should be fine."

Vi held up a blouse and slacks. "So what about this? You could wear it on the drive to Allentown."

"You could," Daisy agreed. "Be comfortable. The most important thing is to just be yourself."

"And if Colton doesn't like me?"

Daisy went over to her daughter and gave her a

big hug. "You can only control what you do and say, how kind you are, how understanding, how friendly. Colton's reactions are *his* problem."

"I don't want there to *be* a problem," Jazzi complained.

"Then just be you."

On Thursday afternoon, Daisy thought again about the advice she'd given Jazzi as she stood in Margaret Vaughn's pantry, readying tea service. Could she do more to protect her daughter from rejection or acceptance or whatever else might happen when she visited Portia and Colton?

Shaking Daisy from her reverie, Cora Sue said, "We're ready to serve the first course."

Daisy nodded as she and Cora Sue, along with Tamlyn, crossed to the dining room and set piping hot bowls of split pea and ham soup in front of Margaret Vaughn's guests. The aroma wafted along the long table, coaxing most of the guests to pick up their soup spoons.

Margaret said to Daisy, "This looks and smells wonderful."

Glenda Nurmi, the playwright, across the table from Margaret, nodded in agreement. "I've never had split pea and ham soup. Is that a local dish?"

Daniel Copeland, the assistant manager of the bank, who was sitting at the head of the table because his ego demanded it, waved a hand over the bowl as if to cool it off. "Split pea and ham is one of those things you make when you don't know what else to make. It's one of those Amish dishes that tourists go crazy for."

Cora Sue exchanged a look with Daisy that said she'd like to clobber the bank manager. Suppressing a smile, Daisy knew he could be irritating. But he was smart and had good organization skills. He'd contributed much to Chamber of Commerce meetings and the town council. He had a say in any of the projects that were either completed or forgotten in Willow Creek.

Arden Botterill, Heidi Korn, and Jasper Lazar, a resident of Willow Creek whom Daisy didn't know and who didn't have much to say, dipped into their soup.

While the guests enjoyed the first course of the tea, Daisy and Cora Sue returned to the butler's pantry to ready the second course—a ribbon salad that included pears and pecans.

At the electric water urn, Tamlyn asked, "What tea should I prepare next?"

Since Margaret had wanted a selection of teas to be available, they had served Daisy's Blend—a decaffeinated green tea infused with raspberry and vanilla—first. "Let's try Winter Surprise," Daisy answered. "It's peppermint with a slight cranberry note."

"I never knew there were so many teas," Tamlyn admitted as she opened a jar that Daisy had labeled.

"More than you can ever imagine with the blends," Cora Sue added. "Daisy mixes some of her own, but our supplier has unusual ones too. There's actually a chocolate tea."

"That would be good for the last course," Tamlyn suggested.

Daisy had been watching Tamlyn as she'd helped serve and prepare. "If you ever need another job, just come to me and ask. You're proficient in serving, and you catch on quickly to the tea garden foods."

Nodding her head, Tamlyn blushed. "Thank you." In a low voice she added, "Mrs. Vaughn doesn't often give compliments."

Without hesitation, Cora Sue smiled. "But *we* do. That's why we work together so well."

Arden, who had just entered the butler's pantry from the dining area, overheard Tamlyn's last statement as well as Cora Sue's. With a frown, she practically whispered, "I don't know how this group is ever going to put on a production. Everyone has ideas on how we should do one thing or another." She looked at Daisy. "God bless Jonas for taking over set management. If he hadn't done that, we'd never get a set to work."

With a twinkle in her eye, Daisy reminded Arden, "At one time, Jonas had to deal with criminals."

Arden burst out laughing. "That's true. This group can't be much different. I do wish Margaret had invited the New York duo as well as the volunteer crew, but I guess that would have been too expensive."

Noticing Arden glancing around, Cora Sue asked, "Do you need something?"

"Yes. We need more honey."

"Coming right up," Tamlyn assured her as she picked up the honeypot and Arden followed her into the dining room.

Daisy looked over the checklist she'd laid on the counter in the butler's pantry. Back in the kitchen, she realized tea service was moving along well. Good food seemed to calm everyone's conflicts. The savory course had consisted of mini-quiches, crab puffs, and a barbecued chicken bite wrapped in bacon. No one seemed to have any complaints, and Daisy breathed a sigh of relief.

Now Daisy, Cora Sue, and Tamlyn were preparing dessert plates with apple gingerbread with clotted cream when Daisy suggested, "Tamlyn, will you help Cora Sue and me serve this? It's their last course, and everyone can be served at the same time that way."

"No problem," Tamlyn assured her.

However, when they returned to the dining room to freshen the table before bringing in dessert, Daisy noticed several chairs were empty. With raised brows, she looked to Heidi for an explanation.

Heidi let Margaret answer. Margaret let out a long, frustrated sigh. "Daniel needed a smoke. Can you believe a man that smart doesn't understand he's killing himself?"

Heidi said, "He's addicted, Margaret, and he doesn't want to change."

Margaret rolled her eyes. "Just like a man. Arden decided she needed fresh air, even though it's as cold as the North Pole out there. She and Glenda had a few words."

Heidi explained, "I think Arden wants a bigger role or at least more words to say."

"And Jasper said he wanted to take a peek into Rowan's library."

Tamlyn had returned to the kitchen and now brought out a tray with three teapots. She set them on the table.

"And where's Glenda?" Daisy asked.

Margaret explained, "She's wandering about somewhere. Something about back strain, and she needed to stand and walk every once in a while."

Cora Sue sidled up to Daisy. "I'm going to take a powder room break."

Daisy picked up the water pitcher and began refilling glasses on the table. She heard the ding-dong of a phone chime and realized it was coming from somewhere on Margaret. Margaret reached into the pocket of her midi-length camel skirt and pulled out her phone. A deep worried expression crossed her face when she checked the screen.

She tossed to Daisy, "Since everyone's taking a break, I'm going to answer this." Her voice was terse as she left the room.

It wasn't any business of Daisy's whether Margaret took the call or not.

After Daisy finished filling the water glasses, she used a crumb remover and cleaned up the table-cloth. She wanted the last course to be perfect and one they would all remember.

Tamlyn removed soiled napkins and laid down fresh ones.

"I'll get clean spoons and forks from the butler's pantry," Daisy told Tamlyn. She'd also look over her checklist one last time.

"I can't wait to start on your dessert," Heidi announced. "If you expect everyone here for the last course, you're sadly mistaken."

Daisy, hoping that wasn't true, spoke with Heidi for a while, willing the other guests to return soon. Then she walked through the huge farmhouse kitchen to the butler's pantry without hurrying.

However, when she reached the butler's pantry, the paneled door was closed.

Was Margaret inside on the phone?

She put her ear to the heavy wood door but could hear nothing.

She rapped, but there was no answer.

Daisy slowly turned the knob and the door creaked open.

She froze.

Cold chills raced up and down her spine.

Margaret Vaughn lay on the floor. The sight of the blood that had poured from the area of Margaret's heart choked Daisy. The sight of the clotted cream spilled over Margaret's chest filled her with nausea and horror.

Her gaze shifted to the brushed nickel knife holder on the counter. The middle knife—which Daisy suspected was the largest in the set—was missing.

As if she couldn't help herself, her eyes darted to Margaret again as she rushed forward to check for a pulse. She pressed hard against Margaret's neck, but she couldn't find one.

As she reached in her pocket for her phone, she realized she could never use clotted cream again . . . for anything.

Chapter Four

Daisy had closed the door of the butler's pantry. She knew better than to touch a crime scene. No one else should go in there, at least not until the police arrived. She'd called 9-1-1 and emergency services should be on their way.

Everyone was in shock, speaking at once over each other. Cora Sue had found Daisy at the butler's pantry door. After Daisy stammered what she'd found, Cora Sue had called everyone into the dining room.

Daisy was still shaking. It was hard to believe someone had apparently stabbed Margaret and she'd bled out so quickly.

Daisy put her phone to her ear again. Still in shock, her mind not firing on all cylinders, she realized she had to press Jonas's number for him to answer. Once she did, she was mute.

"Daisy, is that you?"

When she still didn't answer, he said a bit louder, "Daisy. Answer me."

His voice in a directive must have done it. "I've never found a body before," she murmured.

There was a beat of silence.

"It's awful, Jonas. It's just awful. How did you do this for a living?"

"Tell me where you are," he suggested gently, as if she were on the verge of breaking down.

She was. She still hadn't recovered from her last encounter with a murderer. Jonas had diagnosed her with PTSD symptoms. After reading about the syndrome, she'd realized he was right. Her major symptom—she couldn't stand to be in a confined space.

"I'm at Margaret's for the tea. We were almost finished. I was going to serve dessert. But Margaret received a call and then I went to the butler's pantry. I think she'd been stabbed, Jonas. There was so much blood and clotted cream all over her."

"You're sure she's dead?" He sounded as if he hadn't wanted to ask the question, but did anyway.

She looked down at her hand where clotted cream had congealed. "I checked her pulse. There was none. It looked like a knife was missing from the set on the counter. There was so much blood," she said again.

"If the knife wasn't embedded . . . if the killer took it with him or her, that's why she bled out so fast," Jonas said, almost to himself. "You called the police?"

"Of course."

"I'm on my way. Keep talking to me."

She didn't know what to say. So as Jonas got into his car and drove to her, she told him who was at Margaret's house, what she had served, and what everyone had talked about.

Finally, when Jonas arrived, he rushed past everyone to the butler's pantry.

Daisy had placed a kitchen stool there to sit on and guard the room. Now she rose to her feet and stepped into his arms. When she circled his neck, he held her tight.

Glancing over her shoulder, he asked, "Is that where it happened?"

Cora Sue was beside him in a minute. "In there. That's where it happened. None of us heard anything. Wouldn't Margaret have screamed when someone stabbed her?"

Daisy was shaking so hard she knew Jonas could feel it. She felt his deep breath when he took it. He'd left Philadelphia exactly because he hadn't wanted to be involved in crime scenes. Now here he was . . . because of her.

Others began asking questions of him. Daniel Copeland called loudly, "Are you in contact with the police? Who's handling this?"

Glenda said shakily, "I can't believe she's gone."

Heidi asked, "Do we all have to stay here?"

Daisy knew the answers to most of their questions, but she was in no condition to give out information. With his arm around her, Jonas took her to the dining room and told her to sit.

Then he said to the others, "None of you can leave. The police will want to question each of you and take your statements."

Daisy heard the protests.

"But I don't know anything."

"I wasn't even in the dining room."

"I wasn't anywhere near the butler's pantry."

With his hand on Daisy's shoulder, Jonas announced, "Anyone who was here in this house is going to be questioned. So make yourselves comfortable and don't go near the butler's pantry."

As he was about to go to the butler's pantry door again, Daisy could see him stop and listen. He heard the sirens and she did too. Not long after, both Detective Rappaport and Detective Willet came rushing in.

Detective Morris Rappaport began barking orders as soon as he walked into the house. Practically before Daisy could blink, he put Zeke Willet in charge of the crime scene, separated all the witnesses, and demanded that Daisy follow him to Margaret's study. He wouldn't let Jonas accompany her.

Her legs still felt a little bit wobbly. She sank into the first chair inside the door. It was a steel gray leather club chair, but she hardly took notice.

Instead of taking a position at the desk, Detective Rappaport pulled another club chair directly opposite her. "You're awfully white," he noticed. "You aren't going to faint on me, are you?"

In spite of her resolve to stay strong, she felt as weak as one of her underbrewed teas. "Do you carry smelling salts?"

He scowled. "No, but from all that paraphernalia out there, I could probably get you a cup of tea."

In spite of not wanting to be a problem for him, she said, "That would be good. Hot and strong."

Rappaport took out his phone from his suit jacket, scrolled to his contacts, and quickly sent a text message. With a gentler expression he tucked his phone away. "Do you think you could answer some questions?"

Although she felt cold to her core, and somewhat removed from reality, she nodded.

Removing a small notebook and pen from his inside jacket pocket, he directed, "Start at the beginning. Tell me why you were here, your impression of everyone else who was here, and what happened."

Daisy's thoughts raced until she looked into Rappaport's keen eyes and began. The first part was easy. Margaret had hired Daisy to prepare a tea service for herself and the cast members. Daisy easily gave her impressions of the service and the tea, the food they'd served, and how everyone had enjoyed it.

A patrol officer, Bart Cosner, brought her a cup of tea. "I didn't put anything in it."

Daisy tried to smile and thanked him. Hot and strong, she suspected. Cora Sue had brewed it for her.

Rappaport continued with questions now and then, such as "Was there any tension around the table?" "Did anyone argue?" "Was everybody at the table when the murder happened?"

This part of the interrogation was more difficult. Daisy had to remember who was where. With her head beginning to throb, she told him that she and Cora Sue and Tamlyn were at the table along with Margaret until the hostess received a phone call. Daniel Copeland had gone out for a smoke. Glenda Nurmi had excused herself to stretch back muscles. Heidi Korn stayed and Arden Botterill had gone outside for fresh air. Cora Sue had gone to the powder room but came right back.

"And Jasper Lazar?" the detective asked, looking at his notebook.

"I think he went to Rowan's library."

"I suppose this house has several entrances."

"It does, including a back entrance into the butler's pantry. But the thing is, there are steps going upstairs at the butler's pantry too. So anyone could have taken the front stairs, gone up and around, and come back down the back stairs into the pantry."

"And left by the back door."

Daisy nodded. "Right. This is complicated," she told Detective Rappaport.

"Murder usually is. And how does Jonas figure into this?" Rappaport asked.

"He doesn't. While I was waiting for you, I called him."

"Why?"

"You have to ask?"

Rappaport stuffed his notebook back into his pocket. "No, I suppose I don't. Besides being your significant other, he's helped you solve four other murders."

At that moment, Zeke Willet walked into the study. He didn't knock first. With short blond hair and dark brown eyes, his arrogantly square jaw said he didn't have to knock.

"Don't you think that's kind of weird?" he asked Detective Rappaport. "Mrs. Swanson has been involved in four other murder cases, and now this one. Finding bodies and being around killers seem to be her MO."

Daisy had had arguments with Zeke Willet before. Suddenly she felt all her fight come back. "This is the first body I've found."

"You sound proud of that," he returned. "As if it's some kind of accomplishment."

She knew her cheeks were reddening because her face was getting hot.

Rappaport must have seen that. "Willet, are you faulting Mrs. Swanson because she has good deductive skills, maybe better than we do?"

"She's been lucky," Zeke Willet returned.

But Rappaport just rubbed his chin. "I'm not sure *lucky* enters into it. She knows how to ask questions, and she doesn't treat everyone she meets as if they were hostile witnesses. You might be better served to do the same."

Zeke Willet's face turned ruddy. "Why are you encouraging her?"

"I'm not encouraging her," Detective Rappaport protested. "I've warned her more times than I can count to stay away from our cases. But the truth is, now and then, she provides us with good information. So don't look a gift horse in the mouth. How's the crime scene coming?"

Still scowling, the detective answered, "It's going to take a while. We can't move everyone outside because it's simply too cold. Officer Schwartz has interrogated a few of the witnesses in his patrol car and kept the heat running. We let them go home."

"Which ones?"

"Cora Sue Bauer and Mr. Copeland. Tamlyn went to her quarters upstairs. Schwartz is finishing with Miss Korn now. Speaking of hostile, Arden Botterill is acting as if she had something to hide . . . Glenda Nurmi too. I questioned both of them. They're all coming down to the station tomorrow to sign their statements."

Daisy doubted Arden had anything to hide. She simply didn't like being questioned.

Suddenly Jonas stood in the doorway to the study. His gaze took them all in at a glance. "Are you finished with Daisy?" he asked Detective Rappaport.

"I might have to question her again tomorrow, or Zeke will."

Daisy felt her phone vibrate in the pocket of her

apron. It had a reverberating tuba sound that let her hear it even when the tea garden was busy. Throughout questioning, she'd kept the phone on vibrate. Now she took it from her pocket and started when she saw the caller ID on the screen. It was Vi.

"I have to take this," she said.

Rappaport motioned Zeke outside the door into the hallway. Jonas stood by Daisy's chair.

"Mom, I've gone into labor. I called Willa and she's on her way. Can you come?"

"How far apart are the contractions?"

"Four minutes. Does that mean the baby's going to come soon? They're really strong."

"Maybe. Maybe not. I'll be there in under ten minutes. Hold tight, honey."

When Daisy looked up at Jonas, he asked, "Is Vi in labor?"

She nodded.

Holding her arm, Jonas led her past Detective Rappaport and Detective Willet. He explained, "Daisy's going to be a grandmother. If you have any questions, you'll have to call her tomorrow."

Both men looked surprised . . . but neither uttered a word.

In spite of his former law enforcement training, or maybe because of it, Jonas sped Daisy to the apartment over her garage while she texted Jazzi to come home directly from school. They parked in the driveway, then Daisy jumped out of the car, ran inside the garage and up the stairs. Her heart pounded and not just from running.

Foster met her at the head of the stairs.

The apartment was decidedly tight on space. It

was one open room really, except for a bedroom that
had a connecting bath with a sink, commode, and
walk-in shower. When the architect had consulted
with Vi and Foster, they'd decided to design a bigger
bedroom rather than to try to wall off space for a
nursery. A screen separated the couple's area from
the crib. They were hoping that by the end of the
baby's first year they could rent a bigger place somewhere else.

"How is she?" Daisy asked breathlessly.

"She's asking for you," Foster said, looking
stressed out.

"But Willa's here?"

"Yes, and she said everything's normal, whatever
the heck that means."

"Let's go find out." Daisy headed for the bedroom
area.

Jonas reached the apartment as Daisy was ready to
head into the bedroom. He called to her. "Do you
want me to stay or go?"

Would Jonas rather go to his own place and wait to
hear about the baby, or did he really want to stay
here with her? "It's up to you," she said when their
eyes met.

"I'll stay," he said. "I can be handy if you need
something special."

"Thank you." It was all she could manage before
she turned to go to her daughter and the baby she
was about to deliver.

Daisy knew that Willa had attended the midwifery
program at the University of Pennsylvania. She had two
certifications, one given by the American Midwifery
Certification Board, and another to be a women's
health nurse practitioner. Vi had asked Willa a variety
of questions before hiring her: *Do you have experience*

with turning babies? Do you do gestational diabetes screening? What is your hospital transfer rate?

Vi had also asked herself questions to see if Willa was a good fit. Would she want Willa to be her friend? Did she allow all the questions Vi and Foster wanted to ask? Did Vi enjoy being with Willa? How did Foster respond to her? Vi had ticked off all the boxes with Willa and decided she'd be more than comfortable with her. Foster had been positive about their interactions too . . . as well as Daisy.

Daisy liked Willa. She found her intelligent, experienced, compassionate, and caring. But she was still worried. She knew birth was a natural process, but Mother Nature had her quirks.

At Violet's side now, Daisy's attention transferred away from the murder, away from the awful sight of Margaret's body, to what was happening in the present moment. The pain on her daughter's face and the anticipation of seeing her first grandchild born was all that mattered. As expected, Willa was monitoring everything about the baby, from its heartbeat to its position to its journey through the birth canal.

To Daisy's surprise, Jonas was a big help. For the next few hours he made and brought ice chips to the doorway so Daisy could have them ready for Vi. Jazzi came in, eager to help too. Using the stackable washer and dryer in the back of the garage, she made sure her mom and Willa were constantly supplied with clean towels and linens.

Jazzi tried to distract Vi by talking about anything and everything.

Foster stayed by Vi's side for the first three hours. She clung to his hand during contractions until he lost circulation in his fingers. Daisy could see Foster was awed and unnerved by the birthing process. She was afraid Vi was holding back her reactions because Foster was there.

Taking a short break herself, Daisy went to the kitchen, where Jonas was unloading the dishwasher. She said, "It's intense in there, and there's no way to tell how much longer Vi will be in labor. Each time she has a contraction, Foster looks as if he's going to faint. It will get worse before the baby's born."

"What's the midwife doing for her?"

"She's massaging her back, having her walk around the room and sit on one of those big exercise balls. Jazzi is encouraging Vi through all of it. The idea of having a midwife is for her to encourage the family to be part of the birth. But Foster is so emotionally involved, I think he's freaking out."

"What if I take Foster for a walk and encourage him to call Gavin?"

"That would be great. Not too long. Merely long enough so he gets some fresh air and braces a bit and lets Gavin know what's happening."

Jonas tenderly touched Daisy's cheek. "And how are you?"

"As long as I don't think, I'm fine."

He smiled. "Not thinking is an impossibility for you."

"It is, but thinking about the baby—if we have everything for the layette, what Vi and Foster might name him—keeps me from thinking about the scene we left at Margaret's house."

Jonas brought Daisy in for a hug. "You didn't need that after what happened last time."

"I didn't go looking for this, Jonas."

"No, you didn't, and you can stay out of the police investigation."

She nodded, rubbing her cheek against his flannel

shirt. "I will." She raised her head. "I know they're probably going to ask me more questions, but after that and I sign my statement, that's it."

Daisy had brought a carafe with her from Vi's room. Stepping away from Jonas, she filled it with water. "I'm going to go back in. I'll send Foster out. Vi is seven centimeters dilated, so birth can happen fast or it could take another couple of hours."

Jonas nodded his understanding. "I'll let Foster blow off steam and then we'll be back."

Before Daisy moved too far away, Jonas pulled her in for another long hug, then he let her go.

"Thank you," she murmured.

"For what?"

"For being here."

He didn't have to say the words *I told you I would be.* Maybe she was starting to trust him. Maybe she was beginning to believe in him.

About a half hour later when Jonas returned with Foster, Foster's cheeks were red from the cold, but he looked steadier. He looked as if he was ready to face whatever was coming. A baby was going to change his world, and he seemed to realize that. Maybe his talk with his dad, who was pragmatic, had reinforced that fact.

Two hours later with a cry of joy of her own, Daisy watched the infant being delivered. With tears on her cheeks, she realized she was now the grand-mother of Samuel Ryan Cranshaw.

They all had tears in their eyes . . . even Jonas.

Daisy would never forget the expression on Vi's and Foster's faces when little Sammy had been laid in Vi's arms. Willa had stayed until Sammy had successfully breastfed and she'd given Vi other instructions. Gavin had stopped in to give his support but hadn't stayed long. Jonas had left to take Jazzi to school and go to work. He'd only had a few hours of sleep on the couch, but he'd told Daisy he was used to that. As a detective, he caught sleep when he could. Jazzi had insisted she was fine. She'd crash tonight.

Midmorning, Daisy walked into the kitchen, little Sammy cuddled in her arms. She could lay him in the crib. Vi and Foster were sleeping. Still . . . she couldn't stop looking at the baby and drinking him in—the little wisps of medium brown hair, his tiny button nose, his pudgy cheeks, and the definite cleft in the chin that was just like Foster's. He was indeed a miracle.

Daisy's phone vibrated in her pocket. Sinking down onto the sofa, she made sure her arm was propped just right with the baby at a comfortable angle. Maybe somebody at the tea garden needed something. Or maybe it was Gavin. She'd videotaped the birth and texted it to him as soon as Sammy had arrived. He'd said he'd stop in as soon as he could.

After Daisy checked the number on the screen and the caller ID, Zeke Willet's name popped up.

"Hello?" she said tentatively, watching Sammy's eyelids flutter.

"Mrs. Swanson, it's Detective Willet."

"Yes?"

"I need to ask you a few more questions. Can you come down to the station?"

"I'm sorry, I can't." Before the detective could decide that she was being antagonistic, she explained, "My daughter had her baby last night. I'm taking care of Sammy while she and her husband sleep. We were up most of the night."

Detective Willet seemed at a loss for words. "I see. So you don't know when you can get away?"

Daisy really did want to cooperate. "You're welcome to come here. I'm in the apartment above the garage on my property. I had a doorbell installed at the side garage door, but don't bother ringing that. Just text me when you're close and I'll know you're coming."

"Are you sure that will be all right with your daughter?"

"If she's awake and taking care of Sammy, you and I can go down to the back of the garage. It's not a problem."

"I'll be there in fifteen."

Before he'd left, Jonas had brewed a pot of coffee. With one arm, Daisy removed two mugs from the mug tree and set them on the small counter. Before Jazzi had left for school this morning, she'd gone home to feed Marjoram and Pepper and take a shower. She'd also fetched a container of blueberry scones from Daisy's freezer.

Daisy had prepared them for an occasion just like this. After she'd set them on the table, along with two dessert plates, forks, and napkins, she heard the downstairs side door to the garage open.

Zeke Willet called up the steps. "Mrs. Swanson?"

He kept his voice to the bare minimum.

At the head of the stairs, she motioned him to come up. When he reached her, he seemed taken aback by the baby in her arms. He appeared mesmerized by the tiny blue trucks running across the receiving blanket that swaddled Sammy.

"What's his name?" he asked hoarsely.

"Samuel Ryan Cranshaw. Samuel for Foster's grand-father and Ryan for my husband."

Zeke's eyes met hers. She saw something there that was softer, gentler, and more caring than what usually manifested itself. But then he cleared his throat and became all business. "About those questions."

She motioned to the table, went there, and sat. Then she told him, "Why don't you pour us mugs of coffee. Creamer's in the refrigerator if you need it."

"I really didn't come for—"

"I know what you came for, Detective, but I've been up most of the night and coffee will help keep me awake. I thought you might enjoy some too."

His look was a tad sheepish as he went to the counter and poured the two mugs.

"A teaspoon of sugar in mine, please." She nod-ded to the sugar bowl next to the coffeepot.

After he brought the mugs to the table, he kept his gaze away from the baby and began questioning her, particularly about the crime scene. But to her surprise, she couldn't remember much. She had blanks where before there had been vivid pictures. Zeke, however, didn't question her memory. He'd been taking his notes on an app on his phone.

Now he slipped it back into his jacket pocket. "You told Rappaport more in your first interview."

"I guess it was fresh in my mind then."

She rocked Sammy as if the motion could soothe her too. What was wrong with her? She didn't forget important things. "Detective, I'm not trying to keep anything from you. I promise."

He fleetingly touched her arm and then leaned back in his chair. "I know you're not. You're having a symptom of PTSD. Do you know about that?"

"I've read articles. Veterans who return from war have flashbacks. They have startle responses all the time. Sometimes they overreact."

With a serious expression that aged him, he said, "It's more complicated than that. One of the symptoms is blanks in memory. Let's face it. You had a traumatic event and then you had another. Even though the birth of your grandson was joyous, you were up all night."

"Are you saying after I get some sleep that I'll remember? That might not happen for a while."

"You'll be helping your daughter?"

"As much as she needs me. They grow up fast, Detective Willet. Way too fast."

Zeke looked so sad for a moment, she almost asked him what was wrong. But she didn't know him well enough for that. His tension with Jonas affected his interactions with Daisy too.

To her surprise he suggested, "I think you should talk with Jonas. He knows how to handle witnesses with PTSD. Besides, I think there's an element between the two of you that you and I don't have."

"And that is?"

"Trust. You trust him. You don't trust *me*."

She was quick to say, "It's not that I don't trust you. I don't know you."

"No. No, you don't." He abruptly stood and then pushed the chair in. He held up his hand as if telling her to stay seated. "I can see myself out. If you do remember anything else, give me a call."

With that, the detective descended the stairs and left by the garage's side door. His whole visit had been a bit . . . disconcerting, and she wasn't even sure why.

Chapter Five

Rose stopped in that evening to see Vi and the baby. Daisy had made a light supper of roasted chicken pieces, fresh vegetables, and smashed potatoes. Vi had always liked them. But Vi, dressed in her robe and pajamas, hardly ate anything.

While Daisy's mom cooed over Sammy, Vi said, "Since you're holding and watching him, Gram, I'm going to lie down for a little."

Daisy let Vi go to the bedroom without a word. She didn't know what to say. Vi's attitude wasn't that of a joyous new mother.

Foster looked after his wife, leaned back at the small table for four, then let out a sigh. "It's normal that she's tired and needs rest, right?" Foster seemed to be looking for answers of his own.

"Of course," Daisy said. "Willa was here this afternoon to examine Vi and the baby and check everything out. She insists everything's as expected. Even the breastfeeding is going well."

Foster looked a little embarrassed that they were

talking about that in front of him. Changing the subject, he said, "You'll have to show me what you put on that chicken. Then maybe I can make it for us."

"I'll write down the instructions for you." She paused a few moments. "Having a baby is a trauma to a woman's whole body. Besides the actual physicality of it, there are all the hormone changes. You might have heard stories about women working in the fields, having a baby, and going back to working in the fields. But I think those legends are highly exaggerated," she said with a smile.

Foster smiled back. "I don't expect her to go back to work, not unless she wants to, not unless she feels ready. But I thought she'd be . . . happier."

Just then Sammy started fussing. Rose made a shushing sound and rocked him in her arms. He soon stopped. She said, "Vi has to learn the tricks of motherhood."

"Tricks?" Foster asked.

"Once a woman has a baby," Daisy explained, "there's no separation between her and her child. I know you and Vi decided to have the crib in your bedroom. But what that means is, every time Sammy burps, sighs, cries, or maybe even turns over, Vi's going to be awake. She'll have a sixth sense that connects her to him. That's just the way motherhood is."

Rose studied Daisy for a few more moments, and Daisy couldn't understand the expression on her mom's face. Finally, Rose spoke. "Those tricks I mentioned have to do with learning her child's habits and sounds and communication efforts. Some mothers tune in right away, but with others it takes time. Once Vi does, she won't be so anxious. She'll have more confidence. She won't be afraid so much of the time."

"Afraid of what?" Foster asked, not understanding at all.

"Afraid she's not doing everything right," Daisy explained. "Moms beat themselves up constantly because they feel they can be doing better. Make sure you give Vi plenty of sincere compliments, not fake ones. Don't tell her that her hair looks good when it's a mess. But if you see her do something particularly sweet with Sammy, say so."

"This is a lot to take in," Foster murmured, staring at his son. Then he reached out a hand and touched the little boy's cheek with one long finger. "Thank you for the casseroles, Mrs. Gallagher. They should hold us over for a week."

Rose studied him for a few seconds, then suggested, "Why don't you call me Gram like Vi does. After all, you're now my grandson-in-law."

"I'd be happy to," Foster said.

"Don't hesitate to call me if you and Vi need some relief. You're going to continue with your classes, yes?" Rose asked.

"I'll be finished with this semester in December. Actually, I was thinking about taking off the next semester. I could work more and give Vi more help."

Daisy didn't jump into the void of that announcement, but her mother did. "Foster, you need a degree to get anywhere. You take those classes. If anything, cut back on your work schedule."

"But I can't, not if we really want to make a life on our own."

"Being on your own could cause you more problems," Rose advised. "Take this help while it's offered."

Daisy jumped in with different advice. "I think you should make your decisions when the time comes to make them. Don't try to plan out the next year. It could be that by January or February, Vi might want to get back into the workforce. With a baby, there's no knowing what will come up. For now, just do the best you can with your classes, and fill your holiday break with lots of family time as well as work."

Foster's voice was thick with emotion when he said, "You're all being so great about this. Even my dad has seemed to come around! And when he stopped in this morning, I actually thought he was going to cry. My father."

"He might pretend to have a suit of armor," Daisy said, "but I think he's got some marshmallow in his heart."

"I will *not* tell my dad you said that. He would be mortified."

They all laughed.

"If you two don't mind staying with Vi and the baby, I'd like to drive to the convenience store and pick up strawberry ice cream. It's Vi's favorite. We need a couple of odds and ends too. Would that be okay?"

"I can stay as long as Vi and the baby need me," Rose said. She turned to Daisy. "Especially if you want to get home to Jazzi."

"We'd really like to handle the baby on our own tonight," Foster said.

Daisy agreed that was probably best. "I'll stop over in the morning to see how everything went."

Foster took his jacket from a hook on the wall and grabbed his keys from a dish on the counter. With a wave, he went down the stairs.

After Foster left, Rose turned to Daisy. "I know these young folks want to do everything on their own, but if I can't convince them to take help, you have to."

In her mother's voice was a vehemence Daisy didn't often hear.

"Right now," Rose went on, "Foster's still in wonder that he's a dad. Vi is tired from pregnancy and the birth. If Sammy is at all demanding, they both could have rough times."

Daisy had never heard her mom talk this way before, and she wasn't sure what was behind it. "Up until now they've accepted help. I think they'll realize they can't do it all on their own."

Rose let the subject drop after that. As Daisy held Sammy for a while, her mother cleaned up the dishes. Daisy couldn't help but think about what her mom had said. She'd blocked off time from work over the next two weeks to help Vi and Foster if they needed it with babysitting, cooking, and running errands. But after that, they'd all just have to see what came next.

Around nine p.m. that night, Jonas texted Daisy. **Would you like a visitor?**

She texted back, **If it's you. I'm at home. Foster and Vi wanted to take care of Sammy themselves tonight.**

Be there in ten, Jonas texted back.

Daisy automatically went to the kitchen to brew a pot of tea for the two of them. Jonas wasn't particular and she knew he liked White Symphony tea, so that's what she chose. The tea was ready, and she'd cut apple gingerbread slices and placed them on two dessert plates by the time Jonas rang the bell. She couldn't seem to break him of that habit.

Yet being careful as he'd taught her to be, she checked the camera app on her phone. Yep, it was

Jonas. Instead of using the door intercom to talk to him, she ran to the door and opened it.

He took her into his arms and gave her a huge hug and then a kiss. That kiss was better than all the desserts in her tearoom.

"Rough day?" he asked.

Tonight Jonas wore a black T-shirt, blue jeans, and a black leather bomber jacket. She didn't know any other man who could look so protective, dangerous, yet safe at the same time. Raising herself up on her tiptoes, she kissed him again.

He looked surprised but pleased. "It must have been a *really* rough day."

"Take off your jacket and I'll tell you about it over a cup of tea. Jazzi's already ensconced in her bedroom for the night."

After he shrugged out of his jacket and slung it over a chair, he asked, "Where's my feline welcoming committee?"

His smile made Daisy feel all warm and cozy inside. "They're cuddled up with Jazzi. They miss Vi and I just got home a little while ago. My mom was still with Foster and Sammy when I left."

They both took seats on chairs at the island. "Did you and your mom have a heart-to-heart?"

"Not exactly. But I saw a side of her I don't know if I've ever seen before."

Jonas appeared to note the cat-decorated teapot on the island, as well as the slices of apple gingerbread. "You mean the way she handled Sammy?"

"Yes, that. And her concern for Violet as a new mom."

"That seems only natural."

"I suppose. The good thing is, we didn't argue.

That tension that's been there ever since Vi's wedding reception seems to have lessened a little bit."

"Good."

After Jonas poured tea into mugs, Daisy added a spoonful of honey to hers and stirred. "I think Mom's concerned about Vi, and maybe I am too."

Picking up his mug, Jonas took a cautious sip. He set it down. "The midwife was there and checked out Vi today. Did she raise any concerns?"

"No, but Vi doesn't seem to have the joy a new mom should have."

Jonas shifted on his stool. "Can you explain that to someone who hasn't been a parent?"

Relieved Jonas could talk about what had happened to his significant other now—she'd been pregnant against his wishes when she'd been killed in action—Daisy saw he wanted an honest answer to his question. "I can try."

She moved her dish of gingerbread in front of her but didn't touch it. "Where to begin. The birth of a child, even one as uncomplicated as Vi's was, takes every ounce of energy and every speck of emotion that a woman can possibly feel . . . and give. After I had to give that last push when I had Vi, I actually felt like I was going to die. Maybe it's a little too poetic to say, but my old self died. The whole experience was physically taxing and I felt like a wreck. The thing was, though, as soon as Vi was laid in my arms, all I thought about was her. It was like an adrenaline rush—better than riding on a roller coaster, eating whipped cream, or even having sex."

Jonas laughed. "That explains it pretty well."

"It all summed up to be the most joy a woman can feel. I haven't seen that with Vi. Oh, she followed everything Willa told her in order to urge Sammy to breastfeed. And even that went pretty well. Every two or three hours, she rouses herself, takes him in her arms, and feeds him again. It will be that way around the clock unless or until she and Foster decide she can pump breast milk and feed the baby a bottle. If they make that decision, then Foster or a babysitter could take over the feedings." Daisy snuck a peek at Jonas and asked, "Is that too much information?"

He just grinned at her. "Not really." He sobered. "Do you think the whole experience is overwhelming Vi?"

"That could be some of it. She's as young as I was when I had her. But I didn't *have* to get married. Ryan and I didn't have to be careful because we wanted to have a baby. I put my degree aside to marry Ryan and have Vi, knowing I would finish it later. But Vi's in a place where she has no idea what's going to happen in her future. Sure, she can finish her education eventually, but she might not have the confidence, willpower, and motivation to do it. The problem is—I don't know how to help her."

"Vi is a determined young woman like you were. The difference? You knew exactly what you wanted and Vi's still figuring it out. All you can do is watch and listen and do what you think is best. Maybe even in consultation with your mom."

Automatically Daisy frowned. After forking a piece of the apple gingerbread into her mouth, she shrugged. "Maybe."

"So you're worried about Vi, but your visit with your mom wasn't too bad."

"It wasn't. But I had a visit from someone else today. Zeke."

"You knew *that* would be coming." Jonas began eating his gingerbread.

"I did. Maybe not so soon. Anyway, he wanted me

to come down to the station and I told him I couldn't. So he came to Vi's and Foster's apartment."

"Was that okay with you?"

"Yes, it was fine. Actually, both Vi and Foster were sleeping at that point, and Sammy slept in my arms the whole time."

"So what upset you?"

"I didn't say anything upset me."

"Daisy."

When he drawled her name, she knew she couldn't hide much from him. "He wanted me to remember what happened."

"And?" Jonas pressed.

"And I couldn't."

After Jonas finished his gingerbread, he laid down his fork and reached out his hand to clasp her arm. "What do you mean you couldn't? You told me what happened."

"I told you what happened *before* I found the body. But I went blank when Zeke asked me what I had seen."

Jonas slid his hand down her arm to her hand. "Now I understand. That can happen. Seeing Margaret's body was a shock. In a way, it froze your brain. But memories are in there if you want to retrieve them."

"You mean like with hypnosis?"

"Oh, I don't think you have to go that far. I don't think they're buried. I just don't think you want to remember that sight, do you?"

"Of course I don't. On the other hand, if I can help the detectives solve this, I'll do anything I can. Zeke made a suggestion."

Jonas's frown cut deep lines around his mouth. "Good or bad?"

She took in a breath and exhaled. "He said if I tried to remember with someone I trusted, maybe the details would become clear. He suggested I try and do it with you."

As if he wasn't surprised by the idea, he asked, "Do you want to?"

"Yes. I want to find out who the murderer is."

"Do you trust me?"

When Daisy hesitated a second, Jonas frowned, but asked another version of the question. "Do you trust me as a detective to do this with you?"

"Yes."

"Okay. Let's go into the living room. I want you to relax."

"I can't relax in here?"

"In here you're thinking about brewing tea, making a snack for Vi or Jazzi, what you're going to serve tomorrow at the tea garden. Correct?"

"Yep."

He stood and beckoned to her. "Come with me."

Instead of taking her to the sofa, he took her to the armchair. "Settle in," he advised in a gentle voice.

She hadn't closed her eyes and she was watching him watch her. "What are you looking for?"

"You're a terrible subject," he joked.

"That kind of flattery will get you everywhere," she grumbled.

His lips twitched up in a smile. "I know what I'm looking for, and when I see it, I'll know you're relaxed. Don't think about me."

"Your voice is a disembodied spirit," she said as if in a trance.

But he took her seriously. "If you want to think of it that way, you can."

"Let's do this," she acquiesced.

After a few heartbeats, Jonas suggested, "Breathe in through your nose and out through your mouth six times . . . slowly."

This time Daisy didn't argue, she just did it. However, on the third breath, he requested, "Slower."

So she slowed it down.

"Now flex your hands, wiggle your fingers, and simply let them rest on the arms of the chair."

It was easy to do that. To her surprise, when she did, her shoulders relaxed a bit too.

"Now I want you to imagine a blue light on top of your head. It has a bit of warmth. It's going to start at the top of your head and slowly, slowly go down your body. As it does, the muscles under the light relax. You can feel your eyes relaxing . . . your cheek muscles . . . your jaw. Take in one of those deep breaths and let it out again."

She did.

"The blue light has reached your neck and shoulders. Take a good long time and let it into every muscle and fiber so they relax well. Now the light is shining down your chest and then your arms . . . your stomach . . . your thighs . . . your knees . . . your shins . . . your feet . . . your toes. All you hear and feel is silence and warmth. The longer you sit here, the deeper the relaxation becomes. Not only your body is relaxed now, but your mind too."

Jonas's voice was still soothing when he added, "This exercise is going to be easy for you. Memories will come sliding back in color. You'll notice details you hadn't noticed before. Take in another one of those deep breaths and let it out."

All Daisy was aware of was following the timbre and the timing of Jonas's voice. Each instruction became easier, and she found she was so pleasantly relaxed, she could probably fall asleep. But sleep wasn't what they were aiming for.

Gently, Jonas said, "You're at Margaret Vaughn's house again. Everyone has enjoyed the tea. You're getting ready to serve the dessert—apple gingerbread with clotted cream. Can you see that?"

Daisy nodded.

"Now you're going to help me with the next part. The guests scattered for a break. Where did Glenda Nurmi go?"

"She said she was going to stretch her back."

"How about Heidi Korn?"

"Heidi stayed at the table and Arden went outside for fresh air."

"Daniel Copeland?"

"He said he was going outside for a smoke."

"And Jasper Lazar?"

"He said he wanted to see Rowan's library."

"Why did you go to the butler's pantry?"

"Before serving dessert, I had to go to the butler's pantry to get clean silverware and to see if I forgot anything. My checklist was in there."

She remembered her intent clearly, but when she'd reached the butler's pantry—

"What did you see when you entered the butler's pantry?"

"I don't want to look."

"I know you don't want to see it again, but maybe a clue you provide will help find the murderer. Try to peek in there again. Tell me what you see."

Swirling gray memories coalesced into specific images. "Margaret was crumpled on the floor, blood at her center. Lots and lots of blood."

"Was she on her back?"

"Yes. I could see her chest and her face and her arms."

"Was the knife still in her?"

"No, but I automatically glanced to the brushed nickel knife holder up on the counter. The middle one was gone."

"Did you notice anything else unusual about Margaret's body?"

"Clotted cream had been spread over her."

"Over what part of her?"

"Over her chest, but mostly over a pin she was wearing. I'd seen her wear it before."

"What kind of pin was it?"

"It was amethyst surrounded by diamonds. It was gorgeous."

"Did she ever tell you where she got it?"

"When I admired it, I assumed her new husband bought it for her. But she told me he hadn't. She told me it had been a gift."

"From whom?"

"I don't know. I don't know if she wouldn't say or we just went on to new conversation."

"You're doing really well, Daisy. Did you notice anything else near her body?"

"There was a towel there."

"What kind of towel?"

"A hand towel from the kitchen with a rooster embroidered on it."

"When you say it was *there* . . . where was *there*?"

"It was sort of lying over the bowl of clotted cream on the counter. My guess is whoever dumped it on Margaret used the towel to wipe his or her fingerprints from the bowl."

"You're very good at this, Daisy. Is there anything else you can remember about the scene?"

"The back door was open."

"Had it been open any time before you were serving?"

"No."

Jonas laid his hand on Daisy's and she opened her eyes.

Leaning toward her, Jonas had a pleased expression on his face. "I think you resurrected a few details that will help Zeke."

She hoped so.

Daisy hadn't expected to be working at the tea garden today. But Iris had wanted some time with Vi and Sammy. Saturday could be busy, so Daisy had come in. She'd been a bit shaken up last night after she and Jonas had performed their little exercise. He'd encouraged her to call Zeke right then and there and she had, telling him what she'd remembered. It wasn't a lot, but it had been something.

Cooking was always soothing to Daisy. Between the aromas of the beef lentil soup, apple gingerbread, and snickerdoodles, she was almost able to forget the scene she'd recalled last night. Almost.

It was midmorning when Cora Sue came rushing into the kitchen, saying a customer wanted to see Daisy.

"Who is it?"

"He says his name is Rowan Vaughn."

Daisy motioned to the snickerdoodles on cooling racks. "They should be ready for the case in about five minutes."

Cora Sue nodded. "I'll take care of them."

"I won't be long," she told Tessa and Eva.

"That's not what I'm concerned about," Tessa murmured.

Tessa Miller, her kitchen manager and best friend, knew how Daisy had become involved in murder cases before this one.

As Daisy went to the tearoom, she recognized Rowan Vaughn, who was standing by the yellow tearoom's doorway. He looked like a businessman through and through. His suit appeared well cut and expensive, tailored to fit him. She recognized him because she'd seen his photo in the local papers many times with the building of the Little Theater. He was tall and thin, possibly six-three or -four. His gray hair was slicked back over his right brow, but the hair on the left side of his head was shorn shorter. It was one of the latest styles that Daisy thought cost a pretty penny to produce. His shirt was silver but he'd left the collar open. His black shoes were shiny. In some ways he looked as if he should be going to a business meeting. In others, he looked a bit lost.

He extended his hand to her. His fingers were long and as slim as he was tall. After she took his hand, she noticed an age spot next to his mouth. He was older than Margaret—older than Margaret had been.

"I'm sorry we're meeting under these circumstances," he said, looking again toward the yellow tearoom. "Do you have a few minutes? I really need to speak with you. I'll order tea or something to eat or whatever I have to do."

"You don't have to order anything. But I'd be glad to get you something." She motioned to the board above the sales counter and the sales counter itself.

"I do like tea," he said. "Margaret turned me into a tea drinker." A look of sadness came over his face. "How about black tea?"

"Milk and sugar with it?"

He shook his head. "Just plain."

Daisy motioned to Jada Green, one of their newly hired part-time servers. Jada's braids were caught up into a ponytail. Her mocha skin and her dark brown eyes complemented her high cheekbones, her full lips, and her oval face. She was in her twenties, only about five-foot-one, but always wore a smile and she knew her tea. She had taken the place of another of Daisy's servers—Karina Post—who had left Daisy's employ to pursue a nursing career.

Daisy told Jada what she needed and said they'd be in the yellow tearoom. Jada hurried away to put together Vaughn's order as well as bring a cup of tea for Daisy.

Once they were seated, Daisy said, "I know you have a lot on your mind. What can I do for you?"

"I just came from the police station and they don't have a clue who killed Margaret. I think even *I'm* a suspect. I was in town when it happened, just not at home."

"Whoever is closest to the victim is always considered first on the suspect list. I'm sorry."

"So it really is like the crime shows depict."

His question was rhetorical and didn't require an answer. He went on quickly, "Vanna told me that you've helped solve four murders."

"I'm not sure how much I helped. The police solved them. I just picked up clues along the way."

"I was going to hire a private investigator but Vanna told me to talk with you. She said you're good at this. *This* meaning solving murders."

"Oh, Mr. Vaughn—"

"Call me Rowan. Please."

"Rowan. To tell you the truth, I'm not sure I've recovered from what happened in the last case I helped solve. You really should leave this to the police. They don't want me interfering."

"You don't have to interfere, Mrs. Swanson."

"Daisy," she said automatically.

"Daisy, I know I might be at the top of their list, but I also know they have a long list. Everybody Margaret worked with at the Little Theater to start. I know about the grumblings. I didn't think it was more than that. I do know Glenda Nurmi and Margaret weren't the friends they pretended to be. They had a history. Since Margaret died, I talked with Glenda but she won't confide in me. But she possibly *would* confide in you."

When Daisy had met Glenda, she'd realized that the woman was guarded. If she had any emotions, she saved them for her acting parts . . . or her playwriting.

"I'll say again, you don't have to interfere with the police, but maybe you could whittle down that suspect list. I'll pay you."

Daisy was already shaking her head and motioning for him to stop. "No. No payment. And I'm not going to agree to help you, at least not yet."

"What will convince you?"

"I understand how desperate you are. I've seen this situation before. What I will do is talk to Vanna. Maybe she had some insights. How about if I start there?"

"The truth is—I don't know Vanna very well. She's never warmed up to me. Maybe you can find out something I can't. That would be a good start."

He took a business card from the inside pocket of his jacket and slid it over to her. "All of my numbers are on there. Please call me if you learn anything."

As Jada brought their tea and accompaniments on a tray, Daisy studied his business card and wondered if she was ready to question *anyone.*

Chapter Six

Daisy and Jazzi had gone over to Vi's apartment after Daisy's Tea Garden had closed for the day. Iris had spent the whole day with her and Sammy. As they climbed the stairs, they heard Sammy fussing. But by the time they reached the apartment, he was quiet again.

Iris was sitting in the living room, such as it was, in a platform rocker. It was small so it would fit beside the sofa.

As soon as they greeted her aunt, Daisy could see that Iris had concern on her face. Daisy went to Sammy and held her arms out for him with a grin. "How are we doing today?"

Iris brushed the stray strands of Sammy's hair over his forehead before she carefully handed him to Daisy. "It's hard to give him up after I've been holding him."

"I imagine so." Sammy had been born at seven pounds three ounces, and he fit into her arms just right. She kissed his forehead.

Iris sat down on the sofa and let Daisy take the rocker. "How's the new mom?" Daisy asked in a low voice.

Iris shook her head. "She's eating minimally. She knows she has to eat for the baby to get nourishment. And she's sleeping a lot."

Iris turned her attention to Jazzi. "Jazzi, why don't you go in and see if you can talk to her. Talk about your day, about the tea garden, about anything. Get some lights back into her eyes."

Jazzi studied her aunt. "Is this something to worry about? Are all new moms like this?"

Daisy shook her head. "Fatigue is normal. Sleep deprivation is normal. But not eating and sleeping all the time isn't normal. Go ahead and see if she'll have a conversation with you."

After Jazzi had gone to the bedroom, Daisy sighed. "I don't know what to think. Has Foster been home at all today?"

"He left after I arrived. He stopped in again before his afternoon class. He's enthusiastic and loves carrying Sammy around. But I can't even convince Vi to get dressed. She says it's not practical with breastfeeding and all."

"I'll have to call Willa and talk to her. If she stops in for a visit, maybe she and I can give Vi some strategies to get back on her feet."

After looking down at her black tennis shoes, Iris flicked a piece of lint off her indigo jeans. "I've done some reading on this."

"On having babies?" Daisy asked with a smile.

"Vi said I could use her computer. It's so much easier to read on there than my phone."

"And what did you find out?"

"If a new mom has terrific mood swings, sleeps a

lot, doesn't want to eat or eats too much, she might have more than baby blues. It could be postpartum depression."

"I've heard of that. Vi's certainly showing the symptoms. Maybe I should just call her doctor."

"I think she might become defensive if you do that. Willa might be a better bet. From what the articles say, if this kind of thing goes on for two weeks or more, that's when the mom should see a professional."

Daisy let out a long breath as she placed her thumb on Sammy's cheek and relished the feel of the purely soft baby skin. "How did you even know to look this up? I was thinking she was just tired from having to breastfeed the baby every two to three hours. Lack of sleep can cause confusion and mood swings too, not to mention hormones scrambling all over the place to rectify themselves."

Iris looked down at her shoes again. "I must have seen a talk show about it."

Daisy and Iris had never lied to each other, as far as Daisy knew. Her aunt was a straight shooter and was kindly when she did it. Now, however, the way she wouldn't meet Daisy's eyes, the way she was hesitating, convinced Daisy that something wasn't quite right. "I'll see how Vi is tonight while I'm here. Jazzi and I will stay until Foster gets home. If I see the symptoms you're seeing, I'll call Willa and set something up with her. Do you think you can handle the tea garden tomorrow if it's busy?"

"Jada wants more hours. I'm sure it won't take much convincing to have her work the afternoon shift, as well as the morning shift. We all work well together. Tessa and Eva can bake and cook, and Cora

Sue, Jada, and Jazzi can handle the tables. We'll be fine. I'll come over and pick up Jazzi in the morning."

Daisy's gaze met her aunt's. "It really does take a village, doesn't it?" Then she tucked Sammy's receiving blanket more securely around him.

"I don't want to see Willa," Vi complained Sunday morning as Daisy and Foster sat across from her at the table.

From the bedroom, they could hear Sammy crying. This apartment was small enough that Vi could hear him easily, but there was also a monitor set up on the kitchen counter.

"I'll get him," Vi said, hurrying. She pushed back her chair and rushed into the bedroom.

Foster rested his elbow on the table and pushed his hair back with his fingers. "She's like this all the time. One little sound from him and she's there, hovering over him."

New mother syndrome, Daisy thought, but didn't say it aloud.

When Vi returned, she was holding Sammy on her shoulder. He looked as if he'd fallen back to sleep.

"It's not time for his feeding yet," Foster said. "He has another hour."

"Babies aren't on a timetable," Vi shot back. "He tells us when he's wet or hungry."

"And what was wrong this time?" Foster asked.

"He . . ." Vi stopped, seemingly at a loss.

Daisy reached across the table and touched Vi's hand. "Honey, do you love Sammy?"

"Of course I do." Vi sounded outraged.

"I mean when you look at him, does a joyous love come sweeping over you? Do you realize that you and Foster created this beautiful little being?"

Tears came to Vi's eyes and she couldn't speak. When Foster put his hand on her shoulder, tears began to leak down her cheeks. "I love him. I do. But I'm so worried about him all the time. You know they talk about SIDS and laying a baby on his back so he doesn't choke, and what if he's not getting enough to eat? And what's going to happen when I have to go back to work?"

The tears ran freely now, and Daisy could see how complicated all this was for her daughter. "Vi, I'm going to say something you're probably not going to like. You're still a child yourself when it comes to life." Vi was shaking her head and Daisy squeezed her hand. "What I mean by that is you're not used to multitasking life. It was hard for me when I had you, but your dad had a good job. I was a stay-at-home mom for the time being. Your dad's mom babysat when she could to give us time alone. You haven't even had time to work up a routine. I want Willa to stop by so she can show you the steps for keeping yourself healthy as well as Sammy. You need to figure out how we can help you. Not take over for you . . . but help. You need to get out of the apartment yourself. You need to get out with the baby."

"With Sammy? He's not even a week old."

"Vi, he won't break. As long as you keep him warm and safe and fed, he'll be fine."

"And what if he has a crying fit while I'm in a public place? Not just that, but how am I going to feed him there?"

"Willa talked to you about this, but I'm not sure

you were listening. You have to become comfortable with yourself as a mother."

"You breastfed me?"

"I did. When I was out and about, and you needed to be fed, I found a nook where I felt comfortable. I knew how to keep myself covered without smothering you," she said with a little smile, hoping to break the seriousness of their conversation. "You'll get the hang of it. I promise you will."

"Have you already talked to Willa about coming over?" Vi asked.

"I did. She can be here at lunchtime. She said she'd bring in takeout for both of you if Foster wants to join you."

Vi patted Sammy's back and rocked him a little back and forth. She cooed into his neck and rubbed her nose in his hair. Daisy could see that Vi was bonding with her son when she wasn't too tired or anxious or doubting herself too much.

"All right," Vi said. She turned to Foster. "Can you be here?"

"I can. I'll tell Arden I'll work on her Web site this week."

This was a first step, and Daisy was so glad to see her daughter take it.

By lunchtime, Daisy was glad to see that Vi was dressed in slacks and a loose blouse. When Willa arrived, Daisy greeted her, asked after her, and then left. She'd eat lunch and wait for Vi to contact her.

In her kitchen at home, Marjoram joined Daisy on the stool next to her. Every once in a while, the feline would pop her head up and lean toward Daisy's sandwich, which consisted of sliced turkey, lettuce, and tomato.

Daisy gave Marjoram a tiny piece of the turkey. "You're not supposed to have people food, but I cooked it myself so I know exactly what is on it. But we never know what's in our food these days, do we?"

Pepper must have heard their conversation because she came in from the living room, carrying her favorite black mouse. She plopped it at Daisy's feet, wanting her to throw it.

"I guess I've neglected you two lately. That happens when a baby is born. Once Vi and Foster get their bearings, we'll invite them over here so you can have some fun too."

Pepper looked up at her plaintively and meowed.

"I have a rule. I don't pick up one of your mice while I'm eating. If you let me finish my sandwich, I'll give you both Greenies."

As if they understood that word very well, Pepper went over to stand by her bowl. After Marjoram ate her tiny bit of turkey, she jumped down and went over to her bowl too.

"I can see how this is going to go," Daisy said, placing her sandwich on her plate. "Greenies for you and then the rest of lunch for me."

Marjoram gave a little *murrp*, and Pepper seemed to be smiling at her smugly. After she distributed Greenies into each dish, she washed her hands, finished her lunch, then picked up her jacket and purse. "I promise I'll brush both of you tonight."

The two cats followed her to the living room, then simultaneously jumped up on the deacon's bench under the window in the sunlight. They began washing themselves, and Daisy knew they'd soon be asleep. They weren't going to miss her one little bit.

As she drove toward Willow Creek Community Church, she knew she probably should have called

Vanna to make sure she'd be there. On the other hand, if Vanna wasn't at her office, she'd just stop at the tea garden and see how things were faring without her.

Whenever Daisy visited Vanna at the church, she parked in the church's back lot and walked around to the side entrance. Chrysanthemums bloomed along the walkway. They were looking a little bedraggled because the colder temperatures had zapped them. Sometimes Thanksgiving in Pennsylvania could even bring snow.

An autumn wreath hung on the side door with ears of dried corn, a few gourds, and a huge orange bow. Daisy suspected Vanna had fashioned it.

She rang the bell, and a few seconds later Vanna appeared and opened the side door.

When she smiled, it seemed forced. "Hi, Daisy. What are you doing here?"

"I thought we could talk."

"This is a good time," Vanna said, and turned to head to her office.

Three steps led inside, and after Daisy climbed them, she walked down the hall following Vanna. Vanna turned right, where her office was located directly outside of the minister's study. His door was open, but no one was inside.

"Did you come to me to talk about Margaret? Rowan told me you might."

Instead of going around the desk to the rolling ergonomic chair, Vanna took one of the ladder-back chairs in front of the desk.

Daisy took the other chair.

Vanna looked uneasy as she asked, "What do you want to know?"

"You've already told me a little about Margaret."

Before hopping into questions that could lead to murder suspects, Daisy treaded easily and gently. "What was Margaret like before she left for New York?"

Vanna rubbed her hand across her forehead and closed her eyes for a moment. "She was always headstrong. When she got into trouble, I tried to cover for her."

"Did she get into big trouble?"

Folding her hands in front of her, Vanna shook her head. "No. Mostly things like coming in late at night. She'd go in and out of our bedroom window. Or if all her chores weren't done, I'd take up the slack."

That sounded normal for sisters. "Did she appreciate those things?"

"I don't know for sure. In a way I think she felt entitled. I was her sister so I should have her back."

"But you didn't feel that she had yours?"

Vanna leaned back in her chair. "There was no need for Margaret to have my back. I followed the rules. I did what I was told. I believed in the values my parents did. Even though I left the faith to marry my husband, we followed the same tenets. But Margaret . . . I don't think she ever believed in anything in the first place."

Vanna stood, crossed to the credenza, and straightened a pile of papers. "She couldn't have run off to New York and not looked back if she had. I heard from her now and then. She was so proud of what she was seeing as if the sights of New York were some kind of awards she'd earned. But she usually didn't put return addresses on the postcards except once or twice. To me that meant she didn't want me to visit. I don't even know what her stage name was. Rowan might know that. I did hear from her regularly after she met him. He was all she thought about and wrote about. From what I could tell, it certainly helped that he was rich. He could give her whatever she wanted. But even after he gave her the Little Theater here, I don't know if she was happy. Rowan travels so much for business, and I think that was starting to bother Margaret. She might have left our life here, but deep down I think she wanted a marriage that lasted forever and someone who would think only about her."

"Was Rowan that man?" Daisy asked, knowing all about little-girl dreams.

"I'm not sure."

Deciding to change subjects, Daisy turned to another topic. "What do you know about Glenda Nurmi?"

After the pile of papers was arranged to her satisfaction, Vanna returned to her chair. "Not much. I simply know that she and Margaret were friends in New York. I think Margaret told me they acted in a play together."

"And Margaret asked Glenda to come to Willow Creek because she was the playwright of the play?"

"Yes. Since they were friends, Margaret thought Glenda would enjoy the honor. Can you imagine writing a play and seeing it performed?"

"Do you know if Glenda had anything else made into a production?"

"I don't know. Margaret only ever mentioned Glenda acting with her. This might be Glenda's first play actually produced. Margaret said it needed tweaks and she could do that. Then it would be just right for a small town like Willow Creek."

Daisy wondered if that was a compliment to Glenda . . . or a dig as to her ability.

Had Margaret made other digs? Digs that could have led to murder?

* * *

That evening, Daisy's mom hosted a Thanksgiving planning meeting with dinner at the family home. Once Jonas had stepped in the door with Daisy, Rose watched Foster enter the kitchen behind them.

"Vi's not coming?" Rose asked Foster as he came in with Jazzi.

"Vi wanted to stay at home with Sammy. He was sleeping and she didn't want to wake him."

"You know, don't you, that babies have to adjust to your schedule, not the other way around," Rose pointed out.

"That may be true when Sammy's a little older," Iris said. She had been in the living room and came out to greet everyone. "But he's less than a week old, and Vi's still getting used to a routine."

The look that Iris exchanged with Rose made Daisy wonder what tension lay between those words. Rose looked as if she were biting back a comment, something like, *But you've never had any children so how do you know?* However, Daisy's mom restrained herself, which was a surprise in itself.

Daisy's dad waved at her from the living room, then started into the kitchen.

Daisy went to give him a kiss and a hug.

"How is Vi, really?" he asked.

"Doing a little better," Daisy said. "She talked to Willa again this afternoon. She's going to join a mommy group."

This couple had a lot to adjust to. They only had a little over three months of marriage before Sammy had been born, and that time had been more about the pregnancy than about them.

There was a knock on the kitchen door, and Rose went to answer it. Tessa had been invited to dinner too.

She shared many holidays with them, and Thanksgiving was no different.

When the oven timer went off, Jonas asked, "Should I get that?"

Daisy nodded, not knowing what would come up at their family meeting. Something always did.

Rose had made one of her famous baked chicken pies, and Daisy knew the chicken, potatoes, carrots, onions, and peas in a thick white sauce surrounded and covered with a pie crust would taste delicious. Another casserole was sitting on top of the stove. Daisy picked up potholders to take that to the table. It was her mom's baked cinnamon apples. They'd enjoy dinner if an argument didn't break out.

A half hour later everyone had pushed their plates aside and were enjoying second cups of coffee or tea.

Rose said, "I'll roast a turkey for Thanksgiving and Daisy can roast one too so neither of us has to handle a large one."

Her father added, "Thanks for inviting us all to your house for the holiday, Daisy. You have a lot more room than we do here."

Daisy's first floor was more of an open concept, so she could easily fit everyone in. She said to Iris, "Can Russ come?"

"He's planning on it," Iris answered with a wink.

"Camellia says she's driving down from New York the day before and she's going to bring her latest beau," Daisy's mom informed them.

Camellia dated often, but she didn't spend more than three months with any one man, at least that's the way it seemed to Daisy. It could be interesting to meet her new boyfriend.

Tessa spoke up now. "I thought I'd ask Cade to come along. Is that okay?"

Cade Bankert was a real estate agent who'd gone to high school with Daisy and Tessa. He'd sold Daisy the property that the barn was located on before she'd renovated it. He'd also sold her and Iris the Victorian where the tea garden was housed. She and Cade had gone on a couple of dates, but that hadn't developed into anything more than friendship.

"Of course he's welcome," Daisy said. She glanced at Jonas, but he didn't seem to mind.

"I'm not the best cook," Jonas told Rose, "but I can bring an extra table and chairs to Daisy's. That way you can make sure everyone has plenty of room and a chair to sit on."

Daisy reached over and took his hand and squeezed it. She felt more comfortable doing things like that now. After all, they *were* steadily dating.

Everyone had signed up for something to bring, so Daisy didn't have to handle more than a turkey and acting as hostess. There would be more than enough food probably even for the week after Thanksgiving. In fact, Daisy was relieved with the interactions with everyone today until . . .

At the head of the table, Daisy's dad was around the corner from her. His voice was low when he asked, "When the police questioned you, was it factual or did they push for more?"

"The police questioned you?" Rose asked. "About that tea at Margaret Vaughn's house?"

Daisy hadn't told her mother that she'd found the body. Before she could signal to cut the conversation, Jazzi said, "Mom found Mrs. Vaughn. She walked right into the crime scene. Of course, the police had to question her."

Looking stunned for a moment, Rose shook her

head. "I didn't know you found the body. Why didn't you tell me about it?"

After demanding that question of Daisy, she turned to Iris. "But she told you all about it, didn't she?"

Without hesitating, Daisy stood and put her hand on her mom's shoulder. "Mom, let's go talk in the kitchen."

When Rose didn't stand right away, Daisy asked, "Please?"

Rose tossed her napkin onto the table, stood, and followed Daisy into the kitchen.

Daisy started right in. "I didn't tell you I found the body because I didn't want you to become upset. You always do when I'm involved."

"You shouldn't *be* involved."

"Mom, I was serving tea for Margaret and the cast of the play. I went to the butler's pantry and there she was. It wasn't like I went looking for trouble. I really didn't want to upset you."

Rose seemed to accept her explanation, but she still looked hurt. "I understand it was just part of your business and you found her. You should be used to dealing with the police by now."

Daisy didn't retort. She bit her lip on any words that might make things worse between them. She didn't know how to make her relationship with her mom better except by always agreeing with her.

But as soon as that thought manifested itself, she also knew she couldn't do that.

Chapter Seven

Daisy had once heard a mausoleum described as a magnificent tomb. On Tuesday morning, Daisy studied the structure where Margaret would be buried, and she didn't know if it was grand or not. It was fashioned of stone. What she did know was that the mausoleum gave her the creeps. Since her last murder investigation, confined spaces almost made her panic.

By her side, Jonas circled her waist with his arm. "Are you okay?"

"I'm not sure."

They were attending this funeral at Winding Vines Cemetery in Lancaster and standing in front of Rowan Vaughn's family mausoleum. As her gaze swept away from this mausoleum to the rest of the cemetery, she spotted other mausoleums and sections of burial plots. Older plots were commemorated with memorials in shapes of angels, crosses, emblems, and towers. Many more recent graves were simply memorialized with flat gravestones.

"Would you ever want your family to be buried in a mausoleum?" Daisy asked.

"Not particularly," Jonas answered with a husky catch in his voice.

They'd both lost loved ones. They'd seen death close up. Since they'd been involved in murder investigations, they'd also seen the repercussions of death.

Daisy couldn't help but say, "They're so gloomy. It's got to be dark and damp inside the building. I like trees and sky and sunshine. Loved ones should be surrounded by that in some way."

"There are so many ways to look at this," Jonas said. "Most of them maudlin. Mausoleums are more of a tribute to a family than to a loved one."

"Maybe only rich families have mausoleums."

"Or families with very long bloodlines," Jonas added. "There's upkeep on a building like this."

Gray columns rose from the ground to the ceiling on either side of the mausoleum's doorway. At the wider side of the structure, there was a family emblem. A bas-relief angel with a wide wingspan soared above the emblem. Arborvitae had been maintained at the four corners and rose higher than the roofline.

Daisy felt chilled to the bone. November had descended with a cold grip, and today was a perfect example of a steel-gray day with the reminder of winter in any wind that blew. A green canopy had been set up a short distance from the mausoleum with Astroturf, folding chairs, and a platform for Margaret's casket.

Jonas gave Daisy a little nudge. "We really should go over there."

As they walked toward the site where a short service

would be held, Rowan caught Daisy's eye. Disengaging himself from the group of men he'd been speaking to, he came toward them.

Stopping when he reached Daisy, he asked, "Did you think any more about what I requested?"

While Daisy studied Rowan, she considered the fact that he looked like a man in mourning. He appeared a little more disheveled than any other time she'd seen him. His expensive suit jacket had a few creases. His tie was crooked. His usually styled hair was windswept.

She took a tighter grip on her clutch purse. "I spoke with Vanna. That didn't lead anywhere important, but I did learn some things I didn't know before. I was surprised that Vanna didn't know Margaret's stage name. Can you tell me what it was?"

"Yes. It was Luna Larkin. Unique, don't you think?"

"I suppose it is." Daisy actually thought it sounded more like a Las Vegas showgirl's name than an actress's. But she didn't say that. Both her gaze and Rowan's went to the group of people standing at the chairs under the canopy. Rowan pointed to a beautiful African-American woman with shoulder-length curly black hair that was pulled back on either side by gold barrettes. Her skin was unlined and her big brown eyes darted here and there.

"That's Keisha Washington, the stage manager Margaret brought in from New York. The man next to her is Ward Cooper. He's the lighting technician."

Ward Cooper was tall and thin with ears that wouldn't look so big if he didn't have his hair cut so short. He was wearing a herringbone-patterned sweater coat, black slacks, and a light gray scarf wrapped around his neck in a style common to many men now.

Other members of the cast were also present—Daniel Copeland, Heidi Korn, Arden Botterill, and Jasper Lazar. Glenda Nurmi was speaking with Heidi.

The minister beckoned to Rowan, who excused himself and headed toward the front row under the canopy. Daisy leaned close to Jonas. "Since Glenda's here, I'll speak to her after the service."

"She might be too upset to talk."

"She might be. If she is, I'll set up another time."

The minister gave a signal that it was time for the mausoleum service. Daisy had never been to a service like this one. But she was learning new experiences happened every day.

The minister didn't simply read from the Bible. He spoke about Margaret as if he had known her, and Daisy wondered if he had, or if Rowan had just given him details.

After the minister finished, Rowan went to the podium. He said, "Margaret probably didn't want a funeral service that was traditional. But I thought in a way her roots should be evident. However, I also know she would like me to recite lines from writers she admired."

After Rowan said that, he read quotes from William Blake, Wordsworth, and Ibsen. After he finished, the pallbearers took the casket to the mausoleum. Daisy stared at the small building. She knew at some point she had to confront her fear of enclosed spaces. Maybe today was the day to do it. She wanted to wait until everyone who was inside the mausoleum left.

While Jonas spoke with someone he knew, she walked the path around the edifice. Somehow a pebble got into her shoe, and she stopped to shake it out. She heard voices and realized one of the windows of the mausoleum had been opened. It was above her head so she couldn't see who was inside. But she *could* hear.

After listening for a while, she thought one of the people inside was Glenda. The other person was a man, but Daisy couldn't quite make out their words. Still . . . she heard Margaret's name uttered.

Was this about the funeral service? Or was it about Margaret herself? Maybe it concerned her murder. Daisy stayed where she was. When the voices stopped, she stepped to the edge of the side of the building. Glenda and Ward Cooper exited. Ward broke off from Glenda, and it was easy to see that Glenda was headed for her car, as were many of the other funeral-goers.

Daisy caught up to her and tapped her arm. "Glenda, can we talk?"

When Glenda turned toward her, her face was flushed but there were no tears in her eyes. It was possible she was still angry from whatever she and Ward had been arguing about. "I'd like to talk to you about Margaret," Daisy said honestly.

Shaking her head, Glenda held up a hand. "I don't want to talk about Margaret. I'm not even going to Vanna's house. Everything's still too raw."

"Yes, I suppose it is," Daisy concurred with empathy. "I'm trying to find out a few facts that might help the police. If you don't want to talk here or today, maybe another time and place?"

Glenda looked around the area as if she wanted to run away.

"Why don't you stop in at the tea garden sometime before rehearsal? I heard the play is still going on."

"From what I know, it is," Glenda said as if she didn't agree with that. "Many of the cast and Rowan believe we can pay tribute to Margaret by making this the best production it can be. That means a lot more rehearsals than we've been having. It means new lines to be learned. I'd like to rewrite a few of the scenes. Margaret wouldn't let me make the changes, but now I'm going to do that."

"You're the playwright so I imagine what you say goes."

"If Rowan doesn't want to manage the cast and crew and everything that has to be done, he'll have to appoint someone. I'm hoping he appoints me. Ward and Keisha are experienced in theater mechanics, so to speak, but I think I'm the one who can pull this together."

Seeing that almost everyone was leaving, Daisy nodded. "We can talk more about this soon, tea and scones on me."

Glenda slowly smiled. "Maybe."

Daisy turned and started back to meet Jonas. Rowan hadn't wanted to have a gathering at the house where Margaret was murdered, so the reception after the funeral was to be held at Vanna's house. It was small but would be adequate for an occasion like this.

As Daisy kept her eyes on the mausoleum, she knew she wanted to recover from the panicky feeling she got whenever she was in a small space. She didn't like the condition hanging over her. She wanted to feel normal again.

Jonas stood under the canopy as if he didn't want to be near the mausoleum either. He'd only worn a suit coat, and she imagined he must be cold. Even in her raspberry-colored dress coat with a scarf around her neck, she was chilled. It was as if those chills came from the inside, though, not outside. She wasn't sure.

Once more at Jonas's side, she said, "I'm going into the mausoleum alone."

"Why don't I come with you?"

She shook her head. "Alone, Jonas. I have to do this alone. I don't want you standing right outside like a guard. Why don't you go sit in your car? It's cold out here."

But he could be as stubborn as she could. "I'm going to wait right here for you. Do whatever you need to do, then come back to me."

She appreciated his sentiment and kissed him on the cheek to show it. But then she walked toward the mausoleum, determination in her step. The granite or concrete or whatever it was, was so cold, not only to the eye but to the touch. It held the cold and seemed to radiate it. Crossing the threshold, she shut the wooden door. Standing perfectly still, she took in a breath and let it out. Then she took in another, deeper, and let that one out. After the third, she felt calmer. She didn't know what she intended to do in here. Maybe just feel the space. Maybe she needed to prove she had enough courage that she wouldn't panic while she was in here.

She studied each crypt, all of which held a brass plate with the name of a family member and also engraved with a quote from a text or the Bible. When she came to Margaret's, the newest one, she stopped. It didn't have a name yet, nor did it have a quote. However, she saw a slip of paper on the ground floor. It was half buried as if someone had dropped it and then stepped on it. Pulling it from the ground, she brushed it off. As she opened it, she saw words were written on it. *The acts of this life are the destiny of the next. Eastern proverb.*

Was Rowan going to put that quote on a brass

plate that would be screwed into the crypt? Had Margaret picked it out herself and maybe included it in her will? Daisy studied the crypt a few moments longer, then she walked to the left until she reached the wall. Turning, she walked to the right. Nothing happened to her. A panic attack didn't overtake her. She was perfectly fine.

Maybe not *perfectly* fine. Her heart was racing. Her palms felt sweaty even in the cold. There was no point standing in here becoming chilled to the bone. She didn't like this place because it was a mausoleum. Perhaps the next time she was in an enclosed space, she'd escape a panic attack. She was so grateful one didn't happen now.

After she opened the door, she felt a whole lot better. As she stepped outside, her heart settled into a regular rhythm. A gust of wind blew as if cleansing her from her experience inside. She ducked her nose down into her scarf.

Jonas had stayed exactly where he'd been under the canopy. He was pacing back and forth, but she imagined that was to keep warm. He spotted her, and their gazes met. She walked in a straight line toward him. Without a word he took her into his arms and held her close. At that moment she felt more peaceful than she had since the last murder investigation had been solved. Could this one be solved? Only time would tell.

A half hour later at Vanna's house, Daisy helped the church secretary distribute the platters of deli meat and cheeses as well as potato salad, macaroni salad, and potato chips to her dining room table. Then she returned to the kitchen to the slow cooker of meatballs, where she transferred them to a serving dish.

Daisy arranged the food in an attractive design on the table out of habit and moved to the end of the table where paper products stood. She moved the Styrofoam cups to a card table with the coffee urn. Then she set the luncheon plates, the dessert plates, the napkins, and the silverware in a row so they could easily be picked up by the funeral-goers. She heard Rowan's voice in the living room, and a couple of minutes later guests began entering the dining room. Apparently, he'd told them that lunch was served. While she finessed the position of the food on the table, she heard various comments.

One woman whispered to another, "I heard Rowan say that Margaret never would have used paper plates. He's so right."

Daisy wove in and out of the guests, making sure no one needed anything. She heard a younger woman say to the man with her, "Margaret was a perfectionist. I think that was because she didn't know whether she belonged in the world of her upbringing or in the new world she'd made for herself."

The man responded, "New York can be vicious. I imagine she carved out the life she wanted for herself. After she found Vaughn, she had it made."

If that was true, Daisy thought, then why had someone murdered her?

Jasper Lazar, an HVAC contractor well known in Willow Creek for his expertise, had also joined the cast. His medium brown hair was dusted with silver. His hairline receded a few inches above his brow. His nose was stubby and his double chin broad. He stared down at the food on the table and raised his brows to Daisy. "Quite a difference from the food *you* serve, isn't it?"

Daisy defended her friend. "I imagine Vanna had

to put this together quickly. I brought an assortment of desserts that are on the table in the kitchen if you'd like some of those."

Jasper slicked back his hair that had some length to it. His golden-brown eyes sparked at her as he agreed, "I'll head that way."

A short woman Daisy had seen at church now and then sidled up next to her. She was probably as old as Vanna and wore her hair blunt-cut around her face. She was plump, dressed in a plain black dress and sturdy black shoes. "Mr. Lazar is just mad at Rowan and looking for any reason at all to criticize him. That is perfectly good country-cut ham on that plate, and those cheeses came from the Stoltzfuses, who make their own."

Daisy had often stopped at the Stoltzfus stand at the farmers' market. "Vanna made the potato salad and the macaroni salad herself. I think she just needed to busy herself to keep her grief at bay. She wanted to feel as if she were doing something."

The woman looked up at Daisy with a small smile. "I see you understand. My name is Gayla Mann. You're Daisy from Daisy's Tea Garden, aren't you?"

"I am."

"It's good for Vanna to have her friends around her. She's mentioned you a few times to me. She said you and Tessa Miller make the best teas and baked goods."

"Have you ever tried them?" Daisy asked.

"My husband and I live on a small property out at the east end but we're pretty self-sufficient. I don't have much need to come into town. But now that I've met you, I might have to try the tea garden. I do like tea."

As guests who had been at the funeral filled their

plates and picked up a soda or a bottle of water, Daisy took the chance that Gayla was friendly enough to ask her a question. "You said Jasper was mad at Rowan. Do you know why?"

"Jasper lives in one of Rowan's apartment buildings and is wrangling with him about repairs."

"Doesn't Rowan take good care of his property?" Daisy asked in a lower voice.

"I don't know if the problem is Rowan per se. He has a management company to take care of his properties. If you don't hire the right managers, the work doesn't get done, or they let things slide. Rowan isn't a handyman himself, and it's tough finding good managers, I suppose. Jasper can do his own repairs, but then he feels Rowan should reimburse him. It can be an ongoing circle of argument and resentment."

Argument and resentment. Daisy remembered the phone conversation that Margaret had had with Rowan.

Chapter Eight

A short time later, Daisy decided to freshen up in the powder room. It was located on the other side of the house from the reception, near the three bedrooms. After she'd washed her hands and freshened her lipstick, she unlocked the door and stepped into the hall. Once there, however, she thought she heard a woman crying. Not knowing whether to go toward the sound or away from it, she stood still for a few seconds.

Whoever was crying was in the bedroom next door to the bathroom. That bedroom door was open. When Daisy peeked in, she could see that the bedroom was decorated in lilac. The wallpaper consisted of tiny little violet flowers and the chenille bedspread, very pale lilac, complemented it. Lace curtains crisscrossed at the windows and swooped over white mini blinds. Vanna sat in a deep purple velvet bedside chair, her head in her hands.

Crossing to the older woman without hesitation,

Daisy sat on the bed across from her and patted her shoulder. "I know today has to be hard for you."

"It's so hard," Vanna mumbled. "But Rowan just made it harder or better. I don't know which."

Noticing that Vanna was fingering a brooch on the lapel of her sweater, Daisy asked, "What did Rowan do?"

That brooch gave Daisy chills because she'd seen it on Margaret's body . . . covered in clotted cream.

Without hesitation, Vanna fingered the piece of jewelry again. A small smile slipped across her lips. She unpinned the brooch and held it in her hand. The diamonds with the amethysts twinkled in the daylight from the window.

"Rowan gave me Margaret's favorite piece of jewelry. I've admired it from the moment I saw it. That was the day I saw Margaret for the first time after she returned to Willow Creek."

A thought flitted through Daisy's mind. If this brooch was Rowan's wife's favorite piece of jewelry, why wouldn't he want to keep it?

Then again, maybe he simply wanted to do something nice for his wife's sister.

"Did Rowan tell you where the brooch came from?" Daisy asked.

"You know, I didn't think about that," Vanna answered. "Margaret never said where it came from. I just assumed Rowan had given it to her because she loved it so much. She wore it often. It seemed to be a talisman for her. She'd run her fingers over the diamonds and the amethysts as if she couldn't believe someone cared enough to give it to her."

"You'll treasure it," Daisy offered.

"Yes, I will." Vanna kept her gaze on her hand. "Margaret never wanted a home and family the way I did. She always wanted to be famous. Acting was the path to that and she wanted to be the best actress she could be. She liked putting herself in different roles. The parts were all sides of herself. She never communicated with our parents. They were angry with her and bitter that she'd left without a second thought or a look back."

"That's such a shame. Maybe they could have reconnected."

"I doubt it. They were so disappointed in her. I was fortunate. When I left the faith to marry, it took a while, but my parents could see that I'd married a good man and that we were going to raise our children in the tenets of our faith. I think they finally saw that Margaret and I had to choose our own paths. If she would have tried to communicate with them, tried to come back, they might have accepted her back in. I don't know. Dad had a heart attack and died while she was incommunicado, and then Mom went to live with her brother's family in Indianapolis. She's infirm now and it's too difficult for her to travel. I'd like to think she would have come for Margaret's funeral if she could. I told Margaret she should call Mom and try to make peace, but Margaret said she was happy with Rowan and wouldn't rock the boat by trying to adhere to our mother's ideas of what was right and wrong."

"I'm so sorry."

"Mom's physically in a bad place. But I also think the emotional toll would have been as hard on her as the physical toll. It was hard enough for her to digest the fact that Margaret had died let alone that she'd been murdered. You know, I loved my husband. He was my partner. The children always came first, and if there's any glue in a marriage, it's children. I'm not sure that Margaret and Rowan had glue. Rowan traveled so much, and even though Margaret had the Little Theater, I think she was becoming terrifically bored with Willow Creek."

With a sigh, Vanna re-pinned the brooch onto her lapel. "I'm going to try to find mementos of me and Margaret and keep the memories alive. We were so close as kids. I'm just not sure what happened."

Daisy knew what happened. Life happened. The two sisters had taken different paths just as she and her sister Camellia had. Those different paths had led them away from each other instead of toward each other.

After Daisy had consoled Vanna as much as she could, Vanna wiped her tears away and they returned to the reception. Daisy spotted Zeke Willet speaking with Jasper Lazar and she wondered why. Something to do with the problems he'd had with Rowan about his apartment? Or maybe just making conversation to find out whatever he could.

Jonas and Detective Rappaport both had told her that Zeke was a good detective. However, during the last murder investigation, he had missed clues. He hadn't been thorough enough. Because of Jonas?

Jonas was standing at the window in the dining room and peering outside into a yard that was abundant with flowers until this time of year. He could be checking out whoever was coming and going, or . . . he could be thinking. Daisy went to him, studying his strong back and his broad shoulders. He looked good in a suit, but he rarely wore one. There was no need for him to. She had to admit he looked as good in a flannel shirt and jeans. Jonas was one of those men who could wear any clothes with ease. At least that was her opinion.

When she laid her hand on his shoulder, he smiled though he didn't turn around.

"How did you know it was me?" she asked.

"Because I noticed you were wearing those black flat ballerina shoes this morning. I know the sound of them on the wood floor."

His detective instincts at work again.

"And I know the scent of your shampoo," he went on, "not to mention the way you touch me when you want to know what I'm thinking."

"Sometimes I believe you're psychic," she murmured.

Now he did turn toward her. "Not psychic. I know body language. Sounds kept me alive in the field. I could hear when and how someone approached."

"In other words, spidey senses."

He chuckled. "If you want to call them that. Mine are duller now than they used to be. Where have you been?"

"With Vanna. You know how grief overtakes you when you least expect it."

"I do. Is she grieving, or is she having regrets?"

That was a perceptive observation, the kind she'd come to expect from Jonas. "I'm not sure. I don't think she has regrets, because their estrangement when Margaret was away wasn't Vanna's fault. Except for a communication or two, Vanna didn't know where Margaret was or what she was doing. Marrying Rowan seemed to change all that."

Jonas shifted away from the window. "From what I understand, Margaret was a fiercely independent woman. Do you really think marriage changed who she was?"

Daisy noticed the scar on the left side of Jonas's

face looked lighter today, as if it was fading into the past along with his career as a detective. Returning to the question he'd asked, she said, "Maybe it changed Margaret's sense of security. She no longer felt alone in the world even though that aloneness was of her own making. Maybe she needed someone outside of her family to love her for who she was, not for what they wanted her to be."

"That sounds like experience talking."

"Perhaps. When I met Ryan at college, I was away from home. He loved me not because he had to, but because he wanted to." Daisy was surprised those words had come out of her mouth. She and Jonas let the import of them settle over them.

"Do you believe your parents loved you because they had to love you . . . the same with your aunt Iris?"

Daisy lowered her voice. "I always felt Dad and Iris loved me, but my mom and Camellia? Sometimes I felt everything about our relationships was forced."

Jonas leaned his head toward hers. "I'd like to delve into this conversation more, but I'm not sure this is the place. Somebody is headed our way." Jonas circled her waist, pulling her close to him. For some reason, at that moment she felt she needed his support.

Rowan approached them, his gaze on Daisy's. "I want to thank you for bringing all those delicious desserts."

Desserts were much easier to talk about than murder. "It was the least I could do for Vanna. She's been a good friend to me. Grief can be hard to navigate."

"Yes, I suppose it can," Rowan agreed. "She seemed touched when I gave her a brooch of Margaret's."

"She was. I have mementos from my husband that

mean a lot to me. Memories are precious when a loved one passes. Anything that can make their smile or their voice or their look come alive again is important. I'm sure she'll wear Margaret's brooch often."

Without a segue, Rowan asked, "So you will be speaking to Glenda soon?"

Daisy became annoyed that he kept checking with her about that. But if he was afraid that he would be charged with murder, she could understand why.

"If Glenda shows up at the tea garden, I'll be sure to make time for her."

"Thank you, Daisy. I'd better mingle with the other mourners. I do appreciate their coming and I want them to know that."

As Rowan walked away, Daisy asked Jonas, "Can you find out more about Rowan?"

"What do you want to know?"

"Is there a way you can find out if there are any lawsuits against him?"

Suddenly a voice sailed over Jonas's shoulder. Zeke Willet looked angry. He targeted Jonas first. "You should become a PI if you want to snoop for Daisy. On the other hand, maybe Daisy should forget about background checks and concentrate on brewing tea."

It was easy for Daisy to see that Jonas was angry. Color came to his cheekbones. She could see a temper he wasn't letting loose. Usually he refused to be baited.

She kept her mouth shut. Better if she refused to be baited too.

Zeke pointed his finger at them both. "Stay out of my investigation." Then he walked away, his stride angry, his expression seriously frustrated.

Jonas let out a pent-up breath. "There are times lately when I just want to shake him."

"That's because you still care what he thinks. It's hard to let go of a friendship that was once good."

"He has me wondering if it was *ever* good. Maybe I was deluding myself in thinking we had each other's backs . . . that we cared about making the world a safer place. I'm not sure that's Zeke's purpose anymore."

"Sometimes I think he's lost his purpose and he's just going through the motions," Daisy observed.

"Morris Rappaport is wrong when he thinks Zeke and I can make peace. I can put the past in the past, but I don't think Zeke can."

Although Daisy wanted to check in with Violet often, she didn't want Vi to feel she was hovering or controlling. Vi had seemed to be doing better after her talk with Willa. But Daisy was not at all sure about that.

After returning home from the funeral yesterday, Daisy had called one of their temp workers, Pam Dorsey, to see if she could spend the day helping out at the tea garden. She'd agreed to meet Iris there at five a.m. to start cinnamon rolls and other breakfast goodies. At home, Daisy prepared a baked blueberry and oatmeal casserole as well as a ham, cheese, and potato casserole to take to Vi. Jazzi sampled each before she took a walk down the lane to meet her school bus. As soon as Jazzi had left, Daisy wrapped both casseroles and inserted them in an insulated carry-all that would keep them warm.

Since Daisy usually left before Jazzi most mornings, Marjoram and Pepper seemed surprised when she was puttering around the kitchen, ready to walk over to Vi and Foster's above-the-garage apartment. From her observation, her felines usually accompanied Jazzi down from her room upstairs after she was dressed and they settled on the deacon's bench near the living room window. However, this morning the aromas from the kitchen must have drawn them there. Daisy was setting some of the dishes she'd used to prepare the casseroles into the dishwasher when Marjoram came over to her and sat on her foot. Pepper moseyed over to her dishes on the floor and gave Daisy a disdainful look when she found them empty.

"Jazzi fed you, didn't she?" Daisy asked, conversationally.

From her position at her cat plate with little kitty ears, Pepper meowed. It was one of those impatient I-don't-care-I'd-really-like-a-treat meows. Marjoram stood and circled Daisy's legs, her tail brushing against her calves.

"So you're both trying to tell me treats are dessert after breakfast?"

Marjoram joined Pepper as both cats stood at the bottom cupboard where Daisy kept the treat bag.

"You two are so smart you should be able to serve yourselves." However, when Daisy thought about that she shook her head. "Scratch that idea. You'd have my cupboard empty in no time. All right, what's it going to be this morning, chicken and cranberry or duck and cranberry?"

Since the felines couldn't seem to make up their minds, Daisy put a few treats of both in each dish. Then she went to the closet under the stairs for her fleece jacket, picked up the insulated bag with the casseroles, set the security alarm, and headed for Vi's.

At the garage, Daisy pushed the bell. From the intercom she heard Vi's "Come on up." There was a click and the lock opened.

A few minutes later she'd climbed the stairs and entered the apartment. Sitting at the small table, Vi was still in her robe, her hair disheveled, large blue circles under her eyes.

"How about a spoonful of blueberry oatmeal and a scoop of a ham casserole I made for breakfast? You'll have the casserole for tonight's supper if you don't feel like cooking."

"I'm not hungry, Mom."

When Daisy gave her daughter a look, Vi capitulated. "All right, just a small spoonful of each."

Daisy hurried to unpack the casseroles before Vi changed her mind. Suddenly Daisy heard a cry from Vi's bedroom.

"He didn't sleep hardly at all last night," Vi murmured.

"What's going on?" Daisy asked, concerned.

"I called Willa and she thinks it's newborn fussiness. We tried to give him a bottle last night and he wouldn't take it. Besides that, I don't know if bottle feeding will help. Foster needs his sleep too."

"You could take turns. Foster could take the feeding before bed so you could go to bed earlier. Then you could take the middle-of-the-night ones. Or something like that."

Vi was already on her way to pick up Sammy. Daisy followed her and peeked in the bedroom. Vi was smiling down at Sammy on the changing table as she changed his diaper. When she finished, she swaddled him in a receiving blanket and brought him into the living room. Sammy, however, still seemed unhappy as he wiggled and squirmed and wouldn't settle. Vi sank down on the sofa to feed him.

Daisy sat with Vi for the next half hour, listening when her daughter wanted to talk, quiet when she didn't. Vi burped Sammy after he finished eating, almost asleep, and then she sighed.

Daisy reached for the baby, always willing to hold and cuddle him. She said to Vi, "I put portions of each casserole in the oven to keep them warm. Go on and eat."

"Don't you have to go to the tea garden?"

"I will. I want to make sure you're okay here. When will Foster be home?"

"Not until after five. I just have to stay awake until then."

"No, you don't. I'm going to drive in to the tea garden when I leave here, just to make sure all is going smoothly. But this afternoon, I'll come over about three. I'll take care of Sammy while you go to bed for a nap. If you're still sleeping when Foster gets home, so much the better."

Already shaking her head, Vi protested, "Sammy will need to be fed."

"Foster and I will try the bottle again. Did you ever think that your anxiety might be making Sammy upset? It's not your fault. It's a new mom thing. But that can happen. He feels your agitation and he's agitated too."

"I was feeling better, Mom, really I was. I went for a walk yesterday when Foster was here. And I do love Sammy, but I just feel so down all the time."

"When Foster gets home, he and I will see if we can coax Sammy to take the bottle. If he won't, I'll go shopping for a new type of bottle and nipple. Sometimes that's the simple solution."

"Do you know about all these things because you had a bad experience with me or Jazzi?" Vi wanted to know.

"Let's just call it experience. Babies definitely don't come with a manual. I remember your pediatrician telling me more than once to try everything I could think of to make life work. Something always does." Daisy smiled. "That had to do with eating, feeding, discipline, and activities. He was usually right."

"Is this ever going to get easier?" Vi asked.

"I asked him the same thing, and you know what he said?"

"Do I *want* to know what he said?" Vi said acerbically.

"Probably not. He told me when you were about four everything would ease up."

Vi's eyes widened. "Was that true?"

"Actually, it was—for you *and* Jazzi. At four you both had minds of your own, but I could reason with you most of the time. By four you were a little more self-sufficient. You have to look at each phase of Sammy's babyhood as an adventure, something new. You'll be amazed at what he learns each week. Keep a record of it and you'll see what progress you're making too."

"In becoming a mom?"

"Yes. Your skills will increase day by day. I promise."

But Vi still looked dejected and sad. If Vi's moods stayed this dejected much longer, she'd have to make an appointment with her GYN and consider what options were open to her.

Chapter Nine

Daisy's tea supplier had brought her a new shipment. She was sorting teas and pouring them into their proper tins when Cora Sue tapped her on the shoulder. Daisy jumped, startled.

Cora Sue said, "Someone's here to see you. It's the woman who wrote that play. You know, the one that got Margaret killed."

Daisy didn't believe the play had gotten Margaret killed, but one of the people involved in it might have.

"I asked Ms. Nurmi what I could bring her. She said she'd enjoy a pot of Winter Surprise, but she seemed fidgety," Cora Sue related.

Fidgety like she didn't want to be here? Or fidgety because she knew Daisy was going to ask her questions? Daisy would find out soon enough.

"I have all the teas stowed away. Maybe later you could make up bags of it to sell. I checked inventory and we're getting low."

"No problem. I'll brew Winter Surprise. Should I bring anything else?"

"Maybe a plate of snickerdoodles. They're hard to resist."

Cora Sue's brows arched and she gave Daisy a sly smile. "Are you trying to soften her up?"

"Not soften her up exactly. I'd like to make her comfortable so she doesn't feel like I'm interrogating her."

"Even if you are?" Cora Sue asked knowingly.

"I'm not getting involved in the case this time."

Cora Sue gave her a long look.

"I'm just going to ask her a few questions to please Margaret's husband. I don't expect to get anywhere."

"That would be the first time," Cora Sue muttered.

"I have a lot on my plate," Daisy murmured. "Vi and the baby, Thanksgiving, Jazzi and her birth mother. I don't have time to step into murder mud, so to speak, and get swallowed up by it."

Cora Sue pulled the tin of Winter Surprise from the shelf. "Do you want a cup of tea too?"

"Sure. Drinking with a friend can create a bond."

"I wish you luck," Cora Sue said as she went to make the tea.

It wasn't long until Daisy was sitting across the table from Glenda, sipping tea. Glenda stirred sparkling sugar into her cup, then set down her spoon. The utensil clinked on the side of the saucer. "I'm not sure why you want to talk to me. I certainly had nothing to do with what happened to Margaret. Arden told me you help investigate murders, but I know nothing. So this is a waste of time."

Daisy believed Glenda was one of those women who knew she was beautiful. She wore her black hair parted down the middle. It fell into waves along her face past her shoulders. Her makeup wasn't dramatic but expertly applied, from eyeliner and mascara to an absolutely flawless matte-surface complexion. Primer and foundation gave the impression of doll-like porcelain. Her lips were outlined and filled in with one of those nude colors that made most women look like zombies.

On Glenda? She resembled a runway model. At five-ten with a slender, almost too thin figure, she could have worn anyone's new line. However, today she wore skinny designer jeans and a silky off-white blouse that tied at her right waist. Her plaid wool cape lay folded over the back of her chair.

"From what I understand, you were a good friend of Margaret's," Daisy said. "Is that right?"

Glenda gave a little lift of one shoulder. "We had one of those friendships that was on and off. I'd get too busy or she'd get too busy and we wouldn't talk for months. In addition to that, I'm ten years younger and we didn't often think in the same way."

Trying to interpret what Glenda was saying, Daisy decided that Glenda and Margaret were surface friends most of the time. "How did you meet Margaret?"

"We met at an actors' workshop. We were both much younger and trying to become experts in our craft. We were both waitressing at the time." She lifted a shoulder again in a shrug. "Many of us did that to pay the bills."

Daisy nodded. "I couldn't find much information about Margaret's acting career. I understand her stage name was Luna Larkin."

After a slight hesitation, Glenda answered, "Her stage name *was* Luna Larkin. She used it when we were both taking bit parts at the time of that workshop. Margaret mostly acted off-Broadway."

"How about you? Off-Broadway too?"

"On and off. But when I started screenwriting I felt that was my passion. I'm not sure Margaret ever found hers. She hit the jackpot when she connected with Rowan."

Jackpot. Is that the way Glenda thought of a rich husband . . . and Margaret too?

"How so?" Daisy asked, wanting more of an explanation.

"She could live more than comfortably with him. He'd promised her that Little Theater before they were married. I think that's one reason she married him. He was intrigued by her. She saw him as a man who could give her everything. The thing is—that thinking doesn't work."

"What do you mean?"

"No man can give you everything. You have to have it within yourself," Glenda determined vehemently. "People think money can make you happy. Money can make you more comfortable, but not happy."

When Daisy offered Glenda the plate of snickerdoodles, Glenda took one. "Do you know anyone who might have wanted to hurt Margaret?"

Glenda shook her head, still holding the cookie. "Rowan had more enemies than Margaret ever did. He doesn't keep a close enough eye on his properties. One of them burned down because of a faulty sprinkler system. I heard him and Margaret arguing over it a couple of times because of the financial repercussions as well as mud on his reputation. She was afraid that would affect the Little Theater production."

Either Glenda was tossing out information to put Daisy on a different track, or it was info that could lead somewhere.

Glenda took a bite from her cookie. "These are good."

Daisy smiled. "We consider them a Pennsylvania Dutch treat. Lots of women I know make them for Christmas."

"These would be good anytime. Cinnamon is my favorite." Glenda waved the rest of her cookie at Daisy. "You ought to come to the theater and watch rehearsals."

"The man I'm dating, Jonas Groft, is working on the sets, so maybe I will."

"In honor of Margaret, I'm determined to put on this play in the best way possible. It will be a success just as she planned."

Daisy frowned. Whatever Margaret had planned hadn't worked out. It had gotten her killed.

True to her word, Daisy climbed the steps to the garage apartment around three, ready to help Vi. But Vi and Sammy weren't there. Had something happened? No sooner had she thought the thought when she heard Vi's steps on the stairs. She was walking up slowly, carrying Sammy in his car carrier. She wasn't wearing a coat and she had crib sheets thrown across the carrier.

Daisy rushed to her to take Sammy and his carrier from her clasp.

"I never expected you to be downstairs," Daisy said, surprised.

"I can't leave Sammy up here by himself, and I had to do laundry. The diapers don't fit him quite right and I want to keep his sheets clean for him. He was getting low on onesies too. I wish we could have a stacked washer and dryer up here but there's just no room."

"We talked about it when we were planning the apartment," Daisy reminded her. "Downstairs just seemed to be the best idea."

"I'm not complaining, Mom, really I'm not. It's just . . ."

She threw the laundry on the sofa, then scooped Sammy out of his carrier. "The garage isn't as warm as the apartment. I don't know if I can keep him down there very long."

"You could put him in that cute little bunting that Cora Sue gave you."

"He's not real thrilled with getting in and out of it."

"I know how that goes. As he gets older you can make a game of it. Right now, it's just a matter of wills. As long as he's dressed, if you throw a blanket over him, that would be sufficient."

"Would it? Maybe I could put a hat on him."

"The back of the garage is heated. It had to be so the pipes wouldn't freeze."

"But it's damp. I don't want to take any chances with him."

As Vi held Sammy, Daisy could see her daughter's hand shake.

"Did you eat lunch?"

Vi thought about it. "No. I gave Sammy a bath, then I had to sort the laundry and take care of that."

"Do you still have some of the tuna fish salad Gram made for you?"

"I do, but that's kind of heavy if I'm going to take a nap. I'll just grab a couple of saltines."

"Vi."

"I know, Mom. I'll do better. I will. I'll feed him and then I'll nap for a bit."

Settling into the corner of the sofa, Vi opened her blouse and covered her shoulder with a receiving blanket. Sammy began sucking.

Vi asked, "Are you worried about Jazzi going to Allentown this weekend? She said you're going to take her and Portia will bring her home."

"That's right. And if I'm worried, I'm trying not to let her see. I don't want to dim her excitement."

Daisy went to the kitchen to make a cup of tea. Eva had given Foster and Vi a supply as a wedding present. She chose a blackberry rooibos.

"Tea?" she asked Vi as she filled the red kettle.

"Sure. That would be nice. It would be my cup for the day."

Daisy had just turned on the burner when her cell phone played its tuba sound.

Sammy started and began fussing.

"I'm so sorry. I forgot to put it on vibrate." She answered it quickly as Vi settled her son once more. It was Jonas. "Hi," she said, happy to hear his voice.

"Are you at the tea garden?"

"No, I'm at Vi's."

"I see," he said. "I was calling to see if you wanted to go to dinner tonight."

"I don't know what time Foster will be home. I plan to stay so we could try a bottle again with the baby. On my way here, I purchased a few new bottles with nipples that Sammy might take."

"So you'll be tied up for the evening?"

"No. I just don't know when I'll be free."

There was a short silence. "Do you want company while you're babysitting? I could stick around while you and Foster try your experiment. Then we could take Jazzi for something to eat somewhere, maybe drive to York and eat at her favorite burger joint."

With a sigh, Daisy lowered her voice as she leaned against the kitchen counter. "All that's a far cry from us having dinner together."

"I know your grandchild and your daughters come first. Maybe this weekend we can have dinner alone."

"Jonas, you must tell me the truth. Does my limited time bother you?"

He only hesitated a moment. "It doesn't bother me as long as you include me with whatever you're doing. It's been a long time since I had a family or palled around with one."

"You do have a family with us, Jonas. So let me ask Vi what she thinks of our plans."

Daisy related to Vi what she and Jonas had in mind.

Vi said quickly, "I don't mind Jonas being here. He makes me feel safe. I know it sounds ridiculous, but I'm still not used to being alone here, and especially not alone with Sammy."

Before Daisy could say a word, Jonas did. "I heard that. Maybe sometime I could talk to Vi about what would make her feel more secure in her apartment when she's there with Sammy."

"That would be wonderful. Anything to relieve stress."

"Is she still feeling overwhelmed?"

"I'm afraid so."

"I know you can't talk about it with her sitting

there, but we *can* talk if she manages to take a nap. Did Glenda stop in at the tea garden yet?"

"She did. We can talk about that too. I didn't get a whole lot out of her, but I did learn more about Margaret. She and Glenda met at an acting workshop."

"Mom, he's asleep," Vi whispered.

"Jonas, I have to go. How soon can you get here?"

"How soon do you want me there?"

"As soon as your car can make it from there to here."

He laughed. "I'll see you soon."

Daisy considered what Jonas had said . . . that he wanted to be included. And she would do that as much as she could. But no matter how they looked at it, their time together would be limited. She knew how little things in a relationship, little things that could be annoying, began to rankle a lot. Would he tire of their limited time together?

Daisy went to work the following morning secure in the knowledge that Vi had slept yesterday in the afternoon and into the evening. Foster and Daisy had tried the new bottles and nipples and Sammy had taken a good half bottle. That was going to work. Foster had texted Daisy while she and Jonas and Jazzi were at dinner that he'd given the baby a second feeding so Vi could sleep on even more. She'd gotten a good five hours of sleep and a few more during the night.

Jonas had seemed comfortable as he and Daisy had talked before Foster had returned home. She'd told him all about Glenda, and they'd taken turns holding Sammy. Daisy had watched Jonas bond with another little girl when they were working a murder investigation case, so she knew he liked children. Now she understood he could also handle a baby.

The tea garden was busy this morning, and Daisy didn't have time to think about much else. However, several customers reminded her that Thanksgiving was fast approaching. The turkey she'd be buying and roasting would be a fresh one from an Amish family who raised them. She was beginning to look forward to the day and having a gathering at her house. Since her mother had done much of the planning and organizing, Daisy wanted to buy her a gift just to show her appreciation. She knew exactly what she wanted to purchase.

On her break, instead of eating lunch, she pulled on her fleece jacket, pushed her phone into one pocket and her wallet into the other, and told Tessa where she was going. Quilts and Notions, the Fishers' store, would have exactly what she wanted for her mom.

Quilts and Notions was the kind of shop that made Daisy smile. Colorful quilts hung on the walls and from racks made for that purpose. Shelves on another wall held potholders and placemats. The area with bolts of cloth always drew Daisy to it, even though she didn't sew. Her aunt Iris did, and Daisy had often helped her pick out material, threads, and buttons. A corner rack that spun around held books in subjects from quilts to the historic nature of Lancaster County.

Rachel Fisher was busy at the counter speaking with a woman in Pennsylvania Dutch. She lifted a hand to Daisy to let her know she'd seen her. Rachel was an attractive wife and mother, New Order Amish, who didn't need makeup to make her look beautiful. Her hair, parted down the center and gathered in a bun at the nape of her neck, was covered by a white *kapp*. Their district had decided on a heart-shaped *kapp*, and it certainly fitted Rachel and her girls. She was a loving, kind woman who had been Daisy's friend since childhood.

After Rachel handed the woman a bag with her purchases, she moved toward Daisy, the white strings of her *kapp* floating in front of her. Today Rachel was wearing a dark purple dress with her black apron. A few strands of her blond hair had pulled away from her bun and dangled along her cheek. Her blue eyes sparkled as she came over to stand with Daisy.

"What do you need today?" Rachel asked.

Besides more hours in the day or time to spend with Jonas or a good weekend for Jazzi with Portia and happier emotions for Vi? She shook her head. "Not much."

Rachel laid a hand on Daisy's shoulder. "Too much going wrong and not enough going right, ya?"

She'd always been honest with her friend—no pretense between them. Rachel and her husband, Levi, were as honest as the day was long. Daisy had come to expect forthrightness from most Amish. Their values went deep, and their way of life was humbling. Daisy admired the communal atmosphere they lived in more than she could say. Beyond all that, their faith revolved around the fact that everything was in God's plan.

"I shouldn't complain," Daisy said. "I'm grateful for my blessings. I have so many."

"But as a mom, you worry about your girls, ain't so?" Rachel asked.

"Probably more so than I should." Gazing into her friend's eyes, she shared her major burden. "Vi doesn't seem to be bouncing back since Sammy's birth."

"Is all well with the *boppli*?"

"He's a sweetie." Daisy sighed. "Maybe I'm making too much of everything."

"Moms worry. That is true. But give Vi a little time."

"I came in to buy a few potholders and placemats for my mother."

"Things between you and your mom are better?"

"Better, except when she found out that I found Margaret's body."

"What a terrible thing to happen."

"It was. Margaret's husband came to see me. He wants me to help solve the murder."

Rachel's blue eyes widened. "*Zas in der zelt?*"

Rachel's W*hat in the world?* was exactly what Daisy was thinking. What in the world *was* she thinking? She couldn't help Rowan.

"I told him I'd talk to Vanna and Glenda, the playwright, and I did. But I don't know if I'm going any further than that."

"Do you want to?"

Daisy picked up a potholder with an intricate star pattern in yellow, green, and black. "I didn't learn much. Just some background on Margaret and a little bit about Glenda. My good sense is telling me to stay out of this one."

Touching her hand to her chest, Rachel asked, "But what is your heart telling you?"

"That Margaret was a complicated woman. Nobody deserves to die like that."

Both women stayed silent for a bit while Daisy pulled out a potholder here and another there, and placemats she thought would accompany each other as well as the potholders.

Rachel suddenly stood with her back against the shelves, her arms crossed over her chest. Daisy knew something was coming, but she didn't know what. The Amish didn't like to gossip. It was another trait that Daisy admired.

Finally, Rachel said, "Did you know that Mr. Vaughn has made offers to a few Amish store owners who have apartments above their stores? He wants to buy the buildings and then rent the stores to the storekeepers."

"That doesn't make any sense if they're living there."

"It does when the amount Mr. Vaughn is offering is enough to buy a nice property."

"Has anyone sold to him?"

"Not that I know of. But it could be why his offers are going higher and higher. Someone is bound to sell soon. I guess he's rich enough to make whatever he wants happen."

But was Rowan Vaughn rich enough to subsidize his ambition? What if his ambition was much bigger than the stack of bills in his wallet or the amount of money in his checking account? Perhaps Rowan's finances had something to do with Margaret's murder.

Chapter Ten

The restaurant in York, Pennsylvania—about twenty minutes from Willow Creek—was a lot fancier than Daisy was used to. Jonas had brought her here for a Saturday night date. They sat across from each other at a table for two with a pristine white tablecloth covering the table. The crystal sparkled under a brass chandelier and the silverware definitely didn't have any spots. Daisy had just unfolded the black napkin over her lap when the sommelier brought the wine menu.

Jonas asked Daisy, "Would you like to order or should I?"

"One glass would be fine for me." She wanted him to understand he didn't have to buy a whole bottle.

"And one glass will be enough for me. Order whatever you want, even champagne. We should celebrate Sammy's birth, don't you think?"

She looked up at the sommelier. "Would you recommend the sparkling rosé?"

He did and she nodded. "That will be fine."

Jonas ordered a cabernet. After the sommelier left, Jonas waved at the menu. "Order whatever you want. I mean it, Daisy. You deserve some pampering tonight."

After she looked over the prices, her gaze met Jonas's again. "Seriously?"

"Seriously. Filet mignon, lobster, or prime rib. I hear the Chilean sea bass is quite good."

"Did you sell a lot of furniture this week?"

He chuckled. "Tonight isn't about the cost. It's about enjoyment—enjoying the food, the wine, and each other." His green gaze held the honest light that she appreciated so much.

"All right, the Chilean sea bass it is. And I've always wanted to try asparagus risotto. What are you having?"

"The seafood combo—crab cake, scallops, shrimp, filet of haddock. You can try some of mine if you'd like." His eyebrows wiggled a bit and she laughed. It felt so good to laugh. Violet wasn't the only one who'd been a bit tense . . . more than a bit.

"I suppose we're going to make light conversation all evening?" she asked.

"I think light conversation will go better with the wine and the food."

"It may take me all evening to think of something light."

He grinned at her, reached across the table, and took her hand. "I know what you have on your mind right now. Portia, Jazzi, and Colton. When you dropped off Jazzi in Allentown last evening, I know your worry about this weekend began."

"It did," Daisy said, but didn't have a chance to add more as the sommelier brought their glasses of wine. They raised their glasses, and when Jonas clinked his against hers, he said, "To Sammy and a life full of every good thing."

As they sipped their wine, Daisy felt almost giddy and it wasn't from the alcohol. "I know you said we should have light conversation, but I have a question. If I want to learn more about Margaret's life in New York, who do you think I should talk to?"

"Somehow I knew this topic would pop up." He squeezed her hand.

"That's as light as I can think of right now."

With a shake of his head, he dramatically sighed.

Jonas was different tonight, and she couldn't put her finger on exactly how. Although to her he always looked rakishly handsome, tonight he was wearing a charcoal suit with a pale gray shirt open at the collar. When she looked at him, she knew the man underneath that attractive exterior was filled with integrity and compassion for others. She'd never been attracted to good looks, but rather to a man whom she could form an emotional bond with. When she'd fallen in love and married Ryan, she'd been impetuous, filled with a penchant for a future with him and eager to learn about marriage and life and independence she might have never felt before. Now she wasn't impetuous. Now she knew dreams were wisps like smoke, and today was the reality.

"Are you looking forward to seeing Camellia over Thanksgiving?"

"I haven't spoken with her since Vi's wedding reception. If she's bringing along a boyfriend, hopefully she'll be too occupied with him and fending off Mom's questions to disapprove of *my* life."

"Do you feel that's what she does?"

"As much as Mom does. It's that disapproving *I-wouldn't-do-it-that-way* syndrome. Ever heard of it?"

"In fact, I have. I think it afflicts most families."

They both smiled.

"Have you asked Zeke to have a beer and go watch a game?"

"Not yet. The time just hasn't seemed right. And I know what you're going to say—that the time might never seem right. But I have to follow my gut on this. If I push him too soon, I think he'll just become more antagonistic. I don't want that."

Jonas studied her pensively and returned to the question she'd asked about following leads. "Why don't you stop in at the Little Theater for one of the rehearsals. If you just talk to everyone in general, I'm sure you'll learn more about Margaret. People open up to you. Keisha and Ward might know something that Glenda didn't know."

"And Glenda might know a lot more than she told me."

"Speaking of light conversation," he said with a bit of humor, "did you start Christmas shopping yet? I think it could be great fun going toy shopping for Sammy."

Jonas was probably right about that. After that gambit, they did keep the conversation lighter. The food arrived and they were more quiet while they ate, appreciating each bite. The food really was sublime. Daisy had known they were going out to dinner tonight, but she hadn't expected this. It was as if Jonas was courting her. That was an old-fashioned term that was used a lot in this area. In the Amish community, when a girl and a boy were interested in each other with dreams of marriage and a family ahead of them, they courted. For the Amish that usually meant a buggy ride after a family dinner or after a church service. Courting was a time when the two people could spend an evening alone together. The couple was vigilant about not many public displays of affection, but in private holding hands and kissing were considered appropriate.

She could outright ask Jonas if that's what they were doing, but putting the question into words could spook either of them. She preferred to simply enjoy the dim lights, the delicious food, and the sight of the man across from her.

They'd decided to share a generous slice of Black Forest cake when Daisy's phone played its tuba sound. She quickly dived for it in her purse. When she brought it out to the table, she could see Jazzi was calling.

"It's Jazzi," she said to Jonas.

"Go ahead and take it. I'll save you plenty of whipped cream and cherries."

"I appreciate that," she teased, but she really wasn't in a teasing mood. If Jazzi was calling her, then something was wrong.

"Are you at home, Mom?" Jazzi asked, her voice a bit shaky.

"No, I'm at a restaurant with Jonas."

"Sarah Jane's?"

"No, a restaurant in York. He's treating me to candlelight, chandeliers, and white tablecloths. What's wrong?"

"I don't know if you want to take this call where you are. Can you go somewhere to talk freely?"

"Sure. There's a glassed-in porch. I'll go out there. Talk to me while I'm on my way."

"Don't you have to explain to Jonas?"

"He understands." When she pointed to the enclosed porch, Jonas nodded.

"I'm sorry I'm ruining your dinner."

"Honey, you're not. We're almost finished. Now tell me what's wrong."

She opened the door to the glassed-in porch and stepped down the two steps onto the flagstone floor. A wrought-iron bench sat on one side and she settled on that, looking out into the night through the big windows across from her.

"Colton and I haven't clicked. He's trying and I'm trying, but it's like there's this tall wall between us."

Listening was the best thing she could do for Jazzi. "Go on," she advised, knowing there was more.

"Portia thought it would be a good idea if Colton and the girls and I all went to the mall."

"Does Colton like to go to the mall? Most men don't particularly like shopping."

"I don't know if he likes shopping, but he enjoys being with his daughters. They often end up at the video arcade."

Daisy could see a dad liking that part of the activity. "So what happened?"

"One of his daughters, Missy, wanted to go into a jewelry boutique. You know, one of those cute ones where everything's affordable. They have barrettes and makeup and bracelets and necklaces that really show up."

Immediately a store in the Park City Mall came to mind. Daisy knew what Jazzi was talking about. "And what happened?"

"Trying to be helpful, I said I'd take the girls in and he could go into another store if he wanted. But he got all huffy. He said we should all stay together. He didn't want his daughters spending all of their allowance on junk. He called it *junk*, Mom. That pretty jewelry enhances clothes, and I don't think it was the jewelry or his daughters spending their allowance.

He just doesn't like me. I don't know what to do, Mom. What can I do to make him like me?"

Whoa. Thoughts like that could get Jazzi in trouble. But what should she say that would make a difference? "Honey, Colton is Colton, and you are you. Do you remember when Dad would bring home business friends, and you just didn't like them? You'd go up in your room after dinner and find something else to do. But then there were others that you enjoyed talking to. They'd play a board game after dinner, and you didn't mind staying with us old folks."

"Aw, Mom. That's not the same."

"It is in a way. You and Colton are in an awkward situation. Maybe he doesn't want anyone to influence his daughters except for him or their mother. Maybe he thinks you'll encourage them to buy Goth jewelry." Daisy's voice was filled with a bit of amusement.

She heard Jazzi sigh and knew her daughter was probably rolling her eyes. "Mom, you know I wouldn't do that."

"Sure, *I* know you wouldn't. But *he* doesn't. See if this blows over. What did you do after the kerfuffle?"

"One of his daughters suggested we get gelato so we went to a stand that sells it, walked the mall some more, and then went home."

Home. Daisy didn't want Jazzi thinking of Portia's place as home. "There's something you could do."

"What? Leave?"

"No. You could try to talk to Colton about what happened."

"I can't do that. It would be too embarrassing."

"Maybe, but if you push past the embarrassment, just doing it might show him how adult you are. All

I'm saying is think about it, and don't expect all good or all bad to happen this weekend. You both need some time, Jazzi. You can't get to know a person in a day."

"I suppose not," Jazzi admitted. "Thanks, Mom, for listening. I hope I didn't ruin your romantic date."

"It's early. We still have time to be romantic."

"Mom." That frustrated drawl was in the word again.

"Be kind, stand up for yourself, but most of all, just try to listen. You'll learn about Colton that way."

"Good night, Mom. I'll see you tomorrow."

"Good night, honey. I love you."

"Love you too."

After Daisy returned to the table, Jonas studied her. "Trouble in Allentown?"

"Jazzi thinks there is." She explained what her daughter had told her.

"There's no knowing what's going through his mind," Jonas admitted. "Do you think Jazzi will talk to him about it?"

"She can be forward sometimes, but in this situation, I think she's just scared she'll mess things up even more. And Portia really can't intervene. Not in this."

Jonas pointed to Daisy's plate with the whipped cream, chocolate cake, and cherries. "How about if I feed that to you and we go back to your place and make a pot of tea?"

"I might have a bottle of wine."

"I need to be clearheaded when Jazzi's not in the house as chaperone, don't you think?"

"There's always Marjoram and Pepper," Daisy joked.

But the smoldering look in Jonas's eyes told her

he wouldn't be drinking too much wine tonight. He might even stick to tea. Their lives were just too complicated to take the next step.

Daisy wanted to talk to Ward Cooper privately, not within a group of people at a dress rehearsal. Sunday would go slowly waiting for Jazzi to come home. And she didn't want to intrude on Vi, Foster, and Sammy too often. So after church, she headed for one of Rowan's condo buildings, where Ward was staying.

She found the building easily. It was a four-story brick structure that had at one time been a warehouse. Once it had had historic value. Now, however, the brick building had been renovated. It was a square building without much adornment. She'd heard that there were two condos on each floor.

Granite steps led to a double door that opened electronically. Daisy didn't see any sign of cameras or security, but then this was Willow Creek and security costs could be expensive. As the supermarket-type glass doors opened for her, she stepped inside to a foyer with mailboxes on either side of the corridor. They were small cubicles with a key lock and slots above each box where a postal clerk deposited mail. There were bins underneath each box, apparently for small packages.

She found the box with Ward Cooper's name. He was in condo #302. Before she turned away, however, she noticed the name under the box beneath Cooper's. Jasper Lazar. He was also in the play, and she wondered if maybe he was a permanent resident. There was an elevator to the left of the corridor and stairs to the right. She decided to take the stairs. Her lack of an exercise routine bothered her. She went for hikes around her property when she could, but with winter setting in, she knew she should sign up for an exercise class.

To her surprise, she really was breathless when she reached the third floor. Serving tea just wasn't aerobic exercise, though lifting serving trays might have something to do with weight training. She easily found apartment 302 and she rang the bell. No one came to the door. She rang again. Still there was no sound from inside.

Remembering Lazar's condo number, she headed back down the stairs to the second floor. Wandering down the hall, she found condo 201. What were the chances Jasper was home? She'd heard he'd retired from his HVAC business. In fact, he'd sold it to another heating and air-conditioning firm who had combined the two businesses, one in Lancaster and one in Willow Creek. It was all supposition on her part, but she imagined he'd received a pretty penny for the business.

She rang his doorbell and waited, studying the door that she expected to be of high quality. It wasn't. Granted, it was an interior door and didn't have to face the elements. On the other hand, if someone could put a foot through the door, how secure could it be even when locked?

She could hear footsteps and a moment later the door opened. Jasper looked about a decade older than her dad. In the play, he was playing a grandfather, which suited him. Right now, he had a bit of stubble along his beard line. He was wearing a green sweatshirt with a flannel shirt underneath. His navy cargo pants were heavy too. The outfit was definitely fashioned for cold weather and she wondered if he was going out.

His brows lifted and his brown eyes widened when he spotted her. "Mrs. Swanson. What are you doing here?"

"Please call me Daisy. I wondered if I might talk with you about Margaret and the play."

"Come in," he invited, waving his hand to motion her inside. "I'm afraid it's cold in here. The heating unit for my condo isn't working again, at least not the way it should. I'm an expert at that kind of thing. I should know."

His voice sounded impatient, as if this weren't the first time this event had occurred.

"I imagine it is frustrating to be an expert at something and then have to live with repairs of it."

"Repairs? I only wish that were so. I've been calling about my lack of heat ever since the cold spell hit two weeks ago."

"Rowan Vaughn owns this building, doesn't he?"

Jasper gestured to the gray corduroy sofa, and she sat there while he took the black leather recliner across from her. "Yes, he does. But reaching Mr. Vaughn isn't so easy. He has a management firm to take care of his properties. I've been hoping he'd stop in at rehearsals and I could talk to him there. Maybe *accost* him would be a better word. Isn't it terrible that you have to make a scene sometimes in order to get anything done?"

Daisy really would rather avoid scenes if she could. She had intended to unzip her jacket, and she did so now more as an attempt to be casual with Jasper than anything else. The condo *was* chilly. "How long have you lived here?"

"Ever since Rowan renovated and took over the place—about two years. But there have been problems from the beginning."

"You mean like the heat?"

"Or the air-conditioning. My guess is he had sub-par systems installed. You can't cheat on your HVAC units. It just doesn't pay in the long run."

"I suppose not."

"And it's not just the units, of course. Just look at those windows."

Jasper's condo was located at the front of the building. The windows were about six feet high and four feet wide.

Daisy tried to be positive. "I suppose you're lucky to have a front-facing condo. These windows let in a lot of light."

"Maybe. But see how the one's cloudy? They are supposed to be double sealed for heat efficiency. Maybe the glass is but the way they were installed . . ." He shook his head. "Cold air comes in around the whole window in the winter, and in the summer it's the same with heat. They look great from the outside and they'll draw in customers to rent. But living here is another matter."

"Why do you stay?"

"Because I signed a lease, and breaking the lease would cost more than I'm willing to pay. So I'm on the phone most days just trying to make this place comfortable. I don't have it as bad as Ward, though."

"You mean Ward Cooper, the lighting technician from the play?"

"Exactly. Rowan offered him an empty condo to stay in while he was in town. But Ward's condo has different problems than mine."

"Does he have insufficient heat?"

"Oh, yes, but he doesn't seem to mind that. What he does mind is that his appliances don't work as they should. And he hears scratching in the kitchen wall at night. You know what that means—mice. But he can't complain because he's staying there free. I have to admit Rowan did replace the microwave but the oven on the stove doesn't work. I think one of the heating elements went out."

"Is Glenda staying in a condo too?"

"Heavens no. I guess Margaret knew about the problems with these condos. She found Glenda a first-floor apartment in an old house on Spruce Street. The whole place has been completely renovated, and the landlady lives in the upstairs apartment. From what I understand, Glenda is quite happy with it."

"Do you know if Ward, Keisha, Glenda, and Margaret were all friends in New York?"

Jasper gave a shrug. "I don't know for sure. But apparently there are bars and restaurants where the artistic types go. My guess is they ran into each other someplace like that, though I did overhear Margaret and Glenda talking and I think the two of them have a history."

"A pleasant history?"

"Again, I'm not sure. They bickered a lot but that was mostly about the play. Both insisted on having control so neither of them did."

Thinking about the building again, Daisy asked, "Do you know if other renters have problems with their condos?"

Jasper crossed one leg over his knee. "I've heard rumors. Scuttlebutt says that some of the renters have been paid off not to file lawsuits."

When Jonas had looked into public records, he hadn't found any information about lawsuits against Rowan. "That sounds serious."

"An older woman slipped on a wet floor and she threatened to sue, but the matter was settled out of court. It just seems ridiculous that someone with the amount of money Rowan Vaughn has can't find adequate repairmen to take care of his properties. Keisha Washington is staying in one of his other buildings but I don't think she's had any problems. My guess is it all depends on the manager of the building."

"Can you tell me if the local people are getting to know Keisha and Ward and Glenda very well?"

"Keisha and Ward seem to have their own little club. Glenda and Margaret palled around sometimes but now that Margaret's gone—" He looked forlorn for a moment. "I just can't imagine why anyone would do that to her."

"I can't either. She'd been away from Willow Creek for so long, I can't imagine she'd make that many enemies in the few years she was back here."

"It's easier to make enemies than friends, and you've got to admit, she did have an attitude. She acted like she and Rowan were better than anyone else. People with money are often like that."

"Margaret didn't always have money."

"You'd never know that, though, would you? You'd never know she'd been raised Mennonite."

"Do you know her sister Vanna?"

"I do. Vanna is like a sweet spring day. Margaret was more like a tropical storm. Controlled but a storm no less."

"I didn't know Margaret well but Vanna and I are friends," Daisy confided.

Jasper eyed her with consideration. "Why did you really come to talk to me, Mrs. Swanson?"

Before she could answer, he snapped his fingers. "I get it now. I read that story the reporter did on the last murder investigation in Willow Creek. He quoted you several times. I got the feeling you were in on the investigation. Do you work with the police and just don't tell anyone that?"

"I'm not working with the police. But if I do find anything out, I share it with them. *If* I think it's important."

"You date a former cop."

"I do."

"Jonas seems to be an upright guy. He knows his way around a saw."

Daisy laughed. "Yes, he does. And a sander."

Now Jasper cracked a smile. "I admire men who work with their hands. It's a marrying of intellect and creativity. Few people appreciate that."

"Why did you decide to audition to be in the play?"

He wiggled his brows. "Don't I seem like the type?"

"I'm not sure if there *is* a type. I know getting up on a stage terrified me when I was in high school."

"Believe it or not, when I was in school, I liked English. I was good at it. One of my teachers in high school encouraged me to audition for a play. I did, and I liked being part of the cast, putting something together that was much more than the sum of its parts."

"So how did you become an expert in HVAC?"

He uncrossed his leg, put his elbows on his knees, and leaned forward. "My dad started the business. He was a pragmatic man. He told me I could go act in plays all I wanted, but not expect to be paid for it. On the other hand, if I apprenticed with him, specialized and went out on my own, I could make a good living. And I did."

Daisy rubbed her hands up and down her arms. It *was* cold in here.

"I can see you're chilled. How about a mug of hot chocolate? We can talk about everything that doesn't matter."

Maybe it was because Daisy sensed loneliness in Jasper Lazar. Maybe instead of asking him questions, she could just listen to him to find out more about his life. "Hot chocolate sounds good."

Chapter Eleven

On Monday afternoon, Daisy stopped at A Penny Saved, Willow Creek's thrift store. It hadn't been open very long. However, donations of clothes for children and adults had been coming in regularly. The store seemed filled to capacity. There were racks of blouses, one for skirts and one for slacks. Shoes lined up against one wall according to sizes, men's, women's, and children's separated.

Amelia Wiseman was at the checkout desk. In her mid-forties, she wore her dark brown hair layered around her face. Even though she and her husband ran the Covered Bridge Bed and Breakfast, she also volunteered her time at the thrift store. She seemed to have boundless energy.

When she spotted Daisy, she waved and Daisy went over to the desk, commenting, "The store looks great."

"And I was worried about it being necessary," Amelia said. "You wouldn't believe the people who come in here, families that you'd never expect."

"Families like to put on a brave face that they're doing well when they aren't. I've noticed folks around here don't particularly like to ask for help."

"Now they don't have to ask. It's here in plain sight. Once the town council straightens out the plans for the homeless shelter, this town should be better off."

"Winter is a hard time for many farming families," Daisy agreed.

"And for some of the store owners when the tourist trade isn't revved up."

Moving closer to the counter, Daisy picked up a coupon flyer there. "Every day I'm grateful for the residents of Willow Creek who come into the tea garden."

Amelia sank down onto the wooden stool behind the desk. "When the tour buses arrive, those tourists want something hot to drink in this cold weather and you provide it even if they don't buy other souvenirs. They're likely to stop by for a scone and a cup of tea."

"Our special events are working out well too," Daisy added.

"Who doesn't want to build a gingerbread house?" Amelia looked like a child when she said it. "I'm only going to be here about an hour or so. Agnes Hopper will be coming in for the rest of the day and Sarah Jane will be joining her for a few hours."

Agnes, whose husband had died about a year ago, was one of the older residents of Willow Creek. "Do you think working here fills up empty time for her?"

"Absolutely. I'm glad we're filling a need for the volunteers too. Volunteering and doing something for others can lift anyone's self-esteem and spirits." Amelia hesitated for a few moments, but then she asked, "How is Violet doing? I hear she was having some problems adjusting to marriage and mother-hood."

It was on the tip of Daisy's tongue to ask Amelia where she'd heard that, but there was no point. If someone at the tea garden overheard one of the servers talking about Violet, or maybe even one of Jazzi's friends, word could get around. That's the way Willow Creek was.

"The truth is, I'd like to say she's doing better. In some ways she is, but in others I just don't know. I see a dull look in her eyes sometimes that scares me. Her energy is very low even with Foster taking some of Sammy's feedings now. She's getting more sleep but I can't tell a difference."

Daisy had always been honest with Amelia and Amelia with Daisy. They weren't really close friends, but they were friends, and it felt good to vent to someone outside of the situation.

"Postpartum depression?"

"I assume so. She's going to be seeing her doctor."

"Her doctor might suggest talk therapy first, but with postpartum that doesn't always make a difference. The truth is—doctors don't like to take a chance with their patients since more is known about it."

"You've had experience with this?"

"I have with one of my nieces. Let me tell you, the sooner Violet gets help the better it will be. Make sure to encourage her that breastfeeding isn't the be-all and end-all."

Surprised, Daisy asked, "Why do you say that?"

"If she's on an antidepressant, she won't be able to breastfeed, but her well-being and her state of mind are more important for the baby right now than breast milk."

Daisy could easily understand what Amelia was saying. The baby's self-esteem, development, and even physical activity would have a lot to do with Violet— her moods, her level of energy, and her ability to give of herself.

"I'm hoping her doctor guides her in the right direction."

"Doctors are so much more aware of postpartum than they were years ago, though I'm not sure families are. I know Vi has your full support. That helps."

Changing the subject, Amelia pointed to the racks of women's clothes. "You ought to take a look. We even have designer dresses there."

"I don't have much time. But I will."

Daisy started making the rounds of the racks. She really didn't need anything right now, but if Jonas took her someplace special again, she might want to have a new dress for that. She carefully watched how much of her budget she allotted for a wardrobe for her and Jazzi. Buying at the thrift shop, she could stretch it.

She spotted a maxi caftan-like dress that looked as if the blue, pink, and yellow flowers on it had been hand painted. It was her size. She pulled it off the rack and held it up. "This is beautiful."

"That off-white background is popular even in winter. You should try it on. The dressing room isn't very elaborate, but it's private." Amelia pointed to the back of the store, where a cubicle had been built with a door with a latch. Daisy examined the dress again. The label at the back had been removed. It really *was* beautiful.

Ten minutes later she decided to buy it. The colors in it would accompany any season. With the holidays coming up, she was sure there would be an occasion for something not too elaborate but just plain pretty.

She was thinking about how the dress had looked on her when she'd stared in the dressing room mirror as she walked through the racks to the sales desk. She stopped and examined a man's suit. When she checked the label, she saw it was Armani!

"Wow, this is a beautifully cut suit."

Amelia came around the desk and crossed to Daisy. "I don't usually mention who goes in and out of the store, but I can tell you who brought that in."

Daisy couldn't keep her curiosity in check. "Who?"

"Ward Cooper." She pointed to another rack. "Those dress shirts cost him a pretty penny too."

"I know it's none of our business, but did he say why he was donating them?"

"He said he lost a few pounds and they just don't fit like they should."

"I didn't think lighting techs made a bundle, but maybe I'm wrong."

"Or maybe by staying in Willow Creek, he's saving a ton of money and can afford another suit."

Daisy studied the suit again. "I don't understand."

"New York is expensive. Of course, it depends on what part of the city he lived in, but if Rowan Vaughn is giving him a place to stay here for free, that would make a difference with his expenses."

"But he would have kept the New York apartment, right?"

"I don't know how he lives, but I do know stage crews can be on the road a lot. He could lease a place month to month. Who knows? But I do know if you get a good look at the clothes that he wears, they don't come cheap."

If Daisy asked any more questions, she'd be diving deeper into the suspect pool of Margaret's murder. Right now, that wasn't what she wanted or needed.

She handed the dress she'd found to Amelia. "I'll take this and I'll stop looking."

Amelia raised a brow. "Not interested in who killed Margaret?"

"Oh, I'm interested, but I know I shouldn't be."

"By the way," Amelia said. "I decided to help with costume fittings for the play at the Little Theater. They needed someone who could sew. I attended a rehearsal last week and it was pathetic."

Daisy was sorry to hear that.

The front door of the shop opened and Agnes came in. She was a birdlike woman, short with gray wispy hair that fell around her face in a helmet-like style. Wearing a black wool cape and sturdy brown shoes, she looked ready for anything that came her way. She was all smiles as she slipped behind the desk and hung her cape on the wooden coatrack, revealing a sensible white blouse and black sweater.

After greetings were exchanged all around, Agnes said, "You don't know how this volunteer work fills my day. I hope there are a lot of clothes to be unpacked and hung on the racks."

"I guess that's my signal to leave," Amelia said with a smile.

After Daisy had paid her and she'd bagged the dress, Amelia said, "I'm heading over to rehearsal at the Little Theater now. Why don't you come with me? Jonas will be there working on the set, won't he?"

Yes, he would. Daisy could tell herself that was the reason she was going to stop in at the dress rehearsal at Willow Creek Little Theater . . . but if she looked deeper into the idea, she knew that wasn't the *only* reason.

* * *

The Willow Creek Little Theater fit into the landscape. Daisy turned off Hollowback Road onto the driveway that led around to the side of the theater where the wider parking lot was located. The building itself was cedar-shingled with a peaked roof. It almost looked like a large cabin. The land behind it was filled with pines, oaks, and maples. Beyond that, hills rolled around the property.

Although there were other entrances, Daisy and Amelia walked along the flagstone path to the portico-covered main door. Supports for the portico that were also cedar gave the illusion of a porch.

After Daisy opened one half of the double door leading into the theater, she found herself and Amelia standing in the lobby.

With a wave, Amelia said, "I'm going to see if any other volunteers are here."

There were two bulletin boards encased in glass that were supposed to announce the upcoming shows, Daisy suspected. They were empty.

She followed a short corridor where she passed the ticket-takers' stand and entered the rear of the theater. As soon as she did, bright lights assaulted her and she heard noise, talking, hammering, and the shuffling of feet. As she walked toward the stage, she noticed the navy cushioned seats that looked comfortable for viewing whatever the production was. There were steps on either side that led up to the stage. After taking off her winter jacket, she laid it with her purse on a front row seat. She walked toward the steps, her gaze scanning the stage for Jonas.

Spotting him, she ran up the set of stairs on the left. On the stage, however, she stopped, listening to an argument to the left of her. It was easy to recognize Daniel Copeland's voice as he said, "I disagree.

In that scene I should be firm, maybe even cutting with my words."

Daisy heard Glenda answer, "No, you shouldn't. You're a father. There should be some understanding in your tone."

Daisy wondered if this type of argument went on all the time. How would they get anything done if it did?

Before she could reach Jonas, someone on the right called her name. "Daisy, hold up," a male voice ordered.

She mentally groaned. It was Trevor Lundquist, the *Willow Creek Messenger*'s reporter who had the most bylines. Trevor was a good-looking man. His brown hair was longer now than the last time she'd seen him. It had a slight wave and lay over his mint green oxford shirt collar. He had his sleeves rolled up. His brown cargo pants were casual yet up-to-date.

"You're just the person I wanted to see," he said. "And the fact that you're here tells me what I want to know."

"What do you want to know?"

"I want to know what happened to Margaret Vaughn, just like everyone else," he said, his voice lowered. "Isn't that why you're here? You're investigating?"

"I'm *not* investigating. I came to see Jonas." She pointed to the back of the stage. "He's helping with the sets. Seeing me here doesn't mean a thing."

"I know you, Daisy Swanson. You won't be able to keep your nose out of this one. You found her."

Daisy's heart sank. How widespread was *that* knowledge? "Just how do you know that?"

"I have my sources."

She was already shaking her head. "I don't care

about your sources. I'm not getting involved. The last investigation practically took my life. I have too much to live for to meddle again." Her eyes automatically went to Jonas.

Trevor shifted from one foot to the other. "I hear you have a grandson."

She narrowed her eyes at him. "I do, and you brought that up because . . . ?"

"I'm just making conversation. Can't we be friendly?"

Her voice became firm as she looked into his eyes. "I don't know, Trevor. Can we? In the past I've given you interviews after the fact. But I don't know if that's good for me or my family. I don't want Willow Creek's headlights turned onto me or anyone else I'm close to."

Trevor's frown caused long lines on either side of his mouth. "That doesn't mean you can't feed me information when you have it."

"Read my lips, Trevor—I am *not* getting involved."

Trevor pushed both of his hands palm-out in surrender. "I hear you. But I'll talk to you again in a few days." He backed up, then headed down the steps to the seating area of the theater.

Arden was on a ladder helping Jasper hang a new curtain. It looked as if the material was lush and heavy. Jasper confirmed that fact when he said to Arden, "This cost a heck of a lot more than it should have. But Margaret always had to have the best."

"I'm not sure where she learned what was best," Arden returned sharply. "She didn't have that many posh possessions growing up from what I've heard. The Mennonite faith isn't that far from being Amish, is it? She might not have had a phone or especially not music to dance to. Maybe not even a computer."

"I don't know if that's true," Jasper said. "Unless that's the way her parents chose to live."

"Didn't you find it difficult to get to know Margaret? She was so closed off."

Jasper, holding the curtain up in front of his shoulders, answered, "I want to know why she wouldn't talk about her time acting in New York."

"Only Glenda knew her then, and probably all of her secrets. You know how often they had their heads together."

Jonas was fitting two sections of scenery together when Daisy approached him. He was wearing a chambray shirt with the sleeves rolled up and blue jeans worn white at the pockets and the knees. She wanted to go up to him and put her arms around his waist . . . but not here . . . not now.

As soon as he finished with the corner of the scenery, he turned toward Daisy and his face lit up with a smile. When he was glad to see her like that, her heart seemed to do a little dance, at least the rhythm of it did.

"I didn't expect to see you here," he said.

"It was your suggestion, remember?"

"I guess it was. Did you come over to see our progress?" He lowered his voice. "Or to talk to everybody in sight?"

She elbowed him and smiled. "I don't have to talk to everybody to hear things. I just heard an interesting conversation between Arden and Jasper."

"Did you learn anything?"

"Just that Margaret paid too much for the curtain."

Jonas chuckled. "From what I understand, she paid too much for everything, including the oriental rug that's used in the living room scene and those cushioned seats out there. But I've got to admit if I'm comfortable watching the show, I'm more likely to come back."

Vanna, who was standing in the wings, beckoned to Jonas.

"I'll be right back," Jonas said to Daisy. "Are you going to wait?"

"I'll just look around." Arden and Jasper were no longer on the ladder.

Daisy noticed that the left side of the curtain had been hung. She peered up at a brass chandelier that must be part of the living room set. She wandered to the back of the stage. Even though it was a wider area than she expected, it was crowded with cutouts of fir trees in differing heights. That made sense since the name of the play had *North Woods* in it. There was also a sleigh, an old wagon, and a staircase. She imagined that staircase would be used to lead to the second floor of the house in the north woods. Vanna had told her a few things about the play, so she recognized where the scenery would go.

The scent of newly sanded wood, paint, and stain was strong at the rear of the stage. She wandered along the row of trees wondering where the costumes were kept. She wouldn't mind having a glimpse of those.

Just then she saw a shadow above her. Before she could even think about taking a step, a row of plywood pine trees fell on top of her, jostling her onto the floor. The noise was loud enough to capture everyone's attention, she supposed, because she heard footsteps on the side stairs and on the stage.

Jonas was the first one to reach her. Although she was under the wooden trees, she could see Jonas's

feet. She'd recognize those black shoe boots anywhere.

"Don't move," he commanded. "Let me lift these
trees off of you first."

In a matter of minutes, the trees were upright
again and Daisy could see that Jasper and Ward had
helped Jonas lift them.

Jonas crouched down beside her as she sat up. He
warned again, "I'm not sure you should move. I'll
call the paramedics."

She grabbed his arm. "No. I'm fine. Really. Just
give me a minute to catch my breath."

Amelia and Vanna were crouching down beside
Jonas now too. "Were you knocked out?" Vanna
asked.

"No. More than anything, my hip hurts. One of
those trees landed against me."

Vanna said, "Wiggle your hands and feet, then
your arms and legs."

Daisy did that. "Everything works," she said with a
weak smile. "Just let me stand up."

"Can somebody get a chair?" Jonas called.

Keisha pushed out one of the upholstered chairs
that had been sitting in the wings. "Here you go."
She looked concerned.

Vanna and Jonas helped Daisy to her feet, and she
quickly sat.

Trevor was beside Daisy now too. "I'll stay with her
if you want to look around," Trevor said.

Jonas gave him a *can-I-trust-you?* look.

Trevor nodded again as if to reassure Jonas he was
a good guy. He was, Daisy thought. Sometimes he was
just a little pushy. Glancing over her shoulder, she

watched Jonas search behind the trees and then in the wings.

Keisha crouched down in front of her with a bottle of water. "Here, drink some of this."

Taking the bottle Keisha had opened for her, Daisy took a few swallows. She thanked Keisha.

Keisha said, "I didn't think those trees *could* be tipped over. We'll have to remedy that."

A few minutes later, Jonas returned to Daisy and knelt before her. "There's no point calling the police when what happened could have been an accident."

Trevor faced Daisy more squarely. "You don't think it was an accident, do you?"

Daisy's heart had stopped racing and had settled into a regular rhythm. She rubbed her shoulder. "Maybe it was and maybe it wasn't."

Jonas and Vanna exchanged a look.

"You have a brush burn on your arm," Vanna said.

Keisha appeared again with an emergency first aid kit.

Vanna took it from her.

Daisy protested. "Vanna, I can fix myself up when I get home."

"Don't be silly. You need to sit there awhile anyway. Make sure nothing hurts more than it should."

Jonas ducked down again until he was eye to eye with Daisy. "Are you sure you don't hurt anywhere?"

"Just bumps and bruises. A hot shower and Dad's liniment will make me feel good as new."

Jonas took Daisy's hand in his. "I don't want anything to happen to you. I'm going to take another look around." He kept his voice low. "I really don't see how those trees could have fallen on you on their own. Somebody had to have pushed them."

Somebody. A member of the cast or a volunteer? After Vanna swiped Daisy's brush burn with peroxide, then applied antibiotic cream and a bandage, she said, "You sit still while I put this away."

Daisy turned slightly in the chair and looked up at Trevor. "Talk to me about anything but Margaret's murder."

Trevor let out a sigh. "If you insist. There was something I wanted to ask you anyway."

"Something that has nothing to do with murder?"

"Absolutely nothing to do with murder. How long have you known Tessa Miller?"

That was a question she'd never expected. "Tessa and I went to school together. In fact, we skipped a grade together. We had each other's backs and we still do. I couldn't imagine anyone else as my kitchen manager. Why do you want to know?"

"So you'd say she's a lot like you."

Daisy shook her head and the movement pulled on her shoulder that was beginning to ache. She ignored it. "Oh, Tessa and I are very different."

"How so?"

Forgetting momentarily about what had just happened, she explained, "Tessa is an *artiste*. You can tell that just by the way she dresses. She's much more of a free spirit, and Bohemian in her taste."

"Including men?"

Daisy remembered that Tessa had asked about bringing Cade for Thanksgiving dinner. Cade certainly was as staid as they came. On the other hand, a man she'd loved had been the owner of the town's art gallery.

"To tell the truth, I'm not sure about her taste in men. I think that all depends on who she connects with. I'm sure Tessa would say she's a vibrations person. She'd have to receive the right vibe from a man."

"Uh-huh." Trevor looked pensive.

Was Trevor interested in Tessa?

To tell the truth, Daisy would rather think about Tessa and Trevor instead of what had just happened.

Chapter Twelve

"Is your hip hurting you?" Iris asked Daisy as Daisy shifted her weight from one foot to the other at the counter in the tea garden's kitchen the next day. They were checking the produce that Joachim Adler had brought, making sure it suited them. Joachim had taken off his black felt hat and was holding it in his hands. His light brown beard dangled close to the second button of his shirt.

His face took on a little color and Daisy knew talking about anything personal around him would embarrass him. She said to Iris, "I'm good." Then she gave Joachim a nod. "Everything looks top quality just as always. Your greenhouses are really producing." She particularly liked the leaf lettuce.

"*Wunderbaar*," he said. He flopped his hat on his head. "See you next week." With a smile, he went out the back kitchen door.

"Sorry," Iris apologized. "I almost forgot Joachim was there. He's so quiet. But are you hurting? Did you sleep wrong? You keep shifting from one hip to the other."

Daisy wrapped the lettuce in green paper that kept it fresh. "I had a little mishap at the rehearsal yesterday."

Iris stopped inspecting the turnips and carrots. "What kind of mishap?"

"I was careless and part of the set fell on me. Merely a few bumps and bruises. I'm fine, really."

"Was Jonas there?"

"He was."

"Did he call the paramedics?"

Daisy didn't look her aunt in the eyes, but concentrated on wrapping produce. "Don't be silly. I told him not to. Vanna was there and she took care of one of my brush burns."

"Does this have something to do with you asking questions about Margaret?"

"No proof of that," Daisy quickly answered, and went into the walk-in to store the lettuce.

Everyone yesterday had made sure she was okay. She had a feeling Rowan was more worried about liability than her when he'd called her last night. She caught herself. That wasn't nice. Everyone who had been there had been concerned. Jonas had insisted on driving her home. She'd let him. Then she'd put ice packs on the parts that hurt and texted back and forth with Foster about Violet because Vi hadn't answered her texts.

From Foster she'd learned Vi had had one weepy spell in the afternoon. He'd cooked supper, saying Vi had eaten a few spoonfuls of his macaroni and cheese. He'd encouraged her to eat a piece of toast later.

Daisy was worried. Vi's appointment with her doctor tomorrow couldn't come soon enough.

Cora Sue entered the kitchen from their main serving room. Finding Daisy in the walk-in, she pointed to the tearoom. "Arden Botterill's here. She'd like to see you. I showed her to a table and asked what type of tea she'd like and she told me the honey ginseng green tea. Is that okay for you too?"

"That's fine." She checked the clock on the wall. It was eleven. "Did she say if she'd like anything to eat?"

"She insisted she just wanted tea."

Although Daisy didn't know Arden well, she did know her. When Arden just requested tea and nothing to go with it, she was seriously keeping to her diet. The woman didn't need to be on a diet, Daisy thought.

Iris gestured to the produce still lying on the counter. "I'll take care of this. Go talk to Arden. Be careful not to trip over anything."

Cora Sue gave Daisy an odd look.

Daisy just scrunched up her nose at her aunt. "Not funny."

Daisy found that Cora Sue had set up Arden in the spillover tearoom that for now was almost empty. Only one other table for four was occupied. This was the best place to be for privacy.

Daisy smiled at Arden as she sat around the corner of the table from her. "It's good to see you. What brings you in?"

Arden had slipped off her navy peacoat and let it slide over the back of the chair. "First of all, how are you feeling?"

"A little sore, but nothing I can't handle."

"That was quite a fall you had yesterday, or accident, or whatever it was. I do know those pine trees are heavy. I've tried to move them."

"Fortunately, my shoulder and hip took the brunt of it," Daisy admitted.

"It's a good thing it wasn't Vanna. She could have broken something."

Could that accident have been meant for someone other than herself? She hadn't thought about that.

Cora Sue approached them carrying a tray with a pot of tea, two cups and saucers in a purple rose vintage pattern, as well as a small bowl of sparkling sugar and a tiny pitcher of cream. "Just yell if you need anything else," she directed them, and moved away quickly, seeming to know they wanted to talk.

After Cora Sue had entered the main tearoom, Arden stirred sugar into her tea without tasting the tea first.

Daisy tapped her arm. "Remember, that has honey in it."

"Oh, I know. I'm in the mood for something really sweet right now. No one in the cast is being very sweet."

"Did something happen after I left?"

Arden stared into her tea. "Not exactly. I'm just stressed about the whole thing. I don't know how we're ever going to be ready for a performance."

"Don't you think in every production the cast feels that way?"

With a sigh, Arden met Daisy's gaze. "I've heard that. I don't know if I believe it. If everyone knows their lines and where they're supposed to be and when, and they've practiced enough, they should be pretty sure about how it's going to go. But we haven't done any of those things, not often enough. Margaret kept changing the script. Now Glenda's adding notes. To tell the truth, I think she wants to spend time with Rowan more than she wants to work on the script."

Daisy gave Arden a questioning look, a look that asked if she really meant what she said.

"I'm serious," she assured Daisy. "Do you know if Glenda knew Rowan before Margaret did?"

Daisy took a sip of her own tea and carefully set down the cup on the saucer. "Why do you ask?"

"Because I wonder if there was some rivalry between Margaret and Glenda for Rowan's affection . . . or his money."

Sometimes Daisy thought Arden was very much like the vinegar and spices that she sold. She could be tangy and tart. "Did you see any evidence of that?"

Arden picked up her spoon, studied the decorated handle, then set it down again. "I'm not sure. Rowan wasn't there all that much when Margaret was leading the production. After all, he had business concerns to take care of. But now he seems to be there an awful lot. Glenda takes advantage of that."

"How?"

"Daisy, don't question me like that. You know what I'm talking about. When a woman likes a man, she finds a way to get close to him. Her elbow meets his. Her shoulder rocks his. Her head leans near his. She has questions she never had before, only for him. That's the way Glenda's been acting. What if . . ." Arden stopped and put her hand over her mouth. "I'm not going to say it out loud."

"No one can overhear us. What are you thinking? If it rolls around in your head, it will just make you feel worse, don't you think?"

"You're probably right. You've had more experience with this kind of thing than I have. What if Glenda wanted Margaret out of the way? What if she's the one who killed her?"

That question kept rolling around in Daisy's mind as she went through the rest of the day.

Late in the day, Daisy was handling the credit card for an older woman who placed a large order once a week. Daisy had a feeling that Fiona Wilson bought as much as she could carry and stuffed her refrigerator so she didn't have to cook. She'd said to Daisy more than once, "Your foods are healthy and that's why I buy them."

Daisy knew that was mostly true. No preservatives if she could help it, scratch-made for all the baked goods.

In front of her, Fiona studied her. "Are you feeling all right, darling? You're looking a little peaked."

Her muscles and bruises were starting to ache more. She thought of Fiona and being seventy-five or eighty and still stopping in here once a week for her food rather than going to a grocery store.

"Tell me something, Fiona," Daisy said. "How would you feel if Willow Creek had a meals-on-wheels lunch or dinner service? Would you use it?"

"Would the food be as good as yours?"

Daisy chuckled. "I'm not sure about that. That would all have to be discussed in the planning stages. Citizens have brought it up before at the town council meeting but it's always been thrown by the wayside."

Fiona gave Daisy a smile. "We have a thrift store now." She touched the scarf around her neck, a pretty fuzzy material with a taupe and blue pattern. "I bought this there. I forgot where I put my old one and had to come up with something."

Daisy considered whether the town council could actually get a vote for meals-on-wheels and get it up and running for seniors over sixty. Maybe it could consist of good Pennsylvania Dutch food made from wholesome ingredients.

"Fiona, if you ever need food, and you find you can't come in yourself, call in your order. I'll make sure Jazzi or one of our servers delivers it to you. You don't live that far away from the tea garden."

"I moved into one of those senior apartments near the square about a year ago."

"How do you like it?"

"I like having my independence, and I don't have upkeep. Rent is on a sliding scale according to what I can pay. Filling out all that paperwork took a week, but I'm happy I'm there now. We ought to find a horse and buggy driver who would deliver food to people. Wouldn't the tourists just love that?"

As Fiona took her bags of food, one in each hand, Daisy heard the bell at the tea garden door chime. She didn't know if she was sorry or sad to see Zeke Willet come in. She knew he'd want something. He never just stopped for a visit.

Today she could tell by that determined look in his eye that he had something particular on his mind. She found it hard to believe that he was coming to her for information rather than more questions.

They would soon be closed for the day, and she knew her servers could take care of the end-of-the-day business. She waited at the sales counter.

When Zeke approached her, she asked, "Would you like to go into my office? I can fix you a cup of tea if you'd like it."

"You are bound and determined to give a cup of

tea to anyone who walks through that door, aren't you?"

The way he made it sound, that wasn't a good thing.

She simply responded with, "Tea calms the soul."

His eyebrows drew together and he frowned. "And you think my soul needs calming?"

"I've gotten that impression." As soon as that was out, she knew she shouldn't have said it. But she was getting tired and she ached.

"That came out fast as if you'd been meaning to say it for a while."

"Come on, Zeke. Have a cup of tea with me and tell me why you're here."

She could see that he had stopped in for a reason, and she wanted him to ask his questions and leave.

Once in her office, where she kept a smaller heated urn than the one in the kitchen, she pulled two mugs from the stack, filled them with hot water, and settled a tea bag in each.

"We'll go for the quick version this time. This is a Fortnum and Mason's afternoon blend."

"I'm supposed to recognize the name?"

"Probably not. It's good with a splash of milk."

He turned up his nose. "I'll try it straight, if I try it at all."

"Do you ever *not* argue with someone about something?"

He dropped into the chair in front of her desk, put an elbow on her desk, and sighed. "Long night. Short on flatfoots to run down leads. I'm getting frustrated. You seem to have a broad network, maybe even broader than mine."

"Detective Willet, I told you I'm staying out of this."

"I hope so," he said gruffly.

Daisy put a touch of milk into her tea, stirred, and took a sip. "What did you stop in to talk about?"

After he studied her carefully, he asked, "Do you know about the brooch that Margaret was wearing when she was murdered?"

"Yes, she wore it often. It was decorated with amethysts and diamonds."

"Correct. And quite valuable it was too. We had a jeweler appraise it. Rowan insists that he doesn't know where she got it. If I had a wife and she wore something like that often, I'd make it my business to know where she got it."

"Maybe that brooch had nothing to do with Rowan."

"Do you know where it came from?"

"I don't."

When he gave her a side-eye, she said, "Honestly, I don't."

"How about the tennis bracelet of amethysts and diamonds that was torn from Margaret's wrist?"

"Torn from her wrist?"

"It lay under her on the floor."

"I might have seen it when she wore it. Not that day. I think it was the first time we got together to discuss tea. It was beautiful."

"*That* bracelet Rowan did buy for her. It makes me wonder if he thought he was competing with someone. Do you know what I mean?"

"Or just competing. Maybe he wanted his bracelet to be more important to her than that brooch was."

Zeke pointed to her. "Exactly. You follow things quickly."

Since Zeke seemed more receptive than sometimes, she asked, "Do you have more than one suspect?"

His expression froze and she wondered if he'd learned that as a cop or if he'd always hid his thoughts and feelings. Though, according to Jonas, he'd been a different person when they'd been friends. Finally he revealed, "We're tracing backgrounds on a few people."

"And you can't tell me who they are."

"No, I can't tell you who they are."

"It always leaks out," she reminded him.

"Perhaps, but those leaks won't come from me."

The receptive side of Zeke wasn't all that receptive, but it was better than his gruff limited measure on conversation. So she decided to be "friendly," then go for the question she wanted the answer to the most.

"I can get you honey for your tea if you'd like it," she offered.

"Sweeten me up? I doubt it."

After he took a few sips from the mug, she thought this was the best time to ask her question. "Can you tell me why you're so angry with Jonas? I know you're upset because you don't think he protected Brenda, but Jonas was hurt too that night. He was shot and he didn't know if his shoulder would ever be the same. So why blame Jonas?"

Looking as if he wasn't going to answer, his face became hard. Then he started talking. "Jonas has a savior complex. A hero complex. He thinks he can handle everything . . . handle everybody. But he can't. So don't let him tell you he can keep you safe. That's an impossible feat. Safety is an illusion that can be shattered with a long-nose rifle, crosshairs, and a laser light."

Standing without taking another sip of his tea,

Zeke said, "Since you can't give me information about what I needed to know, I'm out of here. But it was a good break. Now I'll be more awake while I sit in my office going through notes, interviews, and suspects."

He crossed to the door of her office. "Remember what I said, Daisy. Jonas can't protect you. Sometimes nobody can."

As Zeke left, she understood that part of their conversation had been about Zeke himself.

Back at the counter, Daisy was surprised when Russ Windom, the retired teacher Iris was dating, approached her. He usually took a seat and whoever served him told Iris he was there. If her aunt had time, they had a little chat. But today he looked as if he had something particular on his mind. Apparently, he didn't need conversation with Iris but with Daisy.

"Hi, Russ," she said cheerfully. He was around Iris's age. His hair was gray with a high receding hairline. He adjusted his titanium black glasses and she'd learned by now that that meant he was nervous. Nervous talking to *her*?

She didn't have any customers begging for her attention, and if Russ was nervous, she wanted to put him out of his misery. "Is there something I can help you with?"

"Yes. I'm not quite sure how to bring this up."

"You want *me* and not Iris?"

"I do. And this isn't about your food here or anything like that. In fact, I don't know if you can do anything about it, but I thought I'd ask."

"Go ahead."

He rubbed his chin. "I've seen you talking with Rowan Vaughn."

Daisy gave Russ her full attention. "Yes. I know him. Jonas is working on the set at the Little Theater and the tea garden served tea at Margaret's."

"Yes, Iris told me what happened. From what I understand, the Little Theater is going to go ahead with the production."

Daisy hoped they were going to go ahead with the production if they could get their act together, so to speak. "Yes, they are going ahead. I stopped in at a rehearsal, matter of fact."

Shifting from one brown loafer to the other, and plucking down the sleeve of his camel sweater, Russ finally told her his issue. "Businesses can take a sponsorship role in the program for the play. I was told individual persons can too . . . that there are different layers of sponsorship for the theater."

"That's right. The tea garden took a business sponsorship."

"I'd like you to tell Vaughn that expecting five hundred dollars from individual residents of Willow Creek is a little much, don't you think?"

Daisy knew the business sponsorships were one thousand dollars. She'd assumed the average citizen could donate whatever amount they wanted, but she must have been wrong. "Five hundred dollars *is* steep for an individual sponsorship."

"Exactly. I can't do that. When I called the number for the sponsorships, someone named Tamlyn answered. She told me it was five hundred dollars or my name wouldn't go in the program. Vaughn does want this theater to succeed, doesn't he?"

"He does. The money would go into the endow-ment fund so the endowment can go on producing more money to run the theater. Is there a reason you're speaking to *me* about it?"

With a nod, Russ went on. "This Tamlyn that I spoke with, she said she couldn't do anything about it. But I thought maybe if you talked to Mr. Vaughn, he'd understand how ridiculous that amount is for the average person in town. I understand if he wants levels of sponsorship, but the least he could do is come up with different levels, something like a gold sponsorship, a silver sponsorship, a copper sponsor-ship. Don't you think that would be a good idea in the long run to generate more money?"

The idea was a good one. "I think you're right. I'm not sure how Rowan sees it, but I'd be glad to give him a call."

Russ looked relieved. He gave her a smile and asked, "Should I place my order here or go sit at a table?"

Daisy beckoned to Cora Sue. "Cora Sue will take your order and serve you. I'll call Rowan before I for-get."

Minutes later in her office, she brought up Rowan Vaughn's contact information for his cell phone and tapped on his name. He answered on the second ring.

"Daisy? Have you learned anything about the in-vestigation?"

"No, Rowan, I'm sorry. That's not why I'm calling. I'm calling about the sponsorships for the play and the theater."

"Oh, those," he said with some disdain. "Tamlyn's taking care of them. I really can't be bothered with that now."

"I understand how you're feeling, Rowan, but you do want to make the theater an ongoing success in Willow Creek, don't you?"

He seemed distracted for a moment, but then he sighed. "Yes, of course I do. I've sunk enough money into it."

Daisy really hadn't expected this half-hearted response from him. "For it to be a success, you really need to include the whole community. One of my customers suggested you have different levels of sponsorship. The lowest level can't be five hundred dollars. It's just too much even if tickets included four plays a year. A working person in Willow Creek just doesn't have that kind of money to put out."

"What would you suggest? Twenty-five-dollar sponsorships?" Rowan scoffed.

"As a matter of fact, yes. Sure, you can try to encourage big donations, court wealthier donors who would like to see their names in the program. But think how many residents you might draw in for twenty-five dollars. They might even buy a few tickets and suggest their friends come with them. You have to make this a community venture for it to succeed."

Rowan was a businessman and he should know this. But he didn't seem to. Maybe a developer who bought and sold properties was only interested in the big picture, not the small one.

It seemed to take a long time for Rowan to think about it. Then he said, "The Lancaster TV station was going to cover the opening. In fact, they're interviewing me about it tomorrow. I could mention levels of sponsorship and see how it flies. If Tamlyn would get a lot of response, then we could go with it permanently."

"That sounds like a good idea. Russ Windom is the one who thought about it and approached me. So if you see him, you might want to thank him. I'll tell him you're going to put his plan into effect."

"That's fine."

Daisy could hear the fatigue in Rowan's voice. "I know this seems like a bother and this production might not even be something you want to continue with, but if you consider it as a memorial to Margaret, it might mean a lot more."

Suddenly a woman's voice came from somewhere nearby. Was that Glenda?

"I know you're right, Daisy, and I'll put your plan in action. But I need to go now."

"Of course."

As Rowan ended the call, Daisy thought about Glenda being there with him. Just where was "there"?

Chapter Thirteen

Since Daisy intended to take care of her grandson whenever she could, she'd assembled a sleep and play crib in her bedroom for him. The following day, he was sleeping on his back while a colorful mobile with cats and dogs and bunnies hung above him. Since he'd fallen asleep, Daisy found she couldn't stay still.

Vi was at her doctor's appointment. Daisy had wanted to go with her. Foster had wanted to go with her. But Vi had insisted she was going alone. She didn't want anyone to persuade her to do something she didn't want to do. This would be a discussion for her and her doctor.

Daisy had an app on her phone that connected her to the nanny cam and monitor that watched over Sammy in the bedroom. After taking one last look at him, brushing her fingers over his arms, which were kept warm in a mint-green terry onesie, she took the bottle that he'd finished to the kitchen. At least feeding him with a supplemental bottle was going well.

After putting together a chicken and rice casserole for supper, Daisy was headed back to her bedroom when she spied someone passing outside the living room window. She realized Vi was back. She didn't know what to hope for. She just wanted her older daughter happy again, filled with the joy a new baby could bring.

When Vi came in, she looked as if she'd been crying. Her eyes were red and swollen and her nose was red too. Daisy didn't hesitate to put her arms around her, hugging Vi's down jacket until she felt Vi underneath. She held on until Vi began to move away.

Daisy was quick to assure her, "Sammy's asleep."

Vi unzipped her jacket, looking for a moment as if she were lost.

Daisy took her arm and tugged her over to the sofa. She didn't push or cajole. She waited until Vi took off her jacket and then began to talk.

"I was so confused, Mom. For a while, I wished you or Foster had been with me for the appointment. But then I realized I had to do what's best for Sammy, no matter how I feel about it."

"That's a decision you're going to have to make often as he grows."

"I imagine so. Dr. Geisler suggested an antidepressant she thinks will help me. There are several to try. She believes I've given Sammy a good start with breastfeeding, but now I'll have to stop. The medicine could contaminate my breast milk. She says she thinks it will take two or three weeks for the antidepressant to kick in. In the meantime, she gave me the name of a counselor she wants me to see, and she wants me to continue to go to the mommy group. She insists I have to talk about my feelings in a safe place in order to work through them. She gave me samples of the drug but she sent a prescription in to the pharmacy too. I'm hoping Foster can pick it up on his way home."

Daisy hung her arm around Vi's shoulders and squeezed. "Are you okay with what you've decided?"

After biting her lower lip, Vi nodded. "Yes. If I feel like I'm spiraling downward, she wants me to take a break. But that's not always possible."

"You can always call me. If I can't come, Aunt Iris or Gram will."

She watched Vi sort through the idea for a moment and frown. "I don't want to tell Gram about any of this."

Certainly, Daisy could understand. Her mom had a way of showing disapproval that could hurt. Still . . . "Vi, postpartum depression has been kept in the dark for so very long. The only way the sun's going to shine on it is if you talk about it. You know Gram. She might not understand at first, but eventually we'll make her see that you're doing what you need to do."

Vi turned to Daisy as her eyes filled with tears again. "Sometimes I feel like a little kid—confused, not sure what I'm doing hour to hour. Is that motherhood?"

With a gentle voice, Daisy assured her daughter, "It can be. Parenting is like any other relationship that you want to grow. Each day you're building on it with your child. You're getting to know him and he's getting to know you. You're going to make mistakes, but hopefully there are ways to correct them . . . and family and friends who will help you do that. You've made a good first step here, Vi. Honestly, you have."

Turning to her mom, Vi hugged Daisy and held on tight.

Vi had just let go of Daisy and gone into the bedroom to blow her nose and check on Sammy when Daisy's phone vibrated in her pocket. Taking it from her jeans, she saw that Rowan Vaughn was calling.

She hoped he wasn't going to try to persuade her to look into further information about Margaret and who might have killed her. But she had the feeling he wasn't going to let this go.

"Rowan. Hi. I—"

He cut her off. "Daisy, I'm at the police station. I've been here for hours. I have a lawyer but I want to talk to *you*."

Daisy still hadn't eliminated Rowan as a suspect. "Why do you want to meet with me?"

"We need to have a private conversation. If they ever let me out of here, I'll be tied up the rest of the day with business. Can we meet tomorrow?"

What Daisy had in mind for today meant she really had to assist at the tea garden tomorrow. "If we meet tomorrow, it will have to be a short meeting over my lunch hour."

"That's fine. Can you come to the house? I don't really want my business to be broadcast to the public, and anything we'd say at the tea garden could be overheard. Plus, it's just as well if no one sees us together."

Why ever not? Daisy wondered. But she didn't ask it aloud. "Will Tamlyn be there?"

"Are you really worried about being alone with me?" he grumbled.

She told him the truth. "I would prefer to know someone else was there."

After a heavy sigh, he agreed. "Fine. Yes, she'll be there. I need someone to take care of the house, and she does a fine job of it. But she'll be in the kitchen. I don't want her to overhear our conversation."

In addition to using Tamlyn as a chaperone, she would tell Iris where she was going. If she was late returning, Iris would know to contact Jonas or the authorities.

"All right, Rowan, how about one o'clock? That's usually a good time for me to duck out of the tea garden."

"One o'clock it is. I'll see you then."

When Daisy ended the call, she wondered what she'd just gotten herself into.

Daisy was on the way to Rowan's house the following day when Tessa called her. It was Daisy's lunch break and she wondered if something was wrong. The morning had been busy at the tea garden, and she and Tessa hadn't had a moment to talk. That wasn't unusual.

Daisy answered through her car's bluetooth. "Hi, Tessa. What's up?"

"I didn't know if you were coming back this afternoon."

"I am. I'm hoping this only takes about half an hour. In fact, Rowan didn't sound as if he had much time for me, though he's the one who asked for the meeting."

"I wanted to let you know that Cade can't come to Thanksgiving dinner. He has other plans. But . . ." Tessa let her voice trail into a pause.

"But?" Daisy repeated.

"Trevor Lundquist asked me out a couple of days ago. We went to dinner last night and had a really good time. Would you mind if I ask *him* to Thanksgiving dinner?"

Daisy considered Trevor sitting at a table with her

family. He seemed to be able to fit in anywhere and could always make conversation. "Asking Trevor to Thanksgiving dinner is fine with one stipulation."

"What's that?"

"He can't ask us any questions about the murder."

Tessa laughed. "I might have to muzzle him if he starts, but I'll tell him. I'll tell him you're the hostess and you're the one handing out the invitations. He has to comply."

Daisy smiled. "Thank you. Anything else?"

"No, we're good. I have to whip up another batch of the fall fruit salad. Do you think I should use the peach yogurt or the strawberry?"

"The peach is a hit. I'd stick with that."

"Got it. I hope your meeting with Rowan is productive."

After Daisy said good-bye, she considered Rowan Vaughn and what she knew about him. He was a businessman and he traveled. However, from the bits of information she'd garnered about his apartments, he wasn't a detail person. He delegated and maybe didn't look over what the people he hired did to execute his orders. Had he delegated something that went terribly wrong? Was he as innocent as he claimed?

Daisy would get another chance to find out.

On Rowan's doorstep Daisy rang the bell. Moments later, Tamlyn opened the door. Her eyes were wide and she kept her voice low as she said to Daisy, "Mr. Vaughn is in an awful mood. I'm just telling you so you can be prepared."

"I'm as prepared as I can be," Daisy assured the housekeeper. "I understand you'll be in the kitchen."

"Yes, I will. But just so you know, there's a button on the wall near his desk. All you have to do is press that and it rings in the kitchen. If you press it and you need anything, I'll come running."

For Tamlyn to say that, Rowan really must be in a state. "Good to know."

As Tamlyn showed her to Rowan's office, they passed the room that used to be Margaret's den. Some husbands and wives shared the same office. On the other hand, she supposed working was easier if a person could close the door.

Daisy stood in the doorway and unzipped her fleece jacket, studying Rowan, who was bent over a printout on his desk. He looked wiped out with furrows across his brow cutting deep. His hair was a bit disheveled as if he'd run his fingers through it recently. He even had beard stubble that said he hadn't shaved in a day or so. Where she usually had seen him in a suit, today he wore jeans and a flannel shirt. Very unlike Rowan as far as she knew.

Either hearing Tamlyn or sensing Daisy's presence, he looked up. He waved to the chair in front of his desk. "Take a seat, Daisy." His voice held a world of weariness.

"What's going on?"

After closing his eyes for a moment, Rowan leaned back in his high desk chair. "That Detective Willet grilled me as if I were a Mafia boss. I couldn't figure out why he was doing it. Yes, I know the husband is always the first suspect, but then after an hour or so, we got to the point."

Daisy put her purse on the floor and waited for further explanation.

"Detective Willet found out that I consulted a divorce lawyer. Between that and the insurance money that I possibly could collect, I'm their number one suspect."

Opening a drawer, he took out a book with a leather cover. When he laid it on the desk, she could see that it was a Bible. He laid his hand on it. "I swear to you, Daisy, I did *not* kill Margaret."

She didn't know enough about Rowan to know exactly what his faith was, or if a Bible really meant something to him. So she did the only thing she could do. She asked questions. "Why were you consulting a divorce lawyer? That usually means a marriage is splitting up. Was that the case with you and Margaret?"

Rowan looked down at the Bible and then at his other hand, which still bore his wedding ring. With a pained expression he disclosed, "Margaret was never forthright with me. There was a gap in her history before I met her, and she wouldn't fill it in."

If Rowan had been the love of Margaret's life, why wouldn't she confide in him? "You never met any friends of Margaret's from that time period?"

He rocked his chair and it creaked. "Not a one. Sometimes I had the feeling her secrecy had something to do with her family's religion."

Margaret's family religion had been strict. Even Vanna would attest to that. "Do you think she was hiding something terrible?"

With vehemence, he pushed the Bible away. "I don't know about that. I suppose Margaret could have been capable of something terrible. But who defines *terrible* anyway? More than that, I sensed she had guilt about things she'd done. She'd just make a comment here or there, maybe under her breath or to herself, but she wouldn't confide in me. Isn't that what marriage is all about—being able to confide in each other and tell your deepest, darkest secrets?"

Exactly what Daisy had considered. She responded,

"As you know, I was married, and we shared a lot. I don't think either of us had any secrets from the other. But I do know that we probably had deep feelings that we didn't always share. Me about my family and Ryan about my inability to have more children after Vi. We came together in adopting Jazzi, but that didn't mean we shared all our thoughts and feelings. So I don't know if I can really answer your question."

She usually didn't share anything so personal with a practical stranger, but she was trying to bore down to her gut feelings about Rowan and whether he could have murdered Margaret. She couldn't seem to go deep enough to find that answer.

Nevertheless, she did have an idea. "Does Margaret still have anything packed away that might have been from her younger years?"

He easily admitted, "I haven't looked through all of her things yet. It's just too painful. There might be a box or two in the attic."

"That might be a place to start if you really want to have answers."

"You might be right." He looked a little calmer than he had when she'd walked in. "I can look for answers. But *you* have a reputation for finding answers. Please, can you find some answers about Margaret? Find out what got her killed and who did it."

Daisy jumped in immediately. "Rowan, I can't interfere in the police investigation."

"So don't interfere. Skirt around the edges. From what I understand, you know how to find the personal tidbits and I think that's what we need here. If the police are just looking at me, they're not going to find the murderer and I could end up in jail!"

She knew Detective Rappaport and Detective Willet were good detectives, but would they settle on that one person? It had happened in the past. It could happen again.

"I'll do what I can," she told Rowan, knowing that Jonas and her family probably weren't going to be too happy about that.

When Tamlyn appeared out of nowhere, Daisy wondered if Rowan had rung the bell alerting her that he needed her. After they said their good-byes, Daisy followed Tamlyn along the hall to the foyer. Once there, though, she stopped. Daisy was going to be honest with Tamlyn because she sensed a genuineness about the housekeeper.

"Tamlyn, did you care for Margaret?"

Tamlyn's eyes widened and she went a little pale. Daisy considered this the moment of truth. She thought she'd be able to tell if Tamlyn lied.

After a hesitation when her eyes turned down, she stared at her flats, then gazed at Daisy. "She was my employer. I cared for her in that way. I didn't want anything bad to happen to her."

"But as a person, she wasn't your cup of tea, so to speak?"

Tamlyn shook her head. "She had a way . . ." Tamlyn started. Then she flitted her hand through the air as if she couldn't quite explain it. "She had a way of shutting people out. Once in a while, a glimmer came through. I knew she liked how I took care of the house. She cared that I didn't have any family. On the other hand, she could shut me out with a glance. She could give me a look that made me realize she didn't want me in the room. Mrs. Vaughn wanted to be alone a lot of the time."

"I know you had nothing to do with the murder,

and so do the police. You were bustling around the table when the murder happened. But because you were working here, I would think something you know might help figure out who wanted to hurt Mrs. Vaughn. Did Mrs. Vaughn ever speak about her past?"

"Not to me. She didn't confide in me," Tamlyn explained. "But when she was with her friends, she told many stories about when she was acting. They were funny stories about missed lines, missed cues, falling over her own feet. The others would laugh and she would brush it away. She entertained them. That's the only time I saw her really smile. You know, one of those genuine smiles and even a laugh."

"So acting had made her happy."

"I think so. One time she told me that being a housekeeper was honest work and I should be proud of it. I never expected that coming from her." Tamlyn waved to the whole house in general. "Look what she had. How would she even know what housekeeping felt like?"

"Unless maybe she'd done it?" Daisy asked.

"She mentioned waitressing, but never housekeeping. I guess a waitress would feel the same way. It *is* honest work. Most jobs that pay the bills are honest work."

Could that have been what Margaret thought? Had she carried values from her past into her adulthood? Or at the other end of the spectrum, had she had regrets of something she had done to earn a living? That would take some digging.

Tamlyn looked toward the hall where they'd come from. Daisy knew what she was thinking. "I won't keep you much longer, but I'm going to try to help Mr. Vaughn by finding another suspect."

"Won't the police do that?"

"We hope so. But if they want to mount evidence just against him, they might not look at other possibilities."

"That's terrible," Tamlyn said, as if she'd never thought of that.

That was the innocence Daisy saw in her. Tamlyn looked at the world through eyes that considered things the way she thought they should be. She probably believed in fairy tales too.

"Do you remember the amethyst and diamond brooch that Mrs. Vaughn wore?"

"Sure, I remember," Tamlyn admitted. "It sparkled in the sunlight. That purple was so deep and dark. And when she wore it, she touched it as if it meant a lot to her. Do you know what I mean?"

"I do know what you mean. My husband gave me a strand of pearls. Whenever I wore them and whenever I wear them now, I touch them and think about him. Did Mrs. Vaughn ever explain where she got the brooch?"

"She never did. I didn't ask her personal questions. She would have snapped, or maybe even fired me. I didn't want her to do that."

"How about the amethyst and diamond bracelet she wore? Did she wear that often?"

"Not as often as that pin. When she dressed up, she wore both. One time she told me that it caught on things if she wasn't careful, you know, like the lace tablecloth or gloves. I'm pretty sure Mr. Vaughn gave it to her. That bracelet . . ." Tamlyn suddenly closed her mouth and didn't say more.

"Go ahead. You can be honest with me."

"I think that bracelet was just a piece of jewelry to Mrs. Vaughn. But the brooch, that meant something special."

And someone had spilled clotted cream all over that brooch. There was symbolism in that, and maybe even something personal.

Where had the brooch come from?

Chapter Fourteen

Making pumpkin pies the night before Thanksgiving was a tradition among Daisy and her girls. Tonight, Tessa had joined them too. She'd insisted she'd put together her vegetable casserole in the morning and bring it along to dinner. Tonight, she'd help roll pie dough.

They'd closed the tea garden early today, and tomorrow it would be closed too. Everyone deserved a holiday with their families. What had really thrilled Daisy was that Vi had come over to join them. It didn't seem to be a chore for her tonight. She looked as if she wanted to mix up the filling for the pies. They weren't ready for filling yet, so Vi was pulling the recipes out of the binder Daisy kept in the pantry. They were going to roll shells for three pumpkin pies first. In the meantime, Jazzi would be experimenting with a flourless chocolate cake.

When the doorbell rang, Daisy guessed Jonas had arrived. He was bringing over the table and chairs so they could set them up. She'd told him to drive Elijah's truck up to the sidewalk near the house. The ground was frozen over and the tire tracks wouldn't hurt it. Elijah was an Amish friend of Jonas's who often helped at the store and also supplied some of the furniture.

After she rushed to the door, she threw it open and there was Jonas with a smile on his face. "Ready for another table and six more chairs?"

"Ready for something else first," she teased.

Wrapping his arms around her waist, he brought her close and kissed her. "Is that what you had in mind?"

"You read my thoughts."

"Not always an easy feat," he joked.

She rapped him on the shoulder and took a step back. "Tessa and I will help you bring it all in."

He frowned. "That's not necessary."

"We want to help. After we do, maybe you could go to the garage and bring in the box I set outside the garage door that has the flour, sugar, and canned goods in it. When I got home, Vi was coming down the stairs from the apartment and I just wanted to concentrate on her, not worry about carrying everything inside. And we needed to make pies."

"Will do."

Tessa joined Daisy at the door. "Where are Marjoram and Pepper? You won't want them to get out."

"They're upstairs in Jazzi's room, away from all the noise and bustle. They hate that their peaceful home is disrupted," she said with a grin. "But I'm sure tomorrow when they smell the turkey, they'll come down and greet everyone. Just call to Jazzi to go up and close her bedroom door. Then we'll be sure they're safe."

Daisy could hear Tessa call to Jazzi as she went outside to help Jonas.

It didn't take long to carry everything inside. Daisy showed Jonas where she wanted the table in her living room. It wouldn't be far from her dining area, and conversations could roll around both tables with ease.

Once Jonas had set the boards in the table, he went outside to pick up the supplies at the garage.

"This is a beauty," Tessa said, running her hand over the grained wood.

"Jonas told me it's walnut with a dark chestnut finish. It is gorgeous."

"Someday I dream about owning an old house with a dining room where I could use a table like this," Tessa mused.

"My guess is you don't want an open concept floor plan like I have here."

"I prefer nooks and crannies and separate rooms."

Daisy realized Tessa had put a lot of thought into this and maybe dreams too. "Do you imagine sharing that house with someone?"

"Maybe." After she trailed her fingers over the table again, she admitted, "I'm a little nervous about Trevor coming tomorrow."

"Why nervous?" Daisy asked. "You said dinner out went well."

"I know. And he was nice enough when he did that interview with me in January after the murder investigation. I guess I never thought about dating him."

"You don't have to jump in with both feet," Daisy said. "You could just dabble with one toe."

Tessa laughed. "I suppose you're right. Are you going to set the tables tonight?"

"No, I'd better not. I have two felines who might decide they'd like to be the centerpieces. I'll wait until tomorrow about an hour before everyone is going to arrive. Hopefully, the fur kids will be taking their evening naps."

Jonas brought in the carton where Daisy had put extra supplies that she'd purchased to bring home from the tea garden.

After Jonas kicked shut the door with his foot, he asked, "Kitchen island?"

"Put it on the counter," she directed. "That way we can roll out the dough on the island."

Jonas headed that way, but turned back to her to say, "You *are* going to give me something to do other than rolling out pie dough. I have a feeling I wouldn't be very good at it."

"I have two food processors," she assured him. "You can help me keep those going."

At the kitchen counter, he called, "Deal."

Tessa leaned close to Daisy. "You and Jonas seem to be doing well."

"I'm afraid to talk about it," Daisy admitted. "I'm afraid I'll jinx it."

Jazzi and Vi stood at the stand mixer, mixing the chocolate mousse filling for the cake, when Daisy moved to the counter to unpack her carton. She'd ordered twenty pounds of extra flour—one ten-pounder to use and the other to fill up her canister—as well as five pounds of sugar, two large cans of pumpkin, and three jars of Emma Zook's tart cherry pie filling. With all of them helping, they might have time to make the cherry pies too.

However, as she lifted the first bag of flour out of the box, she realized there was a hole in the bottom of the bag, and flour started sifting out into the carton. She made a frustrated sound. Sidling around her girls, she picked up the canister and brought it to the carton. There she poured the flour into it. After she finished with that, she picked up the second bag and the same thing happened. All right, one bag could be a fluke. Two bags was no fluke.

Jazzi had turned off the mixer. Tessa was talking to Daisy's daughters about the cake and what containers would be best to bake it in. Daisy was concentrating on the other elements in the box. When she picked up a jar of cherry pie filling, she couldn't believe what was in front of her eyes. The glass had a crack along one side of the jar. Every jar did.

Trying to keep her mind from reeling, she turned to the island, where Jonas was assembling one of the food processors. "Jonas, did something happen to this box?"

He tilted his head with a perplexed expression. "What do you mean—did something happen to it? I just picked it up off the bench outside of the garage and brought it inside."

"You didn't drop it?"

The little quake in her voice must have alerted him that something was wrong. Quickly he crossed to her. "Why do you think I dropped it?"

"The flour bags . . ." She picked up one bag. "And the sugar," she murmured, "have torn sacks. The jars of cherry pie filling are cracked."

Jonas stared at all the elements in the box as if she were telling him they were on fire. With a gruff sound, he said, "I didn't look in the box before I carried it in."

"If you had looked, I don't think you would have seen anything. The sacks were set up so that nothing escaped as long as they were in the carton. And the cracks in the jars are on the sides. You couldn't have seen those either."

By now Vi, Jazzi, and Tessa were listening in. Finally Tessa said what everyone else might have been thinking. "Somebody sabotaged your ingredients. How could that have happened?"

Considering how she'd taken the ingredients from the pantry at the tea garden, how she'd packed them in the carton, and then . . .

Leaning against the counter, Daisy sighed. "I set the carton outside the back kitchen door of the tea garden. Then I went back inside for my purse. I was the only one there. When I was in the office, pulling my purse from the drawer, my phone rang. I answered it because the caller ID was a client. She was explaining to me exactly what she wanted at her tea, and I took notes. Then I left those on my desk, retrieved my purse, went outside, and picked up the carton. I loaded it in my car and drove home. That's the only place anyone could have tampered with it."

"I don't like what that means," Jonas muttered.

"What does it mean?" Vi asked, not following his line of thinking.

Jazzi quickly picked up his thought pattern. "It means somebody was following Mom or knows her habits and is out to play a prank on her."

Daisy remembered those wood trees falling on her at the rehearsal at the Little Theater. Was this a prank? Or was it something more sinister?

Daisy had all morning on Thanksgiving Day to cook, reassure Jazzi that someone had just played a prank on her, and text with Jonas that she was okay.

He hadn't seemed to believe her and he'd arrived early, ready to do anything that needed to be done.

She'd given him the job of setting the table. The white tablecloth with gold threads interwoven into a geometrical design fit her table. She'd found another white tablecloth in her hutch to cover the table that Jonas had contributed. She decided to mix her set of white ironstone plates with a set of dishes her mother had given her so they'd have enough place settings for the tables. The mixture of her mother's garden-painted china and the white ironstone went together well. So did the mugs. The silverware was a combination of a rose-pattern stainless steel set her mother-in-law had given her and Ryan when they'd married and the everyday silverware she used with Jazzi. Tessa had provided orange-and-gold-patterned paper napkins to add even more color to the tables. The artistic one, Tessa had created two arrangements, a small pumpkin, gourds, and Indian corn for each table. She'd brought them over that morning along with the napkins because Trevor would be picking her up to bring her to dinner.

Daisy had stabbed the turkey with a meat thermometer and closed the oven when Jonas came up beside her. "Have you spoken to Camellia yet?"

Daisy hadn't thought much about her sister with everything else going on. "No, I haven't spoken with her, but she and her guy got in last night to stay at the Covered Bridge Bed and Breakfast."

"How did your mom feel about that? Didn't she want them staying with her?"

"She did, but Mom wouldn't have liked it if they were sharing the same room. This is Camellia's method of getting her own way, yet pleasing Mom too. They stayed late last night and played cards with Mom and Dad. I did find out her boyfriend's name is Robert—Robert Corning."

"And that's all you know?"

"Actually, I think he works in an advertising company. But that's it. I've had my mind on other things."

Jonas leaned so close that their shoulders were touching. Then his arm was smack up against hers. It gave her a measure of comfort just to have him here. "Have you given any more thought to who might have sabotaged your baking supplies?"

"Put that way, it sounds like a prank, doesn't it?" She lowered her voice. "If it is the same person who killed Margaret, then my guess is Margaret's death wasn't premeditated."

He leaned away to study her. "How did you come to that conclusion?"

"The holes in the flour and sugar bags and the cracks in the jars just seemed like something he or she did on the spur of the moment. No one could have known that box would be sitting outside. No one could have known I'd be gone for more than a minute to retrieve something I'd forgotten. That phone call just happened to tie me up longer."

He pushed his hand into the pocket of his black jeans, and Daisy suspected he did that to keep from clenching his fist. "So you think somebody is following and watching you?" he asked, tight-lipped.

"They may be trying to lead me off the scent. I don't know, Jonas. I've been so preoccupied with Vi and Sammy . . . and just running the tea garden. I haven't noticed if anybody is following me. We're so rural out here that anyone could park their car in a stand of trees and follow me when I leave."

"That's a chilling thought." Jonas glanced at the

sliding glass doors that led out onto the patio in the back. "Glass doors are never secure, at least not se-cure enough."

"When I renovated the barn into a house, I wanted convenience to the backyard. I hadn't even planned on a security system at that point."

"I know you have a camera at the back as well as the front, but it wouldn't hurt to have more motion detector lights on the property."

"This place would be lit up as if it were Christmas with all the raccoons, possums, and cats, not to men-tion deer, who run through the backyard."

"Let me look into it, will you? Even low-level lights around the garden and the patio wouldn't be obtru-sive, but they would give anybody the idea that there are technological eyes on the whole place. You want to give the illusion of being guarded."

"How about solar lights?"

"There are some garden solar lights that also de-tect motion. But depending on the weather, they're not always reliable. If you want that kind, that's fine, but I'd suggest a few electric ones for the sake of de-pendability, in addition to the others."

"That sounds like big bucks."

"That sounds like security, Daisy. If you're going to be involved in murder investigations, you need to protect yourself and your family."

Jonas was right, of course. She could squeeze the budget and dial back her own purchases. She didn't want to skimp with Jazzi. But if Jazzi understood the situation, she might not mind. Since she wasn't pay-ing tuition for Vi now, she'd intended to put that money into a savings account for Jazzi for college. She'd portioned out some of the insurance money that had been paid to her after Ryan died for the girls' educations. They all really had everything they needed as long as they were healthy and happy.

The doorbell rang.

Jazzi called, "I'll get it. I used my phone app. It's Gram and Aunt Camellia. Gramps and Camellia's boyfriend are following behind. He's pretty hot, Mom."

"She's going to be dating soon, isn't she?" Daisy asked Jonas woefully.

"Have you talked to her about boys lately?"

"No. With her learning to drive, we've had enough to discuss."

"My guess is she has her eye on one."

She gazed at him aghast. "Jonas Groft, what do you know about teenage girls?"

After another look at his smug expression, she shook her head. "Never mind. Don't tell me. As a detective, you saw way too much."

"Everything I saw as a detective shouldn't even be talked about in the same room with Jazzi. You've got a gem there, and in Vi too."

She leaned her cheek against Jonas's shoulder just for a moment. Then she went to the door to greet her mother.

Somehow, once everyone arrived, Daisy and her many helpers carried the food to the table. Daisy had briefly met Camellia's boyfriend. He was about five-foot-ten, looked as if he worked out, and had a nice smile. His hair was short and spiky, his nose narrow, and his jaw pointed. He was wearing a tan oxford shirt, brown dress slacks, and a sports jacket with a small plaid design in burgundy and dark brown.

Daisy was hoping she'd get a chance to talk to him later. Right now, however, her dad was carving the turkeys. He was an expert at it, and Rose was holding Sammy, cooing to him while Vi looked on. Tessa and

Trevor seemed friendly enough as they conversed with each other and Daisy's other friends and family.

After Daisy's dad finished carving the turkeys and they placed the trays with the meat on the tables, he stood between the two tables and gave a short prayer of thanksgiving. Then they started the meal, and Daisy kept her fingers crossed that all would go well.

Conversation swirled around the table as everyone ate turkey and all the trimmings. Those trimmings included sweet and sour red cabbage, green beans with bacon bits, cranberry, walnut, and orange salad, sweet potato casserole with a crumb topping that was more like a dessert, and of course, bread stuffing from both inside and outside of the turkeys. Daisy heard Foster explain to Russ and Iris that his dad and brother and sister went to have dinner with one of his father's friends who was also one of his crew managers.

Daisy tried to hold a conversation with Camellia, but Camellia seemed more intent on listening to Robert's conversation with her father. As they were growing up, Camellia had ignored Daisy whenever she'd wanted to. Daisy had gotten used to it. Unless she had something really important on her mind, or Camellia's attitude seeped under her skin, she took a back seat. She considered catching up with her sister to be important, but apparently Camellia didn't want the same kind of bond in her life that Daisy did. However, the conversation that Camellia was listening in on between Robert and her father caught Daisy's attention too.

Robert was saying, "This is the new way of advertising."

Daisy's father apparently didn't agree. "New way of advertising. It seems a waste of time and money to me. By the time the commercial's over, I don't even know what the product was that was advertised. How can that help sales?"

Sean's disagreement didn't seem to bother Robert. "I'll grant you it's subtle. For instance, you have a well-known star in a car commercial. He's in every commercial for that make of car. There's no need for the name of the product if the public automatically associates that star with the product. It's subliminal advertising."

Daisy couldn't help but give her two cents. "That might be the case if the public will recognize the product just by hearing the star's name. That doesn't mean they'll buy the product unless they specifically *want* that product. Even a teenager isn't foolish enough to think if she rides in one of those cars, she gets the star driving next to her."

Jazzi chimed in now. "Mom's right. I'd never buy a car because of a person advertising it. I buy it for the color and what kind of tech conveniences it has."

Daisy's gaze locked with Robert's. "I imagine you have focus groups. What are they saying?"

"Mixed reviews," he kind of mumbled. "We try everything that we think will sell a product. Focus groups aren't always on the mark."

"If a company knows their product," Daisy offered, "there's no need for subterfuge. The company just points out its good points and presents it to their customers."

Camellia gave Daisy an argumentative glare. "It's not that simple anymore, Daisy. Ads have to be slick, fast with music that will attract the right demographics. All you do for the tea garden is put ads in magazines and maybe some on the Internet. It's not the same thing as going after a national audience. Robert does that with the products he has in his client load, and I do it with my company's wines."

Camellia's remarks felt like a put-down. Jonas covered Daisy's knee with his hand. She didn't know if that meant she should take Camellia's comments seriously, or if she should let them slide. But she wasn't in her *let-it-slide* mood.

"Since the tea garden is making a successful profit, I assume I'm targeting the right customers, and advertising in a way that brings them in. Can your company say the same? Or even the car company? It might be worth millions of dollars but has a red profit line." She knew exactly the car company that Robert had been talking about. After all, she didn't live with her head in the sand.

"I still say a small business in a small town isn't the same thing as selling a national product," Camellia protested.

Sean and Rose exchanged a look. Sean said, "Okay, daughters, how about if we pull out the desserts. Everybody can change seats around the table and talk to someone they haven't talked to yet today. Sound good?"

Daisy felt a bit embarrassed. She shouldn't let this sometime tension between her and Camellia come out into the open. She was actually surprised her mother hadn't jumped in.

"Sure, Dad," she said quickly. "We'll stack these dishes, bring in more coffee and tea, and move around a bit."

Tessa was holding Sammy, and he was sleeping in her arms. As Trevor stood behind her, the look in his eyes gave Daisy pause. He was staring down at the baby as if he might want one of those little beings in his lifetime. He hadn't approached her with even one question about Margaret's murder. Just maybe he and Tessa had more in common than Daisy had ever imagined.

At one point, as Daisy, Camellia, and Tessa took desserts to the table, Daisy noticed her mom and Aunt Iris had their heads together. They were looking at Vi, and Daisy wondered what that was about. Maybe they were just concerned for her. Maybe they were figuring out a babysitting schedule.

After everyone was seated again, with a slice of their favorite pie or the gluten-free chocolate cake along with their beverage of choice, Daisy found herself next to Vi with her mother on the other side of her daughter.

She heard her mother ask Vi, "Do you think the medicine is working?"

Vi didn't take offense. She easily answered, "I'm sleeping better at night. I also seem to have a bit more energy. Not only that, but when I hold Sammy now, whenever I just look at him, I feel this bubbling joy and happiness inside of me. It feels like it could burst. It's like bubbles in a champagne bottle. I feel joy."

When Daisy heard Vi's words, tears came to her eyes. That's what motherhood should be—days of joy and caring so much about the little one that you knew you'd be connected forever through space and time and eternity.

When Daisy caught a glimpse of her mother, however, she didn't see happiness on Rose's face. She saw pensiveness that didn't belong at the Thanksgiving table today. Rose glanced over at Iris, and Daisy wondered what the two of them shared that no one else knew.

Jazzi and Foster began a game of Scrabble as Iris

took hold of Sammy next. Daisy organized the cleanup and insisted her mom didn't have to help. Again, in an agreeable manner that wasn't like her, Rose didn't argue. Daisy expected her mom wanted another turn with Sammy. Vi and Trevor seemed to be having an animated conversation about the state of the newspaper industry and whether or not the *Willow Creek Messenger* would go online permanently and stop printing a newspaper.

At the sink as she washed the roasting pan, Daisy was aware of Camellia coming up beside her. Her sister had cared about hair and makeup and the latest styles. She wore her brunette bob in a sleek cut.

Camellia picked up a dish towel. "You didn't have to put Robert down like that, you know."

Daisy stopped scrubbing. "I wasn't putting him down."

"It sure felt like it," Camellia shot back. "He's too nice to come back at you with statistics and argument."

"Camellia, we were having a discussion, pros and cons, what works and what doesn't."

"That's just the thing, Daisy. He *is* an expert, and so am I. We live in New York City. You have a tea garden in Willow Creek."

That was a put-down if Daisy ever heard one. "Yes, I have a tea garden in Willow Creek. Do you have a problem with that?" Letting the roasting pan sit in the sink, she faced her sister.

"You could have done anything with the life insurance money that came your way after Ryan died, but you decided to come back here, renovate some old barn, and start up a business that could go under in a year." Camellia sounded as if that was exactly what was going to happen.

"The tea garden has been open over two years now and is in the black," Daisy reminded her.

"Still . . ."

"You sound as if a barn home is a shack. We're quite comfortable here. We designed it exactly the way we wanted it. Have you designed *your* home?"

"You know I live in an apartment."

"I do. So I don't understand why you're suddenly looking down on what I started here."

"You could have helped Mom and Dad at the nursery."

Daisy almost couldn't find words to respond to that observation. But after a heartbeat, she did. "And been their employee? I'm a grown woman, Camellia. I deserve my own life. I had my own life with Ryan."

Camellia didn't seem fazed by Daisy's vehemence. She glanced over at Jonas. "Are you serious about *him?*"

Turning, Daisy gazed at Jonas and smiled. "More serious each day. Is there something wrong with that?"

"He's a cop, and you've been involved in murder cases. Is *he* the reason why? Mom almost has a fit every time that happens. She worries."

This time Daisy *was* stymied for a response. She took her time before answering. "Yes, Jonas was once a detective. That's how Jazzi found her birth mother. He helped. Somehow I've gotten involved in murder cases, and his expertise is valuable. He even has contacts who are helpful. But he doesn't drag me into anything. If there *is* such a person as a knight in shining armor, I'd say Jonas comes pretty close."

As if she was waiting to jab at Daisy again, Camellia responded, "So you're forgetting about Ryan?"

"I'll *never* forget about Ryan." Daisy kept her voice

quiet but firm. "Not a day goes by that I don't remember what we shared. I can't look at Jazzi and Vi without thinking about the times we all had together as a family. But finally my brain can wrap itself around the fact that my life will never be the same again. I've started a *new* life, Camellia, and I don't know why it bothers you so much."

"It doesn't bother me. I'm glad if you're satisfied with what you have. I just don't want Mom to worry about you."

"I'm sure she worries about you too. Are you and Robert serious?"

She gave another shrug. "I don't know."

"How long have you been dating?"

"About three months."

Uh-oh. That was usually Camellia's time limit for a relationship.

Camellia scowled at her. "I know what you're thinking."

"I doubt that," Daisy said.

"I'm just not sure Robert and I fit together like Mom and Dad do."

"Is that what you want?"

"I think so."

"Then you might have to date a man more than three months to find out."

"You're supposed to know right away," Camellia protested.

"Who told you that?"

"Mom did. She and Dad knew right away."

"Maybe so. But there can be friendship first and then passion, don't you think? Or you could have sparks at first, but then you have to figure out if you can be friends."

Camellia considered that idea. "I never looked at it like that."

Daisy gave a little shrug. "You'll figure it out."

"Are you just saying that or do you really believe it?"

Daisy handed Camellia the roasting pan and looked her straight in the eye. "I really believe it." Camellia was smart enough to figure out anything . . . if she wanted to.

Chapter Fifteen

Wasn't the dress rehearsal supposed to be exciting?

The day after Thanksgiving, Daisy thought back to her high school days. She could remember a dress rehearsal for a spring play. She'd been hyped on adrenaline, excited, nervous, anxious, and over-the-top raring to get started. It was all fun, from putting on different clothes to acting in character to watching for Tessa in the wings because she was helping with costume changes. She'd also entertained the hope that the credit in her record would help her be accepted at the college of her choice.

Sure, this dress rehearsal was absolutely different from that. Jonas had asked her to come along to watch just for the fun of it. They needed a few people in the audience to applaud at the right places.

But the mood for *Christmas in the North Woods* was anything but exciting the night before its first performance.

Jonas, of course, would be helping to manipulate the sets into place for scene changes. Jazzi was studying with a friend, so Daisy had invited Tessa along to help applaud. She enjoyed plays and concerts and any artistic production.

Tessa leaned close to Daisy and asked, "Shouldn't they have started by now?"

"Glenda's still running around with the script making last-minute changes. That can really throw off amateur actors."

"What is this play about anyway?" Tessa asked.

"It's about a family who went away for Christmas to a cabin in the North Woods. They thought they'd be alone to celebrate without all the glitter and distractions of the city. Like most families now, they don't have much time to be together."

"I know there's a *but* coming," Tessa said with a smile.

"Oh, there's a *but.* Extended family members and friends show up to surprise the family at the cabin, and they all get snowed in together."

Tessa's face showed a distasteful expression. "I can't say it's a novel premise."

From the first row, Daisy could clearly see the cast scurrying around. "It doesn't have to be novel to be satisfying and heartwarming. But the actors and actresses have to dive deep into their parts and make it real. Right now, they're all running around looking as if they don't know what they're doing."

"I can imagine what you're thinking," Tessa said.

"What's that?" Daisy couldn't help watching Jonas, the play of his muscles under his flannel shirt and the fit of his jeans as he moved a piece of scenery into place. He was a man worth looking at.

Tessa continued, "You're thinking that if Margaret

were here, she would have whipped everybody into shape. They'd know exactly what they were doing, where they were supposed to be, and how they were supposed to act."

"I wasn't thinking exactly that, but you're right."

Tessa settled deeper into the cushioned seat. "How's Vi feeling?"

Daisy relaxed against the seat back. "I think all of our strategies are coming together. Postpartum depression has so many components. I've given Vi advice on nutritional supplements. They can build up vitamin deficiencies and help moods too. We're trying to hit all the angles."

"It sounds as if having a baby depletes a woman's body and puts every hormone in a tizzy."

"It doesn't do that with *all* women," Daisy explained. "But apparently Vi is one of the susceptible ones. Speaking with Vi's gynecologist, I discovered there's actually a new drug that's an infusion treatment for postpartum depression. But it has to be administered in a hospital setting and the woman monitored. You won't believe the cost."

"How much?"

"Twenty-five to thirty thousand dollars. What insurance company will pay for that?"

"So only the rich can afford to be treated?"

"If one of the big drug companies takes it on, it could become cheaper. Or it could stay in the stratosphere. For now, new moms just have to be aware of what's happening to them and reach out for help wherever they can. I think Vi misses breastfeeding. Some research says antidepressants won't hurt a baby, or they won't be transferred in breast milk, but Vi and Sammy's pediatrician don't want to take any chances."

Jonas and another volunteer moved a stairway to give the illusion of a second floor onto the stage.

Daisy pointed to the chandelier near the stairway. "Jonas showed me the pulley apparatus for the chandelier. Keisha Washington, the stage manager, arranged all the props."

"Is she the one who chose that oriental rug? It's gorgeous."

"Actually, Margaret chose that. Keisha said it blew their budget but she managed."

As Daisy kept her gaze on Jonas, he moved an imitation fir tree into position while Jasper lined up another one.

"Are those the trees that fell on you?" Tessa asked.

"They are."

"They have a solid base on them. Could they have fallen over on you?"

"The trees did what?" a male voice asked right over Daisy's shoulder.

Daisy had taken a seat at the end of the aisle, and now she looked up straight into the eyes of Detective Rappaport. "I didn't even hear you come down the aisle," Daisy said.

Detective Morris Rappaport looked a bit rumpled, as if he'd had too much coffee and not enough sleep. He was wearing a black suit tonight with a white shirt. If he'd been wearing a tie, he'd long ago discarded it. The top two buttons of his shirt were open. He scowled at Daisy. "Detectives walk on cat feet, didn't you know that?"

Daisy knew exactly what that meant. Her two cats were fast, and most of the time she didn't hear them come into her room or leave.

"You learned that at the police academy?" she asked with amusement, trying to remove his scowl.

She and Detective Rappaport had somewhat of a friendship, but tonight that wasn't in evidence.

"*You* are trying to change the subject. I want an answer to my question."

Looking as innocent as she could, Daisy asked, "What question?"

"I'll arrest you for being coy if you don't level with me."

Tessa elbowed her. "You better tell the man what he wants to know."

Tessa moved over a seat, and Daisy stood and did so too. Then she gestured to the aisle chair. "Why don't you have a seat and watch the show. If you sit, I'll tell you what you want to know."

Still with a scowl, Detective Rappaport sat heavily on the padded chair. "Spill it."

"It was an accident," she said softly.

His eyes narrowed. "So tell me about the accident."

"I dropped by to see Jonas and he was working on a set. He got called over to help someone and I was wandering around backstage. I probably shouldn't have been. Two of those trees fell over on me."

"They're eight feet tall," the detective noted. "Were you hurt?"

"Just a little banged up."

Tessa interjected, "And a scrape with a bandage."

"Why didn't you or Jonas tell me about this?"

She looked him straight in the eye. "It didn't seem important enough."

He waved that comment away with one beefy hand. "Let me decide that."

"What would Jonas or I have told you? Everybody was milling about. If someone did it, we had no idea who. And it could have simply been an accident."

"But you don't think it was."

"I don't know. Seriously, Detective Rappaport, I don't. I'm attempting to stay uninvolved in this."

"Have you given anyone the impression you're involved?"

She knew she had to be honest with this man who had once been almost an enemy. But now she knew he had her back. "Rowan Vaughn asked me to look into who might want to hurt Margaret. After all, you're looking at him as a suspect, aren't you?"

"Can't say," the detective mumbled.

Daisy almost let out a groan. "Back to that, are we?"

"You were telling me about Vaughn? My guess is he wants you to solve the case in case we don't. So what did you tell him?"

"I told him I'd talk to Vanna, and I'd talk with Glenda. That's it. I did and I didn't learn anything that will help."

"Someone thinks you might have or those trees wouldn't have fallen on you."

"When did you get so cynical?"

"I was *born* cynical."

She doubted that.

The curtains suddenly closed.

A few seconds later, Glenda emerged from the side of the stage in front of the curtain. She made a motion with her hand, probably to Ward Cooper, who was in the lighting booth. The lights dimmed and then the curtain reopened. The dress rehearsal began.

"It's a mess," Rappaport mumbled to Daisy in the middle of the first act. "Most of them can't even remember their lines."

"That's because Glenda changed a lot of them."

Daisy had been watching the play, but she'd also been watching the detective. He hadn't taken his eyes off Glenda, who was still standing by the side of the stage watching every motion and listening to every word.

Rappaport grumbled, "Wouldn't she make you nervous if you knew she was watching what you were doing?"

Tessa must have heard him because she answered, "The whole audience is going to be watching what they're doing. That's the point, Detective."

He gave Tessa a look, then went back to staring at Glenda. Daisy couldn't keep her question in check any longer. "Is Glenda a suspect?"

As if talking to himself, he mumbled, "Margaret stole a juicy role from her."

"When was that?" Daisy asked.

Rappaport just shook his head.

"Do you *know* that Glenda and Margaret were rivals?" Daisy asked. "Do you think Glenda has a motive?"

Again the detective didn't answer.

"Maybe they were rivals once," Daisy said. "But Margaret and Glenda renewed their friendship after Margaret married Rowan."

"What do you know about it?" the detective asked Daisy and Tessa.

"I don't know much," Tessa answered. "Just what I've heard from people coming in and out of the tea garden. They seemed to be friends, like Daisy and I are. They had a history. They reconnected when Margaret asked Glenda to come here to produce the play. Glenda seemed to be thankful for that."

"Really?" the detective asked.

"Why? Do you doubt it?" Daisy wanted to know. He seemed to be eking out information to her, little by little. If she asked enough questions, maybe she'd learn something.

"What's that old saying?" he asked. "Keep your friends close but your enemies closer?"

"Do you think that's what Glenda was doing?"

"What do *you* think?"

"I think you can't always tell someone else's motive," Daisy responded.

Tessa leaned across Daisy to ask the detective, "What's the word on the street about Glenda and Margaret?"

That was an interesting way to ask the question, Daisy thought. Maybe he'd answer.

After hesitating, he did answer. "The word on the street is that maybe Glenda Nurmi had something to gain from her friendship with Margaret. The word on the street is she's become helpful to Rowan Vaughn ever since Margaret died. That's the word on the street."

He hadn't told them anything new. He'd told them about gossip he'd heard. The truth was Daisy had heard that same gossip from Vanna and Tamlyn. Possibly Glenda *did* have a motive. Possibly Glenda *was* the murderess.

The whole tea garden smelled like gingerbread on Saturday, which was no surprise since this was gingerbread house–making day. Tonight, she'd be attending the premier performance of *Christmas in the North Woods* along with Jazzi and Vi. Foster had pushed the idea of his wife going to the opening night of the play. In an aside, he'd told Daisy that Vi hadn't been dressed up with makeup on since before the baby had been born. It would do her good to leave Sammy with him and just be a woman on the town again.

From the moment Daisy had met Foster, she'd considered him mature. This commonsense approach to what was happening in his marriage proved it. Daisy's mom and dad would be joining them at the theater, and it would be a real family night.

But now she had to put thoughts of the Little Theater aside while she accepted the tickets of the tearoom guests appearing at the doorway to the tea garden and show them to their tables. Foster had come in early this morning to help Daisy, Iris, and Tessa make the sheets of gingerbread that would be needed. Cora Sue and Eva had been on icing duty. Now they were distributing squeeze bottles of it to each table to help "glue" the gingerbread houses together.

At the same time, Pam and Jada were filling bowls on each table that the gingerbread house builders could use for decoration. There wouldn't be any judging of the final creations because Daisy didn't want any of her child guests to feel that theirs wasn't the best gingerbread house in the room. The Zook daughters would be helping the children when necessary and also serve tables in the main tearoom when tourists or other tea lovers came in for a scone or a cup of tea. Daisy knew she'd taken on a huge endeavor, but if today was successful, it could become a yearly tradition.

At the door, welcoming her customers, she suddenly gasped. "What are *you* doing here?"

Gavin Cranshaw grinned at her and pointed to his daughter Emily beside him. "Emily thought this would be fun."

Emily didn't hesitate to offer her opinion. "Dad does more stuff with Ben than with me. So I'm just trying to even things out a bit." She winked at Daisy. "Maybe you could teach Dad how to make gingerbread."

Daisy laughed. She'd met Gavin's daughter at the rehearsal picnic for Vi and Foster's wedding. Emily was fourteen and didn't hesitate to say what she thought. To Gavin's credit, Emily seemed to be confident in herself and unafraid to face the world.

Since the tea garden spillover room where they held private tea functions was almost full, no one came in behind Gavin.

"Come on," Daisy said. "I'll show you to your table." She addressed Emily. "Do you mind sitting at a table with smaller children? My guess is, you'll be finished before they will, and you can help them."

"Unless I make our house really complicated," Emily teased. Then she added, "I don't mind. I like kids."

Gavin just rolled his eyes and leaned close to Daisy. "As you can tell, she doesn't consider herself a kid anymore. Turning fourteen did that."

Daisy laughed and showed them to a table for six with two moms and their daughters who were about eight. She introduced everyone and said, "Have fun."

After they all assured her they would, Gavin asked, "Can I talk to you for a couple of minutes?"

Daisy looked around and saw that all was under control. "Sure. Do you want to go to my office?"

"No, Foster would probably see us there and think we're hatching a plot. How about that quiet corner over there?" He nodded to the corner by the bay window where a service cart stood.

"Sure," Daisy agreed, wondering what this was all about.

Gavin put his hand on his daughter's shoulder. "I'll be right back. Draw up the plan you want to use, and then I'll see if we can execute it."

His daughter gave him one of those *oh-Dad* looks.

Over by the serving cart and out of earshot of the general population, Gavin stuffed his hands into the pockets of his jeans. "Foster came to me to talk about Vi and the baby."

"Did he just need to vent?"

"I think so. He's feeling powerless. I just wanted to check with you to see if there was anything in particular either he or I could do to help. I've hesitated to interfere or even to stop in too often. He explained postpartum depression and everything they're trying to do to help Vi. I never realized it was so complicated."

"Did you ever have to deal with it?"

"If Annie ever experienced it, I didn't know about it. But I was working long hours building up the business and exhausted at night. Do you think I was clueless?"

"Many moms go through some version of postpartum depression, but not as serious as Vi's experiencing. Now general practitioners and gynecologists try to catch it early. Willa, as a midwife, was particularly aware of it."

Gavin raked his hand through his sandy brown hair, then rubbed his square jaw. "I hate to think Annie needed help and I didn't notice."

"You would have noticed. You're that type of man."

Gavin looked a little embarrassed and flushed. "I might have learned a thing or two since I was young.

Back then, I'm not sure what kind of man I was. The truth is—I don't think I was as mature as Foster is. What I'm concerned about with him is that he'll take on too much responsibility. He needs an education and I want him to have it, but he can't expect to work one or two jobs, go to class, and help Vi too. Not if he wants to eat and sleep and not get sick."

"I agree. Two jobs?"

"From what I understand, he's spending a lot more time on his Web site business."

"If he builds that up, that could be more lucrative than working here," Daisy admitted.

"Possibly. But I guess I simply wanted you to come on board to make sure we take care of Foster too. If he gets run-down, that's not going to help Vi."

"I absolutely agree. Did you think I wouldn't?"

"Of course not," Gavin protested with a shake of his head. "I suppose I just wanted backup. The truth is, I think he'd listen to you better than he listens to me. After all, you're the one who kept a sane head when they wanted to get married."

"You came around admirably."

He sighed. "Not one of my finer moments at first." He glanced toward his daughter. She was already talking with the two women and children at the table. "I better get over there before Emily plans a community gingerbread house." He started toward the table, then turned around. "I mean it, Daisy. If you need anything to help Vi and Foster, please let me know."

"I will, Gavin. I will."

The laughter, fun, spilled candy and icing, sticky fingers, and the sampling of gingerbread all combined to make a wonderful day. The houses themselves on their cardboard platforms went from cabins to ranchers to double-storied Hansel and Gretel replicas. Everyone seemed to be having a good time. Not only that, but the tea garden's sales cases almost looked bare. They'd rung up more bags of tea today too than on a normal Saturday. Maybe people were getting ready for the holidays.

Some of the children and their parents had already left when Emily showed Daisy her finished house. Daisy could tell that Gavin, a master at construction, had had a hand in it. It was well built, evenly decorated with windows that were even complemented by window boxes. The gingerbread trim had been expertly applied. "You and your dad make a good team."

Emily beamed at her. "We do. This was a whole lot of fun. Do you think it's okay if me and Ben come over to see the baby tomorrow? We've been dying to see him, but Dad kept telling us Foster and Vi needed a chance to get into a routine."

Obviously, Gavin hadn't told Emily and Ben exactly what was going on. Maybe that was best, so they wouldn't act differently around Vi and Foster. "Babies have very unpredictable hours. Sammy's doing better now with his napping and sleeping schedule. The best thing to do is to call or text Vi and Foster and ask them the best time to come over."

Gavin tweaked his daughter's braids. "I think the secret will be to not stay too long. Shorter visits are probably better than longer ones. You can stop in more often that way."

Emily looked to Daisy as if she didn't quite trust what her dad had told her.

"Your dad's right. With shorter visits, no one gets too tired."

Emily leaned close to Daisy. "I have a present for Sammy. It's the cutest little baseball outfit. Do you think Vi and Foster will like it?"

"I think they'll like it, and Sammy will too. Just give them a call and make sure he's not having one of his fussy spells. Then you'll be good to go."

Gavin's shoulder touched Daisy's when he said, "Thank you. We'll see you soon."

Later that day, Iris was at the sales counter and pointed to a table with two of their regular customers. Betty Sue and her sister Rhonda came in to sample different teas, lunch offerings, and baked goods. They were millennials and knew exactly what they wanted.

Daisy crossed to them and asked, "What will you have today?"

Betty Sue, who usually wore something purple— like the jeans and sweater she'd donned today—said, "How about that cocoa rooibos and a slice of apple gingerbread. Do you have clotted cream for that?"

"We have whipped cream. How about you, Rhonda?"

Rhonda, whose blue hair atop her head was usually arranged in a messy topknot, said, "I'll try the peppermint tea. It seems fitting for the season. With that, I'd like two lemon tea cakes."

"Both will be coming right up."

Daisy went to the kitchen to ready a tray. When she returned to the main tearoom, she served both women, adding a ceramic pot of honey and a bowl of sparkling sugar in case they wanted to add that to their teas.

Betty Sue dipped her finger to sample the whipped

cream. "I heard Margaret Vaughn insisted on clotted cream at her tea."

There were so many aspects of a small town that Daisy liked. But there was one aspect she wasn't sure did anyone any good—the gossip running rampant like wildfire. The Amish believed gossiping was a sin. Daisy only wished the rest of the town did too.

"Yes, Margaret ordered clotted cream."

"I knew Margaret," Rhonda revealed. "We met at the farmers' market of all places, and we struck up a conversation. She found out I act in amateur productions in Lancaster. She told me she'd been an actress. I was bewailing the fact that I needed a costume for a part but wasn't sure where to find it. She actually invited me into her home to look in her closet with costumes."

Daisy felt her eyes widen in surprise. "Margaret had a closet of costumes?"

"Yes, she did," Rhonda affirmed. "She took me to a spare room. It wasn't a very big closet. Those old houses don't have big closets unless they're renovated."

"I see," Daisy said, wanting to keep Rhonda talking.

Rhonda lowered her voice. "Margaret wasn't as straitlaced as everyone thought. She acted that way here, wearing skirts and jackets that covered everything up."

"How do you know she wasn't straitlaced?" Daisy asked as Betty Sue looked on.

"From those costumes in that closet," Rhonda answered. "I was playing the part of a hostess at a saloon, and she had just what I needed. It was skimpy with feathers. Bright red."

It was possible Margaret had kept costumes from her acting career for sentimental reasons if nothing else. "Did she say where it had come from?"

"She simply said it was a dance outfit that she had worn for a part."

As Daisy left the women with their tea and desserts, she wondered even more about Margaret's past life, and if that's what had gotten her killed.

Chapter Sixteen

The production of *Christmas in the North Woods* was sold out. It could be that the population of Willow Creek was curious about what had happened to Margaret. It could be that everyone just wanted to see a Christmas play. It could be that the killer was at the show.

Daisy's mom and dad, along with Iris, Russ, and Vi, attended the Saturday night performance. Foster was at home with Sammy. He'd convinced Vi that a night out would do her good. He was trying to help Vi any way he could, and Daisy was glad to see it.

Earlier, Daisy had been backstage with Jazzi. Glenda had decided to enlist the children's choir from Daisy's church to sing carols at the opening of the play and at intermission. Jazzi had volunteered to help keep the kids in order.

To Daisy's relief, and surprise, the first two acts of the play went off without a hitch. Applause was enthusiastic as intermission was announced and the children's choir lined up on either side of the stage a second time.

Daisy leaned close to Vi. "I'm going backstage and see if Jazzi needs any help. I understand they're serving beverages out in the lobby if you want to get something."

Daisy glanced at her mom to see if she'd like to go, but her mother was just staring straight ahead and didn't seem to hear Daisy or Vi. Her mother's reaction made Daisy uneasy. Another time, her mom would have had an opinion about the play so far. She seemed quiet tonight.

Iris stood and called over to Vi. "Do you want to get something to drink?"

Vi nodded and she said to Daisy, "I want to call Foster too and see how he and Sammy are doing."

"Are you worried he can't handle Sammy on his own?" Daisy asked.

"I'm with Sammy a lot more than he is. I just want to make sure."

Daisy gave her daughter's shoulder a squeeze. "Call as often as you want if it will relieve your stress. I'm sure Foster will be glad you're checking in."

Waiting until Iris and Vi had gone up the aisle to the back of the theater, Daisy moved to the side entrance of the stage and climbed the steps, crossing behind the curtain.

Keeping her distance, she watched Jazzi as she stood in back of children dressed in red dresses. They were singing their hearts out. The boys were on the other side of the stage and had worn white shirts and red bowties. Daisy had a feeling Glenda had provided the bowties.

Seeing her mom, Jazzi gave a little wave, then went back to watching the kids.

Keeping an eye out for Jonas, Daisy moved behind the stage sets. Ward Cooper was helping Jonas move new sets. Keisha seemed to be everywhere, checking that props were in their place.

Ward came over to Daisy's side of the stage.

"I thought you'd be in the lighting booth," Daisy noted.

"Manpower is always needed when set changes are necessary." He moved with Daisy to the side of the stage where the children were singing. "These are nice kids." There was sincerity in his voice.

"I know many of their parents," Daisy explained. "They have sisters and brothers Jazzi's age."

Ward asked, "You have two girls, right?"

"I do. Vi is in the audience with me. She just had a baby a few weeks ago, and this is her first night out."

"So you're a grandmother! No one would believe that."

His compliment wasn't in the least bit smarmy. It was genuine and she appreciated it.

For a few minutes, they listened to the choir singing "Joy to the World." After the song was finished, Ward said to Daisy, "I wish I would have had kids but my work never keeps me in one place very long."

"It's hard to make connections when you're constantly moving around," she empathized.

"It is. I've missed out on relationships and family opportunities because of it. But I do love my work. I always have. It comes first."

"I can imagine. I was a dietician before I opened the tea garden, but now the tea garden takes up a majority of my time. We have to work to pay the bills, but the hope is that we can enjoy what we do and put our best energy into it."

"It sounds as if you're doing something you love too," he said with a smile.

"I am." She was about to say she was lucky enough to have experienced marriage and children, but she didn't want Ward to feel worse that he hadn't.

Just as the children started singing again, this time "The First Noel," Jonas appeared beside her and put his arm around her. "How do you think it's going?"

"I haven't seen a mistake yet. Have there been any?"

Ward gave her a signal he had to go back to the lighting booth and she nodded.

"Not that I noticed," Jonas answered. "But I don't have the script in front of me. Glenda does."

"Where is Glenda?"

"She's behind the sets, going over her notes. She won't hesitate to give pointers to the actors and actresses before they go onstage if she thinks it will make the production better. But sometimes I think it throws them off. Jasper almost missed a cue because she told him something before he went onstage. It turned out all right, though."

Daisy supposed too much instruction was as bad as not enough. "Is Rowan around? I didn't see him in the audience."

"He was backstage with Glenda but then I lost track of him. He could be roaming around making sure all is well. After all, he put a lot of effort and money into this place."

"I'm going to slip out to the lobby and get a drink with Iris and Vi. Vi was going to call Foster. I'm hoping everything is okay."

Jonas leaned down to Daisy and kissed her lightly

on the lips. "To be continued later," he said with a wink.

Daisy was looking forward to it.

In the lobby, Daisy was noticing who had attended the play when Iris asked Vi, "Are you ready to go back in?"

With a wide smile, Vi nodded. "Foster's doing fine with Sammy. It *has* been good to get out tonight. I've missed being with all of you by myself. The play is actually good."

With a hearty laugh, Iris put her arm around her niece.

Daisy, thankful Foster and Sammy were doing well, finished the last of her soda. She was ready to follow Iris and Vi into the theater when Vanna slipped up beside her and took hold of her arm.

Daisy said to Iris and Vi, "I'll be along in a minute."

The look on Vanna's face had told Daisy she needed to talk, if only for a few minutes. Knowing Vanna was still immersed in her grief, Daisy wanted to help any way she could.

"Can I talk to you?" Vanna asked.

"You can always talk to me. Come on, let's go over by the window." Many of the playgoers were already heading into the theater at the end of the intermission, though the lights hadn't blinked yet as a warning to be seated.

"I found out something that you should know," Vanna explained.

That comment had Daisy puzzled. "Go ahead," she said.

"I heard from Margaret's lawyer today."

Daisy supposed that could be about one thing. "Her will?"

Her head bobbing vehemently, Vanna confirmed, "Yes, her will. Her funds were separate from Rowan's. I never thought about having a marriage like that. From the moment my husband and I were married, everything we did was together. We put our money together, just like we put our thoughts together and our hearts. But Margaret and Rowan didn't do that."

"Vanna, Rowan probably had much more money than Margaret did. Was there a prenup?"

"A prenup?" Vanna looked puzzled, as if she didn't know what Daisy was talking about.

"Yes. A prenuptial agreement is a contract that two people make before they're married. Basically, it's to protect the person who has a lot more money. It says how the funds are supposed to be divided, or what might happen in case of a divorce."

"I see," Vanna said slowly, staring into space. "Nobody mentioned anything like that. But since Margaret's funds were separate, in her will she designated me as her heir, not Rowan. That means I'll receive everything she saved. It's a tidy sum that might pay a nursing home for a few years if I ever have to go that route."

"Oh, Vanna. I don't think your children would let that happen unless it was an absolute necessity."

"Maybe not. But if I keep good count of it, I can will it to them. It would help all of them."

"I can see that." She could. But she didn't quite understand why this was something Vanna needed to tell her.

The warning lights blinked that intermission was almost over. Vanna took hold of Daisy's elbow. "The police could think that I killed her!"

"Oh, Vanna. I doubt that." Though Daisy wasn't sure. She wasn't sure at all *what* the detectives were thinking.

As Daisy returned inside the theater, she saw her dad standing at the end of the aisle. Her mother must have gone to the ladies' room because she wasn't in her seat or in the near vicinity.

Daisy placed her hand on her dad's arm. "Are you enjoying the play?"

"To my surprise, I am. Even though the actors are local, they're quite good."

"They've made a concerted effort to make this play a success for Margaret's sake." Since she didn't want to enter into a discussion about that with her father right now, she asked, "Is Mom enjoying the play?"

"I think she is. I heard her question Vi more than once about how she's feeling. She's worried about her."

"Mom seems unusually quiet tonight. She has been feeling well, hasn't she?"

"I think she's feeling fine. She's been working hard at the nursery. You know, as the holidays gear up, we have more and more to do. In January we'll slow down and take a vacation again." Her father squeezed Daisy's shoulder. "I'd better go to my seat. Thanks for asking us to join you tonight."

While her father made his way to his seat, Daisy stood glancing around the theater. She spotted Cade a few rows ahead of her. He was standing as if to stretch his legs. He waved and smiled, and she waved back. Tessa had been escorted by Trevor tonight. In fact, speaking of the devil, Trevor was coming down the aisle from the lobby now.

He gave Daisy a wink and said in a low aside, "You better avoid the trees."

Trevor's dry humor didn't offend her. She returned his comment with one of her own. "I've been watching out for more than trees."

Trevor took his seat beside Tessa, and Daisy's mom returned to her seat too. But she didn't glance Daisy's way.

The rest of the performance was filled with holiday relationship drama, more Christmas carols, sleigh bells ringing, and a family reunion that bonded the members of the pretend family together. The cast had taken their curtain calls and members of the audience were leaving when Daisy spied Zeke Willet. He was striding down the side of the theater in what seemed to be a hurry. He aimed toward the stage.

Had the police discovered who'd murdered Margaret?

Her eyes on the detective, Daisy watched him approach Glenda Nurmi, who was standing by the side of the curtain with her clipboard. A patrol officer had followed him down the aisle and stood stationed at the bottom of the steps. If Zeke brought a patrol officer with him . . .

Jazzi pulled on Daisy's wrist. "What's he doing?"

"I'm not sure," Daisy murmured.

She looked for Jonas up on the stage. Suddenly he appeared beside Glenda.

Zeke and Jonas exchanged words, both of their expressions serious.

Daisy kept her eyes on Glenda and saw her take a slip of paper from Jonas. Daisy could guess what that was—a lawyer's phone number.

The expression on Detective Willet's face was so hard that Daisy wondered if he was going to cuff Glenda. However, he didn't. He stood at the top of the steps while she walked down them to the patrol officer.

Suddenly Vanna ran after Glenda, carrying her shawl. She handed it to Glenda and then stepped back as if ordered to do so.

Daisy hadn't seen the patrol officer's lips move, but that didn't mean he hadn't given a command. Glenda slipped the black shawl trimmed with gold thread around her shoulders and followed the patrol officer up the aisle with Detective Willet behind her. A few of the residents of Willow Creek who had enjoyed the performance gawked as the little parade continued up the aisle. Daisy knew Vanna, along with Keisha, had been helping the actors and actresses change their costumes from scene to scene. She'd told Daisy by doing that, she felt she was helping Margaret too.

Now she crossed the front of the theater and came running up the middle aisle to Daisy. "They're taking her to the police station," Vanna said. "They might actually *arrest* her."

"Maybe they just want to question her," Daisy said, hoping. Daisy's instincts told her that Glenda had had a real affection for Margaret. The problem was, she also might have affection for Rowan, maybe a serious attraction too.

Cade came up the aisle to Daisy now and joined the little group around her. "Are you involved in a murder again?"

She didn't even try to give him an explanation. She just said, "I found the body."

His eyes went wide and his eyebrows almost met his hairline.

Trevor, who'd appeared out of nowhere, bumped his shoulder against Daisy's. "Have the police taken in the right suspect?"

"I honestly don't know."

Looking thoughtful, Cade took hold of Daisy's elbow and pulled her aside.

Trevor gave her a questioning look, but she just shook her head for him to give her a moment.

"You're gathering information, aren't you? Just like you did before."

"Cade, if you're going to give me a speech about not interfering—"

"Jonas is the one who should be giving you that. No, that's not what I want. If you *are* gathering information maybe there's something you should know."

"What's that?"

Frowning, Cade hesitated, then went on. "I can't talk about clients. However, since Margaret Vaughn is dead, I see no reason to hold back. She spoke with me about having the house appraised without Rowan knowing."

Ideas and suspicions began tumbling around in Daisy's mind. "Did Margaret buy that house when everybody thought Rowan did?"

"I don't know about that. I didn't have her as a client back then. Maybe she wanted to sell it and cash out. Maybe her marriage to Rowan wasn't what everybody thought it was."

Was the marriage really what everybody thought it was? Romantic and genuine? Outside looking in was different from actually living in the marriage.

Out of the corner of her eye, Daisy could see the curtain was open again on the stage. Jonas had apparently finished with moving the sets back to their stored position because he came out to the center of the stage and peered over the audience. Seeing her, he jogged down the steps and started toward her.

In the meantime, Ward Cooper joined her and Cade. He'd come from the lighting booth. "The performance went off without a hitch."

Vanna crossed to him. "I doubt if that's going to happen again. The police took Glenda to the station."

Ward looked genuinely surprised.

Daisy suggested, "They might have merely taken her to the station for questioning."

"But she's the director now," Vanna said. "The cast is going to be at a loss."

"No, they won't," Ward said. "The cast learned the changes she suggested. They did well tonight. They don't need her if she's going to be unavailable."

In other words, the cast didn't need Glenda if she went to jail.

Chapter Seventeen

Simply put, Jazzi was moping around on Sunday. She hadn't heard anything from Portia since her visit to Allentown. It was hard for anyone to be patient but especially a sixteen-year-old. She wanted to be approved of and liked by the people who mattered to her. So it was advantageous when Vi asked Daisy and Jazzi to come over to the apartment to have supper with her. Foster had gone to his dad's to visit with Gavin, Ben, and Emily. As Vi had anticipated, Daisy offered to make macaroni and cheese and bring cherry tarts for dessert. Vi was going to provide a salad.

When they arrived, Vi had settled Sammy in the swing his great-grandmother had provided as a baby present. It was a wonderful device because Sammy often fell asleep in it when rocking or singing to him didn't work.

Daisy couldn't help but go to Sammy as soon as she arrived. "Can I hold him for a while?"

Vi eyed her mom. "You're spoiling him."

"I'm not," Daisy protested. "I'm loving him. There's a difference." She scooped him out of the swing while Jazzi shoved the casserole into the oven to bake.

Vi had lost at least half of the baby weight. She was wearing jeans and a pale green oversized sweater. Her cheeks had color and she even looked . . . happy.

Walking Sammy into the living room area, Daisy kissed his soft cheek, loving his baby smell. He was so precious. His eyes were clear and wide, and his mouth widened in what Daisy hoped would soon be a smile. Christmas would be here before they knew it and she hadn't even shopped for him yet.

Jazzi pulled out her phone as she settled on the sofa beside her mom.

After drying her hands on a dish towel, Vi joined them in the living room area and sat in the rocker. "Have you heard from Portia?" she asked Jazzi.

Jazzi mumbled, "No, and I don't know if I'm ever going to. Colton thinks I'm frivolous. He believes all I want to do is shop and learn how to drive so I can run around with friends."

"What makes you think that?" Daisy asked, cuddling Sammy in the crook of her arm. Jazzi hadn't mentioned this to her before.

"I heard him talking to Portia Saturday night after I went to bed. She told him how I babysit, work at the tea garden, and am part of the peer counseling program. But I don't think it made an impression. He hardly talked to me on Sunday."

Looking concerned for her sister, Vi said, "You can't do anything about his attitude. We have Christmas to think about, and I have something else I want to discuss with you."

From the tone of Vi's voice, Daisy didn't think it was something serious.

Vi pointed to Jazzi. "You can help me plan Sammy's christening. Mom's busy enough."

"And I'm not?" Jazzi quipped.

"Not too busy that you can't help me plan food and favors and who we want to come."

"When do you want to have the christening?" Daisy asked.

"I spoke to Reverend Kemp on the phone, and we're thinking about three weeks. Can we have the party at your house? That way we can invite more guests."

It warmed Daisy's heart to see Vi excited about the idea of a christening. In the past week especially, she had seemed so much more herself.

As Vi leaned forward in the rocker, she set her attention on Jazzi. "I'd ask you to be Sammy's godmother, but Reverend Kemp said the godmother should be over eighteen."

"I understand that," Jazzi said. "You know I'll look after him with you. Who do you have in mind? Aunt Iris?"

Vi shook her head, keeping her gaze on her mom now. "Do you think Aunt Iris will be hurt if I don't ask her?"

"I'm sure your aunt would want you to choose whoever you want. Who do you have in mind?"

"I'm thinking about Tessa. What do you think, Mom?"

Daisy thought about it. Tessa had a good heart. She knew about responsibility and devotion and loyalty. "I think Tessa would be honored if you ask her. Who do you have in mind for the godfather?"

"Foster and I talked about it, and we decided to ask Gavin." Foster's dad was more than responsible. After the death of his wife, he'd raised his three children. Foster was becoming a fine man, father, and husband, and Daisy was sure Ben and Emily would grow up with the same values and integrity because they watched their dad and that's what they saw in him.

"You've chosen well, honey, and I'd be glad to host the party at my house. I'm sure your grandmother would love to help too."

"She can help," Vi said. "But I don't want her running everything. That's why I want Jazzi to help me plan it. We'll go to her with everything set out and then she'll know the party's going to be like we want."

Over the years Vi had learned how to handle her grandmother probably better than Daisy had. Thinking of her mother again, Daisy wondered if something was bothering her. She hadn't seemed herself ever since . . . ever since Sammy was born.

Daisy's cell phone vibrated. She took it from the coffee table. It was Jonas. He asked, "Do you want to go for a walk?"

She smiled and said, "Yes."

Daisy's property was lit with a motion detector light from the security system. Daisy wanted to talk to Jonas about something and was glad they were going to be alone as they walked.

He tucked her arm in his as they strolled toward the garage. They weren't going to visit Vi and Foster, just take a circle around it. Daisy had worn her short boots for any uneven ground they might come across. She zipped her cat-patterned fleece jacket up around her neck and added a scarf. The maroon cap she wore had a pom-pom on top and earmuff-like side pieces. She'd tied it under her chin.

"Warm enough?" Jonas asked after they'd walked a little ways.

"I'm fine. It actually feels good to be out in the cold air. After we go back in, we could light a fire."

"Have you done that yet this season?"

"No. Jazzi goes up to her bedroom many nights to study or play music, and I usually sit on the sofa with a throw wrapped around me."

"But you want to light one tonight?" His voice held amusement.

"I think it would be fun to snuggle on the sofa with you while the fire's burning."

"Snuggling, huh? We might have to practice the Amish way of bundling."

Daisy laughed and they continued walking. She turned her face up to the sky and felt a sudden wetness on her cheek. "It's snowing! This is early."

"It won't amount to anything," Jonas predicted. "It might frost your lawn, but it will disappear as soon as the sun comes up. I think it's supposed to be forty tomorrow."

"Do you check the weather every night?"

"Is that a man thing or do you do it too?"

"I do it. I have so many apps on my phone I don't know what to do with them, but they come in handy."

Even though snow had started, they kept up their leisurely pace, enjoying each other's company, appreciating the intimacy of the dark night and the cold around them. They were close together as they walked, creating heat, and bonding in their way.

"Have you heard any more about Glenda?" Daisy asked.

"The police questioned her for a few hours. Surprisingly, she didn't call a lawyer."

"I wonder why not."

"She said she was completely open with them and told them everything they wanted to know. I don't know what that everything was, maybe about her past with Margaret, maybe about an affair with Rowan."

"She confessed to that?"

"I don't know that either. Neither Rappaport nor Willet would open up about the investigation. You know how they can be."

"I know. But I wonder how the cast is going to feel with Glenda in their midst if they think she's a suspect."

"They're probably watching each other carefully thinking *everybody's* a suspect. This murder investigation certainly isn't cut and dried."

The snow fell faster now.

Jonas suggested, "Let's walk back to the house and sit on the swing on the porch. I'm glad you haven't taken it down yet for the winter."

"I might not. Even when it's cold, I like to go out there and sit." After they circled the path around the garage, they headed back toward the house.

Once they were seated on the swing, Jonas's arm around Daisy's shoulders, she leaned into him. He took one of her gloved hands into his. He was wearing leather gloves and they couldn't feel each other's heat. But they held on anyway.

"I'd like to ask you something," she said softly.

"Go ahead."

She hesitated.

Jonas shifted toward her. "Are you afraid it's something I'll get upset about?"

"Possibly, but I don't want you to be."

He gave a shrug. "So ask, and we'll see what happens."

Pragmatic to the core, Daisy thought. But that

gave Jonas balance and sometimes her too. "Do you feel left out or unsettled because Vi and Foster chose Gavin to be godfather?" Daisy had filled Jonas in on Vi's and Foster's choices.

She felt Jonas lean away from her slightly, and she turned her head to face him.

He began, "Truthfully, for about two seconds I was hurt. But there were so many good reasons why Vi and Foster should have asked Gavin and not me. First of all, Gavin has a better grasp on faith than I do. I still struggle with it—with my dad's death, my mom's struggles afterward, and Brenda's death. Maybe I'm still angry at God. I don't know. But after I thought about it, I knew Gavin was the right man for the job. He's raised three good kids. He knows what he's doing. He'll take the honor seriously."

Daisy wished she could help Jonas take a leap of faith, but faith was too personal to interfere with. Jonas removed his glove and stroked Daisy's cheek. She shivered, but what she felt had nothing to do with the cold.

"You're chilled," he said. "We should go in."

With a smile, she shook her head. "No, I'm not cold. I just like you touching me. Do you mind that we're going so slow . . . that we haven't slept together yet?"

"Some people would think we're foolish, I guess," Jonas said, still looking straight into her eyes. "But I think we're building. What we're building slowly will last."

In her mind Daisy thought, *I've fallen in love with this man.* But she couldn't say it yet. They were building friendship, trust, maybe even a life together. There would be time enough to say the words, she hoped.

* * *

On her lunch break on Tuesday, Daisy drove to Willow Creek Community Church. The clothes drive they were holding was a special one—*Sleepers for Kids.* Daisy had gone to the baby shop downtown and purchased a few sleep sets from six months to toddler to six years old to ten years old. She hoped they would help a family who needed to keep their children warm at night.

She saw the sign outside the side entrance to the offices behind the church where Vanna's office was located. A square of cardboard announced, ALL SLEEPERS FOR KIDS MUST BE DONATED HERE. KNOCK ON THE DOOR OR RING THE BELL AND SOMEONE WILL GIVE YOU A PLACE TO PUT THEM.

Daisy climbed the two steps at the side entrance and rang the bell. The bags weren't particularly heavy, and she didn't mind waiting. She'd used one reusable tote bag from Vinegar and Spice, and another from the Covered Bridge Bed and Breakfast. They were canvas totes and she often took them to the grocery store or wherever else she needed to use one.

A girl of around ten answered the door. She had red hair and curls to her shoulders, and very green eyes. "I'm Leah," she said, a little shyly. "Do you have donations? Grandma will be so happy."

Soon Vanna was in the hall. "I see you've met my granddaughter. She's usually pretty shy. She has a cold so she's home from school, helping me today."

Leah said, "I recognize that this is the woman you talk about often—Daisy Swanson. You say she has a good heart, so I knew I didn't have to be afraid of her."

"I hope you don't have to be afraid of me," Daisy said.

Leah lowered her voice. "Grandma said you help solve murders."

"I don't spread it around," Daisy whispered.

"She says the only reason you can do it is because you know how to ask the right questions, and you don't make people mad."

"That's a high compliment. I try not to make people mad. Maybe that leads me to the right questions."

"Come on now, Leah," Vanna said, swinging her arm around her granddaughter. "You have to rest a bit."

"Resting is getting boring."

"Spoken like a ten-year-old," Vanna whispered to Daisy as Leah ran toward another room at the back of the church.

"Are you going to let me see your stash?" Daisy asked. "If you don't have enough sleepers, I'll spread the word."

"It's hard to tell yet. We have another few days for the drive," Vanna explained. "But come on. I'll show you the room we're keeping everything in."

The small storage room was chaos. Daisy spotted a couple of volunteers who usually helped at the thrift store. Agnes was one of them.

"Do you already have the names of families who need the pajamas?"

"Sure do," Vanna said. "Reverend Kemp knows which families are the neediest. Along with that, if anyone comes to ask, we'll gladly give to them. Some offer to volunteer with parish chores in return."

Vanna leaned her arm against Daisy's. "I don't

suppose you just came to drop off the clothes for kids."

"You're right, I didn't. Can we go to your office or are you too busy? I don't want to interrupt."

"You're not interrupting. Let's have a cup of tea. With cold setting in, I need several cups a day."

Vanna went into her office, turned on the electric kettle, and waited for it to bubble. A mug tree stood nearby and she procured two mugs from it. One said *Oh, Happy Day*, the other said *Lift Up Your Eyes*.

Vanna had three tins of tea sitting on a tray. She said, "I have a strawberry herbal, a cinnamon rooibos, and orange pekoe. Which would you like?"

"I'd like to try the strawberry—just something light for now."

As Vanna readied the tea, she glanced over at Daisy more than once. "A light tea means you want to talk about a heavy subject."

"I don't know how heavy it is, but I just want you to be relaxed with me, and see if you can remember anything about the time Margaret was in New York."

"So this isn't about the murder, per se."

"No. I just think we need to learn something about Margaret's background."

"Let me think." Vanna set Daisy's mug in front of her while she took her mug to her desk and sat behind it. Daisy needed no complements to her tea, and Vanna didn't seem to either.

As they let the tea cool, Vanna said, "New York. I was so hurt when she left for New York. My mother was absolutely heartbroken. Up until then, she thought Margaret would come back into the fold. I thought she might too when she got a taste of New York. But that wasn't to be."

"And you said you didn't hear from her often?"

"I sat down with a box of memorabilia a couple of days ago. It brought back memories that hurt."

"I understand if you don't want to talk about this."

"It hurts me because I didn't do a better job of staying in touch with Margaret."

"What happened immediately after she left?"

"She did write me letters then, basic ones that I looked through, but they didn't have much information. They were all about her need to get away. She found a job in a bar. My mom would have been scandalized. But Margaret insisted she could make more with tips as a waitress in a bar than any of the day jobs she tried to get. Later, I received a few e-mails, but they were lost. E-mail servers changed. I deleted many."

Vanna suddenly went quiet.

Daisy waited, wondering what the woman was thinking.

"Vanna? Did something you found make you sad?"

"When I couldn't find anything else, I sorted through years of photos of my husband and kids. I found one of Margaret too. She sent it to me about a year before she met Rowan. Do you want to see it?"

"Sure, I do."

Vanna pulled her purse from a desk drawer. She slipped the photo out of a zippered pocket and showed it to Daisy.

Daisy stared at the photo. It was of Margaret in front of a building. She'd written on the back, *Mother and Dad would be proud of what I'm doing now, but I still hope to find an acting job in the future.*

"I wonder what that means," Daisy said. "What kind of job did she have?"

"I don't have a clue. I didn't hear from her again until she married Rowan. She was acting off-Broadway when she met him. There are so many holes in her history. Do you think Glenda knows more than she's saying?"

"I think it's certainly possible." If only Daisy could tap into Glenda's history too. What kind of information would flow out?

Chapter Eighteen

After work Daisy locked up the tea garden, made sure the security alarm was set, and walked the back route to Jonas's store. Jazzi had a peer counseling meeting tonight after school, and Daisy would have to pick her up in about half an hour. That gave her time to talk to Jonas about what she'd discovered with Vanna.

As she walked along the back of the properties, the clear cold night swung itself around her with a breeze. She hadn't worn her hat. Instead of putting up the hood to her jacket, she slipped the band from her ponytail and let her hair blow free. There were times like this when she just wanted to be alone with her thoughts, letting air with the scent of woodsmoke clear any clouds away.

She was anxious to see Jonas for many reasons. One of them was that she missed him when she didn't see him. She was so used to talking to him every day that when she didn't, something in her life just felt missing. Jonas seemed to want to be with her too, dropping in at the tea garden or coming over to the house, not even minding if she was babysitting Sammy. Together just seemed to be better than apart.

The path was wet from melting snow as she walked over gravel, macadam, and grass. Each of the stores had motion detector lights to the rear of their property as well as on the front. As she approached the back of Woods, she could see that Jonas's truck was still parked there. She knew he had collected reclaimed wood recently and was probably building something special with that.

She knocked on the back door to his workshop. If he wasn't in there, if he was in the main store, he might not hear. It was possible she'd have to traipse around to the front.

But she didn't. He opened the door and when he saw it was her, he took her into his arms and gave her a walloping kiss. "I've missed you," he said into her hair.

"I missed you too."

With his arm around her, he brought her into the workshop. "No reason to stand out there in the cold. You have time to kill?"

Often when Jazzi had a meeting, Daisy stopped in to spend time with Jonas. "I wouldn't say I was killing time. I came to see what you're working on."

"How did you know it was something new?"

"You can't look at a pile of reclaimed wood and not imagine what you're going to do with it. What did you do with it?"

He laughed and Daisy unzipped her jacket. She laid it on the bench, then she saw exactly what Jonas had been working on—a beautiful island. He'd used the barn wood for the base of the cabinet. Along with that, he'd added barn doors to open and shut the cabinets. The top of the island was glossy gray and white quartz that looked a bit pebbled with mother-of-pearl glimmers. The cabinet itself was a pale distressed green.

She ran her hand over the top. "This is beautiful, Jonas. Do you have a buyer for it?"

"No one knows about it yet. Elijah and I are going to set it in the window tomorrow morning. We'll leave it there for a week and see if we have any interest. If not, I do have some buyers who want me to call them when I have new pieces. With that combination, we should sell it soon."

She slid the small barn doors back and forth and noticed the shelves inside. Jonas had made the piece not only elegantly rustic but usable too.

"Elijah thinks we should do some kind of special event," Jonas said, "with all reclaimed wood pieces. He thinks it would create an awareness of the history of the area, as well as what can be done with reclaimed wood. He has a finish product that will even re-porcelain old sinks. Can you imagine an old farmhouse sink in a cabinet like this?"

"I can. A complete kitchen of reclaimed wood would be gorgeous. When Wyatt Troyer designed my kitchen, we used reclaimed wood on one of the walls because it had come from the barn. He refinished the boards and no one seems to notice it, but I know. I wanted to keep as much of the old barn in play as possible."

"It makes your kitchen distinctive," Jonas agreed. "I was thinking of making a library table out of reclaimed wood for Vi and Foster for Christmas. Do you think they'd like that? I could even put shelves under it so they'd have a place for books. I know Foster has a lot of them."

"That's a *wonderful* idea, and I'm certain they'd appreciate it. They could even set their computers there when they aren't using them. Foster doesn't always like to go downstairs to the garage office to work because he wants to be close to Vi and the baby. That might change as he knows Vi is feeling better and the baby might not need as much care."

"Do you think Vi really is better? She's not faking it?"

After a serious consideration, Daisy answered, "No, she's not faking it. I saw her at her worst, and I know her moods. When she looks at Sammy, there's love in her eyes. When she looks at me now, sometimes I see the old sparkle back. She's enthusiastic about the christening and I don't see how she could fake that either."

"I just wonder because sometimes depressed people can put on a good front," Jonas offered.

"I know, but I really think she's coming out of the depression. Not overnight, and not every day, but it's happening."

Jonas nodded. "Is Jazzi going to come along with us to the bonfire tomorrow night?" The bonfire was a holiday tradition for Willow Creek the first week of December.

"No, she says she doesn't want to get cold. She'll stay home with the cats or spend the evening with Vi."

Jonas leaned against a bookcase that appeared ready to be moved into the showroom. He crossed one ankle over the other and his arms across his chest. "Have you made any more progress about Margaret?"

"I don't know if I have or not. Vanna showed me something and I wanted to show you." She plucked her phone from her purse, tapped on her photo gallery, and brought up a photo. She'd snapped a pic of Vanna's photo. "Vanna said that Margaret sent her this photo about a year before she met Rowan. With it, she had said something like her mother and dad would be proud of her now but she still hoped to find an acting job."

"That means she wasn't acting."

"That's right. But Vanna didn't know what she *was* doing."

With his fingers, Jonas spread the picture so some elements of it came into closer focus.

"You don't seem to be concentrating on Margaret's face. What are you looking at?"

"At where the photo was taken. It looks familiar." He pointed to one aspect of the photo. "See these brick walls and the arch?" He pointed to something else. "Look at these ball lights."

"Do you think you recognize the place?"

"I've only been to New York City a few times on a case, but I have a friend in the police department there who knows it well. I could send it to him and see what he says."

When Daisy looked into Jonas's eyes, seeing the lines around them that came from his experience in the PD, when she studied the scar down his face and his expression as he studied her, she knew one thing for sure—he wanted *her* to make this choice. With each question she asked, and with each answer she found, she stepped deeper into the case. However, sometimes curiosity did get the best of her. It wouldn't hurt to find out where the photo was taken.

Right now, the photo wasn't as important as what she'd just figured out about Jonas. "You're never going to make decisions for me, are you?"

His mouth twisted into a wry smile. "Would you want me to?"

"No, I wouldn't. I want to stand on my own and make my own choices. I just figured out that you'd let me do that." They stared at each other for seconds that seemed to spin very slowly.

He held her shoulders. "I know you're a separate person from me, Daisy. My thoughts aren't yours. We're in sync a lot of the time. But I'd rather know what you're thinking than guess at it."

She leaned closer to him and laid her hand along his cheek that was marked by the scar. "My feelings for you are growing deeper than I want to admit," she said honestly.

He covered her hand with his free one. "That's good to hear." Leaning forward, he kissed her forehead.

How could that slight show of affection make her quiver so inside?

After he leaned away, he asked her, "So . . . should I send my friend the picture?"

"Yes, send it."

"Are you going on a wild goose chase?"

Shrugging, she said lightly, "Maybe I'll catch a goose."

The bonfire at the community pond was always festive. This December night was drop-below-thirty-two cold but clear enough to spot constellations. Residents of Willow Creek could wander around the pond under the light of a crescent moon. The volunteer fire company had organized the evening. They handled the bonfire, made sure everything fell within safety guidelines, and even set up tables with hot cider, coffee, and hot chocolate. Pine garlands and wreaths with red bows decorated the tables.

As did most of the residents of Willow Creek who appreciated the bonfire and wanted to attend, Daisy and Jonas brought along folding lawn chairs that they set up about ten yards from the bonfire. Jonas set them close together and hooked his arm into Daisy's as they sipped cups of hot cider. Daisy stared into the flames of the bonfire, fascinated by the white yellow to blue colors that hopped and danced over the logs and deadwood branches. She'd worn a calf-length yellow down jacket to keep her warm tonight along with heavy jeans, wool socks, and fleece-lined boots. Wearing a hat under the hood of her jacket, she'd tied the strings under her chin. A long cranberry-colored scarf dangled down the zipper of the jacket, its fringes brushing her jeans.

Glancing away from the bonfire, she breathed in deeply a pocket of the cutting cold air tinged with woodsmoke and the scent of the pines that bordered a section of the pond. She eyed some of the Willow Creek residents who stood by the snack tables, sat on blankets, or walked back and forth around the perimeter of the pond.

The production of *Christmas in the North Woods* had scheduled a matinee today. She'd heard the show had gone very well. Apparently, the cast was in a rhythm that worked without further changes. They knew what they were doing. Arden had told her that Glenda had shown up for each performance and had been very quiet and talked to no one.

Daisy caught sight of Arden Botterill along with Amelia Wiseman and her husband. Ward Cooper wore a long black wool coat and a red scarf tied decoratively around his neck. Red earmuffs covered his ears. She thought she spotted Tamlyn, Rowan's housekeeper, but she wasn't sure. With hats and scarves and coats, everyone looked a bit different . . . except for Jonas. In black jeans, a black leather bomber jacket, a flannel shirt, and a black watch cap, she'd recognize him anywhere.

She looked up at the moon and, after a sideways glance at Jonas, saw that he was doing the same. A breeze whipped the edges of Daisy's scarf.

Jonas unhooked his arm from hers and squeezed her gloved hand. "Are you too cold to stay?"

"I'd like to stay a little longer. Did you ever wonder what the tips of the moon would look like if they froze?"

A chuckle rumbled in Jonas's chest. "You do have an imagination, don't you? Do you wonder if there's ice cream up there too?"

She bumped her elbow into his ribs. "It's just that sometimes the crescent doesn't look as if it has points."

"That's because of clouds."

"Maybe, but that's such a realistic conclusion."

He squeezed her hand again. "Do you and the girls go ice-skating on the pond when it freezes over?"

"We have. I think last year we only came out here once. When I was little, Dad would bring me. It was such fun. He and I would skate until we couldn't feel our feet or our noses."

"Not Camellia?"

"She always had better things to do. Maybe if Dad had just invited *her*, she might have come with him. I don't know. Mom wasn't the type to ice-skate, so she and Camellia would find other things to do. One year when Dad and I got back from skating, Mom and Camellia had made perfume. Mom had bought a kit and they'd had fun doing it for the afternoon."

"Did you feel left out?"

"Not any more than Camellia felt left out of ice-skating. I don't know. It was just the way it was. I think as a child you can accept things easier than as an adult."

"Or else you felt powerless to do anything about it," Jonas suggested. "I felt that way after my father died until I decided to become a cop. That made me feel as if I had some control over destiny. At least it did until Brenda was killed. Then I knew no one had control over anything, certainly not other human beings."

"Did you and Brenda celebrate the holidays with family and friends?"

She felt Jonas tense a bit, but then that tension seemed to dissipate. "Officially we kept our relationship secret. We were partners. It was against policy to be involved. So if we celebrated, we did it alone. Only a few people knew about us—Zeke, Brenda's parents, another good friend of mine who had nothing to do with the police department. Once in a while we went there together and had a night of playing cards."

"The friends who were at the barbecue last year and I couldn't go?" Her cancellation of their last-minute plans had caused a misunderstanding between them. It had happened around the time Violet had found out she was pregnant, and everything had been complicated by that.

Suddenly someone tapped Daisy on the shoulder. It was Tamlyn. "Hi there," Daisy said. "I thought I saw you, but I wasn't sure with you wearing that fluffy hat."

Tamlyn rubbed her hands together. "Anything to keep warm. I'm not sure why I came, maybe just to get out of that house for a while. I think I'm going to re-sign my position and try to find something else. Mr. Vaughn doesn't really need me."

"Does he cook for himself?" Daisy asked.

"Oh, no. Ms. Nurmi was doing some of the cooking, but she hasn't been there the past few days."

Since the night the police had brought her in for questioning? Daisy wondered. If Glenda and Rowan were having an affair, that could be motive for murder. Daisy supposed Glenda was wise to keep her distance from Rowan.

"I thought I'd start looking around before Mr. Vaughn decides to sell the house. I heard him talking to a real estate agent. I can't imagine him staying there all by himself. I'm not sure he even liked the place from the beginning. Margaret's the one who wanted it, from what I understand."

"It's a beautiful old home," Jonas said.

"It needs somebody rich to own it. There's a lot of upkeep. Mr. Vaughn's always calling one handyman or another."

Suddenly there seemed to be a ruckus about ten yards away—raised male voices. One of the volunteer firemen strode in that direction.

"I think that's Zeke over there," Jonas said, getting to his feet. "It looks like Zeke and Jasper Lazar are having some kind of altercation. I'm going to head over that way," he told Daisy.

Daisy wasn't content to stay put, so she followed Jonas, trying to keep up with his stride.

When they reached the area, Daisy saw that Zeke was pointing a finger at Jasper Lazar's chest. "You know more than you're letting on," he said.

Jasper shot back, "You're crazy."

It was possibly true that Jasper knew more, but Zeke shouldn't be having this conversation with Jasper here. If there was any merit to his accusation, it should be done in private. This atmosphere was anything but private.

Her assessment must have been the same as the one Jonas was making. The wind had picked up and was slapping against Daisy's jacket. She was chilled, but the drama in front of her made her adrenaline level accelerate and warmth spread through her. Someone had to stop this before either Jasper or Zeke took a swing. If Zeke was going to take Jasper in for questioning, he could do that quietly.

The firefighter who had been studying what was going on turned to Jonas. They nodded to each other as if they knew each other.

"Hi, Frank," Jonas said. Then in a lower voice, he asked, "What's going on?"

"I'm not sure, but Zeke Willet's been drinking."

"If he's drinking, then he's not on duty. He shouldn't even be questioning a witness."

Frank nodded. "That's what I thought. But I have no authority to do anything."

"I don't either," Jonas admitted.

Daisy slid into position beside Jonas.

Jasper pushed Zeke away from him, saying, "You shouldn't even *be* a cop if you can't hold your liquor."

To Daisy's dismay, Zeke bounced right back. He took Jasper by the shoulders. "You can't talk to me like that."

Jasper was practically shouting now to be heard against the wind. "You've no right to ask me anything without a lawyer present. If I say I want my lawyer, you have to back off."

Apparently, Jonas didn't want this to escalate. He

said to Frank Dowling, "Can you go around the other side? I'll try to talk to Zeke."

Frank did as Jonas suggested in case they had to physically break up a fight.

Jonas approached Zeke with an easy gait, put a hand on his shoulder, and asked, "Need some help here?"

Zeke shrugged off his hand. "No, I don't need help, especially not yours."

Jonas turned to Jasper. "Are you interested in talking to the police?"

"If I was," Jasper said, anger in his voice, "I wouldn't be talking to *this* detective."

"You'll talk to me because I'm on the case," Zeke returned.

"Zeke, do you really think this is the way to have your questions answered?" Jonas asked calmly.

Now Zeke swung around to Jonas. "Stop butting in on my business."

"Stop making a spectacle of yourself," Jonas advised. "Do you want me to call Rappaport?"

"And just what do you think *he* can do? He's not getting any further with this investigation than I am."

Jonas's voice was steady and even. "You know it takes time. You know one clue leads to the next."

"I want you out of my life," Zeke shouted at Jonas.

Maybe frustrated and disappointed with the way Zeke had been treating him, Jonas asked, "Then why did you come to Willow Creek? You could have gone anywhere." Backing off a couple of steps, Jonas gave Zeke space.

"I needed a new job."

"And this was the only one that was open? Did you know I was here?" Jonas's expression was as somber and questioning as his voice.

"Yeah, I knew. I thought maybe we could get things straightened out once and for all. I thought you'd be as unhappy as I was. But, no, you're just moving right along. You've got a new girlfriend and everything."

Daisy took in a sharp breath, knowing no good could come from this public discussion. She seemed to have an even greater premonition of that when Jonas asked, "Why can't *you* move along, Zeke?"

After a long, deafeningly silent moment, Zeke answered, "Because I don't know if Brenda's baby was yours or mine."

Daisy heard Jonas gasp as if Zeke had punched him in his solar plexus. In that one statement Zeke just might have changed Jonas's attitude about life, about love, and about moving forward.

Chapter Nineteen

Daisy was scooping scones onto a cookie sheet the following morning when her phone played its tuba sound.

Eva slipped over next to her to take her place. "Go ahead and take it," she said. "I know your life requires spinning many plates right now."

Spinning plates was putting it kindly. When Daisy checked her screen, she saw that Jonas had placed the call. She absolutely wanted to take this.

She answered, "Good morning, Jonas. Give me a minute. I want to take this in my office where I can hear."

As she made her way to her office across the hall from the kitchen, she thought about the bonfire last night and what had happened. Zeke had quieted down after he'd blurted out that Brenda's baby might have been *his* child. Jonas had turned away from him, his face showing complete control.

However, Daisy knew Jonas's emotions had to be roiling. He'd thought that baby had been *his* child.

Brenda had told him so. Now he had to be plagued with a feeling of betrayal as well as loss.

They'd driven back to her house from the bonfire in a resounding silence. Finally, after Jonas pulled up in her driveway, she'd asked, "Do you want to come in and talk?"

His *No* had been immediate and vehement. But she hadn't let it deter her from the possibility that he'd completely close down his emotions. "Do you want to stay *here* and talk?"

"Daisy, let it go."

That's what he'd wanted her to do. "Are *you* going to let it go?" she'd asked him.

"I don't know what I'm thinking right now. And I definitely don't want to have a feelings talk."

In a slow, gentle voice, she'd protested. "The fact that you think of a possible discussion that way tells me you've already dissociated from your feelings."

With an exasperated tone, he'd advised, "Using that lingo on me isn't going to help either."

She'd reached over and touched his arm. "Jonas."

Turning toward her, he'd let out a long sigh. "All I can tell you is that I need to be alone."

Although she hadn't wanted to, although she'd wanted to hug him, she'd accepted his words at face value.

However, now in the morning light, possibly he was ready to share with her. "Okay, Jonas. I'm in my office. How can I help?"

After silence for a few beats, she knew she'd probably said the wrong thing. She suspected he wasn't going to want her *help*.

Without commenting on her question, he turned to the topic he wanted to talk about. "I heard from my friend in New York."

It took her a moment to remember what that was all about—the photograph that Vanna had showed her and she'd taken a photo of . . . the photo that Jonas had sent to his friend.

"Did he recognize where it was taken?"

"He did. It was shot at Chelsea Market."

"What do you think I should do next? How can we find out if Margaret lived around there . . . and what she was doing then?"

"There is one way," he said as if he'd expected her question and considered it. "It depends on how much Margaret shared with Rowan. They would have had to file their income taxes separately until they were married, and my guess is maybe even after they were married. As precise and responsible as Margaret was, she might have had copies of her income tax forms from even the time before she met Rowan. It's quite possible he could have them at the house. If he does, he could look up her addresses and you could check if any of them were near Chelsea Market."

Thinking about what had happened since she'd last spoken with Rowan, she responded, "I don't know if he'll do that."

"If he wants to find out who killed Margaret, he will."

If Rowan wanted to clear himself, he *would* agree. Even if he wanted to clear Glenda because they were having an affair, that would give him even more reason. "I'll call him and ask. Right now."

She waited a beat to see if Jonas would jump into the awkward silence. Silences hadn't been awkward between them for a very long time. Last night could have changed that. Last night might have put Jonas back on the road he'd been on when she'd first met him—closed off, guarded, not sure he wanted to be involved in a relationship. The fact that he now could feel betrayed by a woman he'd loved didn't bode well for the two of them.

The aroma of cinnamon, vanilla, and sugar wafted into Daisy's office, even with the door closed. Instead of asking a question that Jonas might find intrusive, she jumped into what might be a normal conversation for them. "If you were here, I'd offer you a just-baked cinnamon scone."

She thought she heard a sigh of relief when he said, "I'd tell you to save one for me, but I'm driving up toward Caledonia today to see a man about walnut timber. I'll probably be gone all day. I might even stay over up there. He has a cabin."

Without putting his thoughts or feelings into words, Jonas was telling her that he needed to get away. He needed to be in a different location—away from people he would normally see. He needed to be alone in a cabin with his cell phone turned off. All of that could be what he *thought* he needed.

She didn't agree.

"If you change your mind and you want company tonight, you know where I'll be."

"Thanks, Daisy." His voice was husky when he added, "But I need time to myself."

After Daisy said good-bye, she couldn't think about Jonas without her heart hurting—for him, for Zeke, and for her and Jonas as a couple. They now knew what was at the bottom of Zeke's anger and resentment toward Jonas. They now knew there was little they could do about that.

Somehow both Jonas and Zeke had to find their

way to peace. She had the feeling she would be no help, and maybe she'd even be a hindrance.

Her cell phone still in her hand from her phone call, she tapped on her CONTACTS icon to call Rowan. One way or another, she'd find out where Margaret had lived in New York. One way or another, she'd get to the bottom of her murder.

Since Jazzi had worked at the tea garden after school, Daisy drove them home. She listened as Jazzi told her about a peer counseling session. Jazzi normally kept the information quiet . . . and confidential. But she also knew Daisy wouldn't spill a secret.

"I just feel so sorry for Brielle, Mom. Her parents are rich. She has everything she wants. But they're *never* home. They both go out of town a lot."

"What does she do when they go out of town?"

"They have a housekeeper who stays overnight. If she can convince her parents, she stays with her grammy who's very old-world . . . almost Amish."

Daisy knew there wasn't any *almost Amish*. You either were or you weren't. But she knew what Jazzi meant. The girl's grammy might live with the bare essentials, and ultimately a plain life. Maybe they all should be living a plain life. Maybe the world would be a better place, focusing on faith, family, and community.

Daisy considered her childhood friend Rachel and Levi and their family. Sure, they had family troubles too. But somehow they all pulled together to ease those troubles. Somehow the family nights around the dinner table, evenings filled with homework and possibly board games, gave them family unity. Physical labor with chores, learning to farm,

caring for animals all contributed to teamwork. It coalesced into a happy life for the Fisher family.

A sigh inside of her seemed to build up so big that
she couldn't let it out. She was probably idealizing.
Even Rachel would tell her so.

"Mom, did you hear me?"

Daisy gave Jazzi a sideways glance. "I'm sorry.
What did you say?"

"Nothing important."

"Jazzi, whatever you have to say is important. You
just caught me daydreaming for a minute."

Perceptive, Jazzi shook her head, her long black
hair sliding across her peacoat. "I don't think it was
daydreaming."

Daisy gave her daughter another quick sideways
glance. "Pardon me?"

"You were up at dawn this morning before I
caught the school bus."

Because she had been worried about Jonas, she'd
felt the need to go into the tea garden early, meet Iris
there, and start baking. Her hands kneading dough
always calmed her. "I left you a note."

"Yeah, something lame about helping Aunt Iris
make loaves of apple bread. Since when do you go in
at five a.m. to help with that? Usually Tessa and Aunt
Iris start it."

Daisy was silent. Her daughter was more observant
than she gave her credit for. She wasn't going to lie
to her. "I had something on my mind."

"Something to do with Jonas?"

When Daisy had gotten home, Jazzi had still been
at Vi's and Foster's apartment. After Jazzi had come
home, they'd both gone to bed.

"Mom," Jazzi prompted, drawing out the title.

"I *do* have Jonas on my mind. Detective Willet said something to him last night that upset Jonas."

"But you're not going to tell me more," Jazzi guessed.

"Not now."

"Do you know *why* Jonas is upset?" Jazzi asked.

Daisy turned onto the road that led to her house. "I do."

"Then I know you'll help him."

Jazzi's sureness about that possibility disconcerted Daisy. "That's the problem, Jazzi—I don't know if he's going to want my help."

Both of them were quiet on the rest of the drive. After they walked from the garage to the house, they went inside the house and greeted the cats. Marjoram almost tripped Jazzi as she crossed to the closet to hang up her coat.

She picked up the tortoiseshell and nuzzled her neck. "You're demanding attention. Didn't you and your sister have enough to do today?"

Daisy pointed to the ruffled rug near the coffee table and the few toys—a Ping-Pong ball, a toy turtle filled with catnip, and a fake mouse—that lay in the area.

Daisy had hung up her jacket when Pepper ran to her.

"You don't want to be left out, do you?" Daisy stooped over and picked up the tuxedo cat, scratching her around her ruff. Pepper purred and leaned against Daisy's chest. The warm little body against hers felt good.

Marjoram had already squiggled out of Jazzi's arms. She headed to the kitchen as if to ask, *When's supper?*

Daisy sank down onto the sofa with Pepper, running her hand down her back, relaxing along with Pepper's purrs. She'd heard petting a cat could lower blood pressure. She also thought cuddling with a cat could soothe her soul.

Sitting on the coffee table facing Daisy, Jazzi asked, "Is there anything I can do for you, Mom?"

Daisy flipped off her shoes. "No, honey. I just need a couple of minutes before I start supper. Are tacos okay tonight?"

"They're fine."

"I want to check my e-mail and then we can get started."

"Are you expecting an e-mail from Jonas?"

When Daisy gave her daughter a warning look, Jazzi reached over to pet Pepper too. "All right, I won't press. But why are you checking e-mail? Do you want your laptop?"

"That would be great."

"I'll get it." Jazzi knew Daisy kept her laptop on the desk in her bedroom. Seconds later, she was back with it. Daisy booted up her e-mail program.

Pepper walked from Daisy's lap to the sofa cushion beside her and wriggled next to her leg. Marjoram came back into the living room and sat at Daisy's feet, looking up at her as if to say, *What's the holdup with supper?*

When Daisy checked her e-mail, she found what she was looking for. "Aha! I got them."

"Got what?" Jazzi asked.

"Addresses. Margaret moved around from year to year."

"Can you tell me about that or is that a no-no for discussion too?"

Should she tell Jazzi and let her help? They seemed

to bond when they did research. And it wasn't getting Jazzi involved in the investigation per se.

Daisy explained, "I had a photo of Margaret Vaughn. Jonas found out from a friend where the photo was taken—Chelsea Market."

"I've heard of that place. It's fabulous. It's in Manhattan, right? There's shopping, food, and an office building too, I think."

"That's it," Daisy said. "We think Margaret lived near it in the years before she met Rowan. After I asked, he looked through her old income tax forms to find out what her addresses were back then. He sent me a list of five of them. Do you want to help me check out if they're near the Market?"

"Sure. I'll feed Pepper and Marjoram. Do you want to get a snack to hold us over until we finish?"

Daisy had realized often over the past year that Jazzi was no longer a child but a maturing young woman. "How about carrot salad, farmer's cheese, and some of those multigrain crackers that Tessa baked?"

"With that as a snack, I won't need tacos."

"You'll be hungry for tacos. Looking up addresses is hard work."

Jazzi gave Daisy a smile that told her she was probably right.

Daisy smiled back, thinking that this day had just turned around.

The Amtrak train that Daisy had picked up in Lancaster the following day zoomed on its way to New York City. It had been a long time since she'd been on a train. As this one clacked against the tracks, she tried to read. It was impossible. She thought about texting Jonas, then decided against it. She wasn't sure he really wanted to know *what* she was doing. Apparently, he was consumed by what Zeke had told him. She couldn't blame him for that, but she wondered where it left the two of them. An outsider might say what had happened with Brenda was in the past. Her relationship with Jonas was the present. So true. Yet she knew that the past could dog them whether they wanted it to or not.

Jonas had once believed in Brenda's loyalty. And love. He'd first learned she'd betrayed him the night she'd told him she was pregnant. That night she'd also told him she'd had her IUD removed. She wanted a family . . . with him. They'd argued and, as Philadelphia PD partners, they'd headed to their shift together. After all, they had a murder suspect to question. When they'd arrived at the location where the suspect was holed up, he'd ambushed them. He shot and killed Brenda. While Jonas had tried to save her, the suspect had shot Jonas too.

Jonas's shoulder—the way it stiffened up and he had to work it to keep it agile—was a daily reminder of what had happened that night. As if he needed one. He'd lost his lover and his child.

His child. That's what he'd thought.

Now his paternity was in question. And Jonas was in turmoil.

Yes, she was right not telling him about this trip. It might lead to nothing. It might lead to something. She wasn't in any danger. All she was doing was looking into Margaret's background. She and Jazzi had worked finding the address closest to Chelsea Market. Rowan's list had guided them. Only one address had made sense.

To Daisy's surprise, as well as Jazzi's, they'd used

several search engines as well as address look-up sites. They hadn't been able to find a viable phone number for the address. They had used Google Images and Zillow, finding that Margaret's former address was a four-story, multimillion-dollar town house! Someone with that kind of money might do anything in their power to keep their phone number off the Internet. Today, she was going to find out who lived there . . . and whether or not they'd known Margaret.

After Daisy exited the train on a busy Thursday, she didn't let the people or the city distract her. It would have been so easy to people-watch, to take a walk and shop, to stop at a bistro for a latte and a croissant. But she wasn't in New York on a pleasure trip, and she intended to head home as soon as she could.

She'd brought enough cash to take as many cab rides as necessary. Fares could be expensive. Her money was hidden in a zipper compartment in her fanny pack, which was buckled close to her body. She wore it under her jacket, zippered up to her neck to keep her warm . . . and also to protect her identification, credit card, and cash. She was no fool when it came to New York City. She'd read about all the touristy things a tourist shouldn't do. She'd read about the safety measures a tourist should take.

She hailed a cab that dropped her off at an intersection a quarter block from the town house. She didn't ask the cabbie to wait because she might want to explore a bit. Her main fear was that no one would be home. However, if no one was, she could try to talk to neighbors.

Daisy walked along West 11th Street, finding a row of single-family town houses. Trees bare of leaves now lined the sidewalk. She reached the address she'd memorized and remembered the description of this particular town house. It was built in 1899, a Greek Revival. It was nineteen feet wide with antique brick. Ironwork graced the windows and outer border of the property. When she'd looked up the address on Zillow for more details, she'd read that hardwood flooring inside was cherry. She also knew there were three bedrooms and three baths. Cherrywood paneling also adorned the kitchen. One of the town house's best features, in her mind, was the five working fireplaces. The master suite with a bathroom was on the top floor and it had its own marble-encased gas fireplace. The town house also had a finished basement.

She couldn't imagine anyone buying this town house with its estimated price tag. The price per square foot was over $2500. The price per square foot in Willow Creek could run between $100 and $150. Yes, there was that much difference.

Daisy's heart thumped hard. If it weren't so cold out, she'd probably be sweating. As it was, she was hot, even in thirty-two-degree weather. She climbed up the eight steps to the covered entrance trimmed in white. A ceramic pot with a decorative spiral evergreen stood in the corner of the porch.

After Daisy rang the bell, the intercom crackled and a male voice asked, "Who's there?"

Daisy should have suspected she would have to identify herself before making contact. "My name is Daisy Swanson. I own a tea garden in Willow Creek, Pennsylvania. I'd like to talk to the homeowner, if that's possible."

The silent pause stretched her nerves even more taut.

Finally, the man said, "I need to see ID before I talk to you."

"No problem," she agreed, her voice a bit squeaky.

Not two minutes later, a tall man possibly in his late forties opened the door. He wore designer label slacks, a navy cashmere sweater with a cream oxford shirt beneath. His hair was professionally styled, short on the sides and longer on the top. Daisy had readied her driver's license and held it out for him to see.

"What do you want?" he asked haughtily.

She decided honesty was the only way she'd capture any information. "A friend of mine in Willow Creek was killed and I'm investigating her background. This was the address she used on her income taxes for a year six years ago. Can you tell me if you knew Margaret Vaughn?"

He was already shaking his head before she finished. "I just bought this town house four years ago, so I have no idea who you're talking about. I moved here from Connecticut for business reasons."

"She also went by the name Luna Larkin."

His lips twitched ironically. "A stage name?"

"Yes. She was an actress."

"I'm sorry. I don't recognize that name either."

"Can you tell me who you bought this house from?"

"Not that it's any of your business, but I bought it from a bank. I don't know what the story was behind it. I didn't care because I got it at a discount. I liked it on first sight and that was it."

This trip might have turned into a wild goose chase, but she wasn't finished trying to succeed. "Can you tell me if your neighbors are friendly?"

"You mean, will they give you any information? It's possible. I don't know them well, but my neighbor two houses down always says hello when he sees me. He owns a Scottish terrier, and I see him walking up and down the street quite a bit. You could try him."

"From the real estate records, I found out that your name is Charles Martz. Is that correct?"

"You did do some investigation. I've kept my name and number off of most public records."

"I have a daughter who's computer savvy."

Mr. Martz nodded as if he understood that. But he didn't give Daisy any additional information. She thanked him and he closed the door. She heard it lock.

A few minutes later, she was walking along the sidewalk to two town houses down. She went up similar steps and rang another bell. This time, there was no intercom. A man, much older than Charles Martz, opened the door and smiled. His face was lined with wrinkles and a few age spots dotted his broad nose. Wispy gray hair grew above his ears, but the rest of his head was bald.

A dog barked from another room, then came running into the foyer. It was a cute little black Scottish terrier. Hopping out onto the stoop, it automatically sniffed up and down Daisy's pant legs. She knew it probably smelled cats.

"Well, you've got Topknot's seal of approval," the man noted.

She noticed the dog's topknot and smiled. "Is he safe for me to pet?"

"He loves to be petted. Go ahead."

Daisy let the dog smell her hand that she'd ungloved, and then she scratched the fur around his ears. Afterward, she ran her hand down his back. He yipped at her and then jumped up and down around her legs.

"All right now, Topknot . . ." The man patted his leg. "Come on. Back inside. We'll go for a walk later. Let me find out what the lady wants." The man closed the door on Topknot.

Daisy went through her introduction, then asked his name. She mentioned that his neighbor recommended that she talk to him.

"Why, I'm surprised. Charles isn't talkative on a good day." He stuck out his hand. "I'm Timothy Aberdeen. I gather you're looking for information of some type."

"I am." She told him why.

"Oh, my goodness. I've lived here for fifteen years now. Let me think about this. Charles's town house was in a bit of an upheaval the past five years. Six years ago, a man named Conrad Eldridge lived there. He'd lived there for quite some time and, if I remember correctly, a woman named Luna Larkin worked for him. In fact, she not only worked for him. She took care of him for about a year. You see, Conrad was an actor . . . very popular in the sixties. However, he tired of the LA lifestyle and left a hit series to move to New York. Once, he was well-known for his extravagant parties."

"But his health declined?"

"Yes, it did. Miss Larkin had met him at the strip club where she was working."

"As a stripper?" Daisy asked, starting to put all the pieces together . . . at least some of them.

"Yes. They connected on some level, as people often do. It wasn't a romantic relationship from what

I understand. After all, Conrad was so much older than she was. He helped her get bit parts so she could stop stripping."

"You said his health declined. Did he have a disease of some kind?"

"He did," Timothy said with a nod. "It was an aggressive form of Parkinson's disease and he became reclusive. She cared for him and he paid her well."

"Did Miss Larkin care for him until he died?"

"Yes, she did. News travels fast, especially about people who once had a large audience. Everybody wants to know every little detail. I heard that she inherited jewelry that had belonged to his mother, as well as a substantial financial gift."

Daisy finally felt as if she was getting somewhere. She smiled and couldn't help beaming at Timothy. "This information helps me so much. I don't know if it will have any relevance to the investigation, but I hope it does."

"You say you own a tea garden in Pennsylvania?"

"I do. My aunt and I run it together."

"What's your favorite kind of tea?" His hazel eyes twinkled as he asked.

"I'd have to say that oolong is my favorite."

"A woman after my own heart. I'd ask you in for a cuppa, but I doubt if you'd accept. Am I right?"

She liked this man and felt he was an old-school gentleman. "If the weather was nicer, I'd sit out here on your stoop and have a cup with you. I don't think I should come inside. But it was a pleasure to meet you. I'm going to catch a train back to Willow Creek and try to do something with the information you gave me." She took a business card from her pocket. "How about if you hold on to this and, if you remember anything else, could you give me a call?"

"Certainly. And if you have more questions, feel free to call *me*."

Taking her phone from her pocket, she tapped in his number as he gave it to her. After they said their good-byes and Daisy walked down the street to hail a cab, she wished she had gone inside and had tea with Timothy. It might have been a very interesting experience.

Chapter Twenty

All Daisy wanted to do when she returned home from New York was crash. Jazzi was staying overnight with a friend, but Daisy felt the need to check on Vi and Sammy. She didn't want to miss anything with Vi that, if watchful, she could catch. Preventing her daughter from going into a downward spiral was her main objective. Hence, texts during the day and company when Vi needed it.

So as she drove up the road to the garage and pulled inside, she noticed Iris's car. A short visit could reassure her all was well.

A half hour later, she'd convinced herself that Vi was doing much better. Her daughter wore a smile more than she didn't . . . and it was genuine. After Foster came home, Iris and Daisy decided to leave. All Daisy could think about was a warm bath and bed.

As soon as Iris exited the garage with Daisy, she said, "Do you mind if I come over to the house for a bit? There's something I want to talk to you about . . .

something I should have talked to you about before now."

Whatever did Iris have on her mind? Daisy had no idea. Iris walked beside Daisy to the house. After Daisy unlocked the door, she deactivated the security alarm. Inside, she turned on the wagon-wheel ceiling light, and both Marjoram and Pepper blinked at her from the sofa where they'd pulled the afghan from the back and nestled in it.

Daisy and Iris removed their jackets. Daisy took her aunt's as well as hers to the closet and hung both of them inside. Her aunt looked so serious Daisy didn't know what to think.

"A cup of tea?" she asked her aunt.

Iris responded with a bit of a smile. "Always."

Crossing to the kitchen, Daisy pulled out a tin of Earl Grey. She knew her aunt liked it, especially in the evening. They knew each other so well. They always had. Daisy could remember many cups of tea with her aunt as she was growing up when she confided things she wouldn't confide in anyone else, not even her dad.

Taking a plate of whoopie pies from the refrigerator, with their chocolate cookie outside and their cream cheese whipped center, she set them on the table while the tea brewed. Iris came over to the island and pulled out a stool.

Her aunt took her tea with a spoonful of honey. Daisy plucked the jar of wildflower honey from the cupboard and set it on the table. There were no pretensions between her and her aunt. Iris would spoon it out from the jar and be happy doing it.

At the cupboard again, Daisy found an antique aqua iridescent gilt pedestal teacup and saucer. For her aunt, she chose a vintage Royal Albert teacup and saucer with tea roses in yellow painted on the cup and dish. She and her aunt appreciated porcelain and china, colors and textures, gilt and silver. Maybe Daisy was just postponing the inevitable, but there was no reason they couldn't have a calming snack while they talked.

Daisy took her seat and pushed the honey jar toward her aunt. "I've had many serious conversations at this island. Your demeanor and tone of voice suggest this might be one of them."

"It *is* serious," her aunt confessed as she opened the jar of honey, dipped a spoon inside, and then slid it into her cup of tea. She stirred absently.

Daisy had chosen a slice of lemon to use with her tea. She squeezed the slice with her fingers, wiped them on a napkin, and waited.

"I should have brought this up with you a long time ago. Actually, your mother should have talked to you about it."

Daisy felt her brow crinkle. "Is this a family secret?"

"I'm not sure you can call it a secret, but it's something we all went through together."

Puzzled again, Daisy shook her head. "I don't understand."

Iris took a sip of her tea as if she needed a fortifying drink, then set down the teacup. "It's about time you do understand. Tell me why you think that you and I might have a closer relationship than you and your mother."

"I told Mom the night of Vi's wedding reception that I was closer to you for a reason. You don't criticize everything I do."

"Sometimes Rose only sees what she wants to see. I

believe she's jealous of our relationship and she takes it out on you."

"I've tried to get closer to Mom since that night, but it's not easy."

"No, it isn't," her aunt said. "Let me tell you why."

Daisy tried to brace herself because she had no idea what was coming.

Her aunt bit her lower lip and started. "When your mother had Camellia, it was as if God's blessings shone down on all of us. She was an easy baby. She napped, she smiled, she slept at night fairly early on. Your mother even took her to the garden center in one of those swaddling carriers, and she worked alongside your dad. It was almost as if their life hadn't been interrupted except to have been made better."

Daisy wanted to jump in. She wanted to ask if *she* had been a problem baby. She wanted to ask so many questions. Instead she let her aunt go on.

"When you were born, something different happened with Rose. From the moment she brought you home from the hospital, she was upset. She had more sleep deprivation, which was common in a new mom and now a mom of two. But I could tell she didn't attach to you as she had with Camellia. I don't know the underlying reasons—if it was your mother's psychological makeup or if it was hormones or if it was having two children to care for instead of one. Not as much was known about postpartum depression back then. Mostly it was ignored. It was called baby blues. There was an attitude even among professionals that said, *Pick yourself up and move on.* The chemicals in the brain don't always respond to pep talks as you could well see with Violet. Your dad and I stepped in to take care of you because your mother seemed incapable of it. In that first year of your life when your mother couldn't get her bearings, it affected all of us."

Daisy felt numb and cold and almost bereft. She didn't know what to say. Her mother hadn't bonded with her and that's what had led to their guarded relationship all these years later? That numb feeling started to melt away when she realized how grateful she was that Vi had the support system she had and a doctor who could help her. Vi was bonding with Sammy now, and he'd never have the desolation of feeling he was never close to his mom.

Tears came to Daisy's eyes and she blinked them away. There was nothing to cry about. The past was in the past, and all they could do was go on from here. She took her aunt's hand. "Thank you for telling me, and thank you along with Dad for always making me feel loved."

Iris shook Daisy's hand gently. "Your mother loves you. You know that, don't you?"

"I've always thought her personality simply clashed with mine," Daisy said.

"And it probably does," Iris agreed. "I think she tried to overcompensate for what she didn't feel that first year."

"She does like to hover."

Aunt Iris smiled. "Yes, she does. She does that with everyone, only more so with you. It's her way of taking care of you. If you look at it that way, your relationship with her might be better. I think she has mellowed since Sammy was born."

"Maybe," Daisy agreed. "On the other hand, maybe she's just been quiet because problems with Vi have brought her past back. Do you think she'll ever talk to me about it?"

"There's no way to know. But I felt you finally needed to understand your roots."

Apparently, every family had its secrets. Maybe now she could stop blaming her own shortcomings for the way her mom reacted to her. Maybe now Daisy could see her mother in a new light . . . and just love her.

Daisy needed time to explore a particular site on the Internet on Friday evening. All day, that's all she could think about. But she'd just arrived home with Jazzi, and supper loomed on the horizon along with feeding Pepper and Marjoram. She was about to do that when the doorbell rang. Checking her phone and the app on it, she saw that it was her mother. Had she been at Vi's and something was wrong?

Hurrying to the door, she let her mother inside. "Hi, Mom. This is a surprise. Were you over at Violet's?"

Her mother came in and her gaze scanned the downstairs. "No, I wasn't at Violet's. Is Jazzi around?"

"She's upstairs working on a research project. Do you want me to call her?"

"No. No, I don't."

Puzzled, Daisy said, "Let me take your coat. Would you like to join us for supper? Are you alone? Did Dad have something to do tonight?" Her parents usually did everything together.

"Your father's at home. I told him . . . I told him I needed to talk to you . . . alone."

Warning signals clanged in Daisy's head. Her first thought was—what had she done wrong now? Her mom wasn't acting like her usual self. If she had something to criticize Daisy for, usually her back was straight, her demeanor authoritarian. Now she looked smaller, older, maybe even defeated.

Daisy motioned to the sofa. "Make yourself comfortable and I'll brew us a pot of tea."

Rose again glanced around the first floor. "This open concept . . ." She shook her head. "Can we go someplace more private to talk, maybe your bedroom?"

It was an odd request, but Daisy didn't see why they couldn't. "Sure. Go ahead in. I'll bring you the tea as soon as it's ready."

Rose didn't hesitate. She left her coat on the sofa and her purse on the coffee table, then she went to Daisy's first-floor bedroom and closed the door.

As Daisy waited for the teakettle to heat, she fed Marjoram and Pepper. They were both finished before she'd assembled the tray to take to the bedroom. "I think you two better stay out here," she told them. "Or go upstairs with Jazzi."

Marjoram turned golden eyes on her and gave a little *murrp*.

"I'm not sure what this is all about, but it's better if you don't distract us. Jazzi will be glad to see you. She'll probably give her pen to play with."

Marjoram turned away as if that idea could be appealing and headed for the staircase.

"You can always take a mouse along," she told Pepper. The feline washed one paw and then the other as if *hurry* wasn't in her vocabulary. Then she stared at the closed door to the bedroom.

"I know you don't like closed doors," Daisy acknowledged. "But I'd appreciate if you don't meow and scratch at it. Take your favorite toy and go upstairs with your sister."

Daisy motioned toward the steps.

Pepper tossed Daisy a slant-eyed look, then with her tail high in the air, ambled toward the steps.

Daisy picked up the tray and went to join her mother.

To Daisy's surprise, her mother looked nervous. She couldn't remember any time when her mother had looked nervous. Her mom's eyes held an expression she'd never seen there before, and they looked moister than usual. Those weren't tears, were they?

Daisy set the tea tray on her desk and pulled out the desk chair. Her mom was perched on the bedside chair.

Daisy offered her mom the cup of tea, but her mother shook her head. "In a minute, okay? I want to talk first."

Rose pushed her hair back over her forehead and clenched her hands in her lap. "I want to talk about us—about you and me."

"Mom, if this is about the night of the reception, I told you I'm sorry. I never should have said what I did." Daisy's voice caught on the last word because the whole situation had upset her too. Sure, she'd always wanted to tell her mom those things, but not in that way, and certainly not then.

"You had every right to say what you did."

Daisy was going to open her mouth to say she was sorry again when she realized what her mother had said. She felt stunned, and she kept quiet because she didn't know what would come out of her mom's mouth next.

Fidgeting with the belt on her slacks, Rose continued. "It's my fault you felt closer to your aunt Iris and your dad. It's all my fault. I wasn't a good mother to you."

Daisy called on heaven to help because she'd never wanted her mom to feel like this. "You're wrong! Of course you were a good mother. You took wonderful care of me. When I was sick, you were right by my bedside. When I went to my first cooking class, you came to the dinner and tasted the food. When I married Ryan, you helped arrange everything."

"Yes, I did those things," her mother said sadly. "By then I had lost an important connection with you, and I was trying to make up for it. I guess I always felt guilty."

She remembered what her aunt had told her about her mother's postpartum depression. She stayed quiet.

"Your aunt Iris told me she confided in you about my postpartum depression."

"Yes, she did. I wish *you* had confided in me. Did you think I would judge you?"

"You should have. After I came home from the hospital, I didn't know what was wrong with me. I didn't want to get out of bed. I didn't want to take care of you. I just let your dad handle everything. Your aunt Iris stepped in to make sure neither you nor Camellia would be lacking for anything. After a month or so, I could still relate to Camellia, but I thought something was missing between the two of us. I didn't know what to do about it. You had just had your first smile, and I didn't feel any of the things I felt when Camellia had smiled."

That comment was a stab into Daisy's heart.

Her mother apparently could see that because she rushed to say, "I'm saying this all wrong. I'm making everything worse, and that's not what I want. I want you to understand that like Violet, something was going on inside me that I couldn't fix, that I didn't know how to fix. And by the time I felt more like myself, you were already walking and I realized that somehow I had lost my first year with you."

For her own well-being, Daisy had to take a step back and look at this more objectively. "Did you ever talk to anyone about this, besides Aunt Iris and Dad?"

"No. I was so ashamed. I didn't even really talk with them. They just saw what was happening. There were no mommy groups like Vi is attending. There weren't even parenting classes anywhere. No, it wasn't the dark ages. Maybe if I had brought it up with my doctor, he could have done something. But he was a *man*. I didn't think he'd understand. Your dad had trouble understanding."

"So much more is known about postpartum depression now," Daisy said.

"I've seen that with Violet. I've seen what the right kind of support can do."

"But you had the right kind of support, Mom. You had Dad and Aunt Iris, and I'm fine. Yes, I always felt you favored Camellia, but on the other hand, I thought Dad and Aunt Iris made up for that. I was never neglected. I was loved."

There were tears in her mother's eyes as she said, "I often wondered if you married Ryan and moved to Florida to get away from me."

Daisy's aunt Iris had come to the same conclusion. "Mom, no. I loved Ryan. Maybe I did want a different kind of life, but that wasn't because of *you*. I was growing up and I needed to find out who I was."

Her mother grabbed Daisy's hand. "You are a beautiful woman. You are strong, and you are a wonderful mother. I've watched you with Vi and Jazzi, and I know that in my soul. I'm proud that you and your aunt Iris started a business, and are making a success of it. Yes, I've always been jealous of your aunt Iris and her relationship with you. I probably still am. I'll work on it."

Daisy looked into her mom's eyes and said honestly, "Your telling me about this will make things better between us. I know it will. Thank you for having the courage to talk to me about it."

Her mother flipped her hand into the air. "It wasn't courage, it was desperation. I was tired of hiding the secret, and I want to be close to you. I always have. Most of the time, I just didn't know how. So I want to ask you something."

Daisy held her breath, not knowing what was coming.

"Do you think you can confide in me?"

"I can try."

Her mother nodded. "Let's have that tea. Do you have any whiskey to spike it with?"

"Mom," Daisy said with a laugh. "I think I do. I'll go get it."

There was suddenly a knock on the door. Jazzi called, "Mom, can I interrupt?"

Daisy quickly went to the door and opened it. "We're coming out."

"I have something so exciting to tell you." Jazzi practically danced into the room. "You too, Gram. Listen to this. I got a phone call from Colton."

"Colton?" Daisy asked, surprised. "Is something wrong with Portia or the kids?"

"No. He told me he's been thinking a lot since my visit. He was sorry about how things happened at the mall."

"Do you think Portia urged him to say that?" Rose asked.

"I don't think so. Maybe I'm just hoping for the impossible, but he actually said that he'd been mistaken when he thought I could be pushed away or put into the past. On Thanksgiving Day, Portia seemed sad that I wasn't there, and their kids even suggested that I should be there too because it was a family day. He made me want to cry, Mom."

Daisy took a deep breath and waited for further explanation.

Jazzi went on. "He said he didn't know it and Portia didn't know it, but I've always held part of Portia's heart. It took him a while to realize that I was what Portia needed to feel whole."

Without hesitation, Daisy wrapped her arms around Jazzi and squeezed her tight. They stood that way for a few moments, and then Daisy remembered her mother was in the room. When she glanced at her, Rose had tears in her eyes.

"Did he say when he wants you to visit again?" Rose asked.

"Yes. He said he knows Christmas means a lot for me here, and what with Vi's baby and all it will be a special Christmas for us. But he and Portia would like me to come up the week after Christmas and have a second Christmas with them. Isn't that terrific, Mom?"

"That *is* terrific."

Rose stood and crossed to Jazzi too. "I don't think he would have said all that if Portia had put him up

to it. With your visit and the holiday, he finally realized you're a special girl, Jazzi, and they would be
lucky to have you as a member of their family."

Daisy couldn't remember when she and her
mother and Jazzi had stood in a circle like this, feeling strong bonds. This is what she wanted for her
family. This is what she wanted Jonas to be part of
someday too.

Chapter Twenty-one

On Saturday morning, Daisy had one thing on her mind. Maybe she was just trying to distract herself from Jonas's situation weighing on her. Maybe figuring out who murdered Margaret would calm the anxiety she'd been feeling for a while now. She was certain of one thing. If she figured out who the other heirs to Conrad Eldridge's estate were, she would possibly have the best clue as to who had murdered Margaret. Maybe it wouldn't pan out at all, but she was going to give it a try as soon as she had a free moment.

A free moment came in the late afternoon. In her office at the tea garden, she went online. She had a few hit-and-misses because she wasn't cueing in the right words. Instead of records of the deceased in New York State and other similar search phrases, she latched onto the word that mattered—*probate*. From there, it wasn't difficult to find the Web site where she could access New York's probate records.

Public records were public records. After fishing

around in the Web site, she found Conrad Eldridge's will. Most of his money had endowed various charities. However, she found the name of a second heir who'd been left less than Margaret. Examining everything she knew, and each clue that she'd found, she believed she knew who the killer was. Still she wasn't positive and she needed to talk to Rowan.

Picking up the landline receiver in her office, she called Rowan's house. She'd try there first.

Tamlyn answered with her usual greeting. "This is the Vaughn home. Tamlyn speaking."

"Tamlyn, hi. This is Daisy. Can you tell me if Rowan's there?"

"He's not," Tamlyn answered easily. "But I can tell you where he is. He went to the theater to make sure everything was ready for the evening performance."

"I'll try to catch up with him there," Daisy responded. "Thank you."

But Tamlyn wasn't ready to hang up. "I saw Mr. Vaughn packing a couple of bags," Tamlyn said. "I really think my time here is going to be over. Do you need another server at the tea garden?"

"I do. But I probably can't match what you're making now."

"I've saved money from working here," Tamlyn said. "And I need something to get me through until I decide whether I'm staying in Willow Creek or moving away. The thing is—I don't know where I'd go if I did move."

"No family?" Daisy asked.

"None to speak of . . . none I'd want to be close to. If I could get enough hours with you to pay for an apartment, I could handle the rest for a while."

Daisy thought about the holidays and how people liked to enjoy Christmas tea services. If she had another full-time server, she could plan holiday teas more often than she thought she could. But she'd have to talk to Iris about it. If they pulled in more profit, she could afford to pay Tamlyn for full-time work at least through the Christmas season.

"I need to talk to Iris Albright, who's my partner. Let me do that, then I'll give you a call, or you call me at the end of the week and I'll set up an appointment."

"That sounds good, Mrs. Swanson. Thank you so much."

"If we can help each other, we'll have a win-win situation. Thanks for the information about Rowan. I'll talk to you soon."

After Daisy hung up, she knew exactly what she was going to do. As soon as she could get away, she'd drive to the Little Theater and speak with Rowan. His answers could be the key to solving his wife's murder.

By five o'clock Daisy had ducked out of the tea garden early, and she was driving down Market Street. She turned off Market onto Hollowback Road and followed it to the Little Theater. She'd told her aunt where she was going. Her cell phone was charged. It wouldn't be too long before some of the cast would be arriving at the Little Theater to get ready for tonight's performance. She should be able to have private time with Rowan first.

Daisy coasted her car into a parking spot. She decided to park at the back door rather than the front entrance. The cast and crew used it, and she imagined Rowan would too. The thing was—Rowan's car wasn't in the front lot or this back one. Could Tamlyn have been wrong? On the other hand, Rowan sometimes used a driver. A driver could have easily dropped him off. Besides, taking a closer look at the windows of the theater, she thought she saw dim lights inside.

Daisy wouldn't find any answers sitting in her car. Climbing out of her PT Cruiser, she shut the door and pressed the remote to lock it. It felt a little odd being out here alone . . . and a little spooky too. Lights that went on at dusk glowed in the parking lot, and branches from trees that had gone leafless swayed in the wind. Dried leaves on the ground picked up by the breeze rolled across her shoes. No, it wasn't spooky. She was just scaring herself silly. She was *not* afraid of a parking lot.

Nonetheless, she hurried across the asphalt and pulled on the back door. It was open, as she'd expected it to be. A few lights guided her way as she went deeper inside.

She called Rowan's name. Then she called again. "Rowan, are you here?"

Unzipping her jacket, she climbed slowly up the steps at the back of the stage. Once there, she realized the stage was already set up for the first scene of the play. That scene was separated into two sets, one for the North Woods at the right side of the stage, and another for interior scenes on the left. A staircase led to a landing that was supposed to be a fake second floor. A chandelier hung over the living room just beyond the stairs. Daisy had been up there when Jonas had been working on the sets and she had seen how the chandelier was attached to the beam across the stage.

Crossing to the middle of the sets, she called again, "Rowan, are you here?"

Rowan didn't answer her. Another male voice did.

"I'm here," Ward Cooper said.

Panic tightened Daisy's chest. Ward Cooper was Conrad Eldridge's nephew. He was the second heir to an inheritance from the Eldridge estate. He was the one Daisy highly suspected was the murderer.

Still she only had her suspicions. She wasn't sure, not yet.

She noticed that Ward was wearing a running suit. Maybe he'd jogged to the theater?

Keep your cool, she told herself. *Act normal.*

Normal. How could she act normal if she was facing a murderer? Ward had seemed so kind. . . .

He must have noticed Daisy's glance sweeping over him because he gave a small shrug and smiled. "I came in early while I was on a run to make sure everything was ready for tonight."

Okay so far. The panic lessened just a mite. "Is Rowan around?" Daisy wanted to know. "Tamlyn said he'd be here."

"I haven't seen him," Ward said. "If it's important, you might want to try his cell. Do you need his number?"

"I have his number," she responded, but the end of her voice shook a little. Trying to make up for that, she explained, "I had some ideas about the sponsorship for future plays. I wanted to talk to him about those." For good measure she added, "I'm meeting Jonas here. That's why I'm here so early."

She stuffed her hands into her jacket pockets, feeling her keys and her wallet. But she was shaking now. She could feel her fingers trembling against the inside material of the pockets.

Something in Ward's eyes changed. There was a

shift. He didn't look so kind anymore. He must have heard her fear and seen her nervousness. "Sponsorships, huh? You're really getting involved."

"Running the tea garden, I have to be good at organization as well as making scones." She hoped her response would lighten the atmosphere . . . but it didn't.

Where was Rowan? She wished she had called Jonas. But Iris did know Daisy was here.

Ward casually took a few steps closer to her. "I heard you took a trip to New York. Was it successful?"

"Of course it was successful," she bluffed. "All a woman needs is Fifth Avenue to be happy, right?" If she could engage Ward, she might discover all her fears were in her imagination. Yet, she had the premonition that all her fears were in her gut where it mattered.

"So you shopped?"

"Yes, and I always wanted to visit Chelsea Market. It has the best food." It wasn't true that she went there, but it was the only thing she could think of.

"Chelsea Market and Fifth Avenue are a bit apart."

"That's why cabs run in New York City." If she could just keep this conversation going where she wanted it to . . .

"Did you make a stop on West Eleventh Street?"

Ward Cooper knew where she had gone. That was obvious. But how did he know? Could he have been following her? Why would he do that unless he had been afraid she was getting closer to the truth?

She finally decided to deal with this head on. "You were jealous of Margaret, weren't you?"

"Jealous? I deserved everything she inherited. She deserved everything that happened to her. And *you* deserve everything you're going to get for poking into this."

Ward lunged at Daisy, but she took off running.

He yelled after her while he chased her. "She didn't deserve Uncle Con's money or my aunt's jewelry. She took care of him for a year. I knew him for a lifetime."

The closest place to run was up the staircase, but when she reached the top, the theater went dark. Ward had shut down the lights. Daisy knew she was trapped on this landing.

She searched her mind for a way out. As they'd been talking, Ward had been standing near the expensive oriental rug that Margaret had insisted on buying.

Suddenly she heard Ward's voice. "Come on down, Daisy. There's no place to go up there. We can talk some more. Or do you want me to come up there after you?" That last question had been asked in a much nastier voice . . . closer to her too.

If she hadn't been practically breathless with fear before, she was now. How could she coax Ward to stand on that rug?

In her pocket she found her wallet. Fingering it, she decided to take a chance. After all, he was threatening her. She deserved to act a little irrational.

"If it's money you want, I can write you a check. I always carry a check in my wallet for emergencies. It's my business account so I can wipe it out."

Pulling her wallet from her pocket, she threw it in the direction she wanted Ward to go.

The stage was as dark as spades, but she was pretty good at sensing direction. Her hand was on the banister at the front of the staircase. Moving slightly to its corner, she stood in the juncture of the two banisters. "Take my money. Look in the wallet for the check. I'll be glad to sign it."

He wouldn't kill her if he knew he could access thousands of dollars and get away, right?

She heard him scuffling around. It sounded as if his feet were on the rug. She reached up and as far out as she could for the pulley ropes that were holding up the chandelier. Her foot slipped in her ballet shoes, and she caught herself before she fell off the small makeshift balcony. Anchoring her foot under the lowest rung of the banister, she reached farther and felt the rope. She unhooked it, and the chandelier crashed down. Ward Cooper screamed.

Using the banister to guide her down the stairs, she ran, jumped over the last step, and headed for the theater's back door. When she ran across the stage, she couldn't see where the steps were that led down to the back hall. She wanted to know if Ward was following her, but she couldn't spare even a moment to listen. It might only take a second to catch up to her.

She missed the first step on the down staircase from the stage and almost tumbled down the rest of the stairs. Somehow she regained her balance, scrambled down the last two steps, and sped toward the back door. She went at it full force and pushed it open.

Spotting Rowan climbing from his sedan, where Glenda was sitting too, she ran toward him yelling his name. Then she took a deep breath, pulled out her phone, and called 9-1-1.

Epilogue

Daisy sat across from Detective Rappaport in a conference room at the police station. They had just begun when Jonas burst in.

Daisy's mind was still reeling from everything that had happened. Truth be told, her legs were shaking too. Detective Rappaport had driven her car to the police station because he didn't think she was able to drive. He'd been kind, which had almost made her feel worse.

As soon as she saw Jonas, she hopped up from her seat and ran to him. He caught her in his arms and hugged her tight. He buried his nose in her neck, and she thought he was shaking a little bit too. From his tight hold, she knew he didn't want to let go any more than she did. But she had to give her statement to the detective.

After what seemed a timeless few moments, yet not enough time at all, Jonas raised his head and looked over Daisy's shoulder at Rappaport. "Is it all right if I stay?"

"As long as you don't interrupt Daisy as she goes over again what happened. We went through this once, but I think she was in shock."

Jonas released her and stood about a foot away, studying her carefully. "Are you all right?"

She gently touched his jaw. "I'm fine. Honest. You've got to believe I never expected what happened. I just went to the theater to talk to Rowan—"

"Whoa," Detective Rappaport said. "Slow down, Daisy. Come and sit down. Let's start this from the beginning so I can record you. I want you to go slow and give me as much detail as you can."

That's exactly what Daisy did.

After she finished, and the detective completed all of his questions, Jonas moved his chair closer to hers and took her hand.

Detective Rappaport's phone buzzed. He picked it up and listened. After he was finished, he told Daisy and Jonas, "Zeke took a few days' personal leave. The police captain is interrogating Ward Cooper at urgent care. From what I understand, he needed a few stitches. You're lucky the chandelier stunned him and pinned him down."

From the expression on Jonas's face, he looked relieved that he didn't have to face Zeke or speak to him here.

"Bart Cosner is with the chief at urgent care . . . or rather he was," Rappaport explained. "He just got back. Apparently, Cooper didn't ask for a lawyer and he spilled his guts. I'm going to go out and see what he's learned." He looked at Daisy. "You have a right to know. Do you want to stay or do you want me to give you a call later?"

Daisy straightened her spine. "I'll stay. I want his story. I want to know exactly why Margaret died."

Rappaport nodded and left the office.

Sitting quietly together for a few minutes, Daisy and Jonas didn't speak. Finally, he leaned back in his chair and sighed. "I know why you didn't contact me when you went to the theater. It's because I hadn't been in contact with you. If I had been with you, Ward wouldn't have tried what he did."

Daisy placed two fingers on Jonas's lips and shook her head. "Don't do that. What happened certainly wasn't your fault. Jonas, I know when you're upset, you need time alone. I was giving it to you. Even if we had been in contact, you can't be with me every minute. You can't stop me when I want to explore. As I told the detective, all I wanted to do was speak with Rowan and try to dig a little deeper into the beginning of his relationship with Margaret. That's all I wanted. When I learned Ward was the second heir, I was pretty sure he was the murderer. After talking to Rowan, I intended to call Zeke. If I couldn't get hold of him, I would have asked for Rappaport. But plans can get derailed, and so can relationships."

Jonas looked as if he was about to say something, but Detective Rappaport returned to the room. With a sigh, the detective sat down heavily in his chair and lowered his elbows to the table. "This is one of those stories that is so senseless and makes you want to cringe when you hear how foolish people are . . . or maybe how fake people can be."

He looked at his notebook, where he'd scribbled notes. "Apparently, Margaret thought Ward Cooper was over his snit that she'd inherited from his uncle. She'd worked for Conrad Eldridge for a year. But she'd not only worked for him, she'd taken care of him until he died."

Rappaport glanced up at Daisy, then back at his

notes. "Apparently, Margaret had been devoted to him. Ward knew he couldn't contest the will for alienation of affection or something like that because it simply wasn't true, and too many people knew it. All of Conrad's old friends thought Margaret was an angel. Ward thought her break with her own father had always affected her, and Conrad became that father figure she'd never had."

"I wondered what happens when children leave the faith like that, especially if they're shunned or cut off. It's so sad," Daisy said.

"It *is* sad," Rappaport agreed. "The problem was— Margaret thought Ward didn't resent her any longer. She hadn't done anything wrong, but she'd wanted to smooth things over. That's why she invited him to join the staff at the theater, hoping they could erase any bad feelings that might still be unresolved."

"And Ward pretended to go along?" Jonas asked.

The detective checked his notes again. He squinted at them as if he'd written in a hurry. "You have to understand from what Ward said, he'd only pretended to care for his uncle in the few visits he'd paid him. Ward had never put in time with him because he was on the road. So he pretended to go along with Margaret in a similar way. But he was looking for revenge."

"How was he going to get revenge? Had he planned to murder her?" Daisy wanted to know.

"I don't think he thought it would go that far," Rappaport said. "But that's for somebody above my pay grade to decide. From what he says, revenge consisted of revealing Margaret's past as a stripper. He'd decided to blackmail her. They argued about what she should pay him more than once."

"They must have argued the day Tamlyn told me

Margaret was in a bad mood. Margaret had argued with someone before I had a meeting with her."

"Ward was frustrated with Margaret putting him off. The day of the tea, he came in the back door of the house at the butler's pantry. He planned to barge in and tell everyone assembled there that Margaret was a stripper, not an actress. He knew she'd be embarrassed. But their argument in the butler's pantry got out of hand. His anger boiled over. When she wouldn't give in to his demands, he stabbed her. When he realized what he'd done, he'd gotten even more enraged. That's why he'd tossed the clotted cream over the brooch. He'd pulled the tennis bracelet from her wrist but dropped it and didn't have time to retrieve it. My guess is he'll be arraigned on the second-degree murder charge for Margaret, and an assault charge and attempted murder charge for Daisy. By the way, he said something about pushing over those trees on you at the theater. And something odd."

"What?" Daisy asked.

"Something about damaging flour and cherries?"

Daisy explained what had happened to the supplies at Thanksgiving.

After making a few final notes, Rappaport shuffled papers on his desk, signaling the end of the conversation.

Jonas must have realized it too. "I have something to ask you," he said.

"About this case?"

"No. I'd like to know if what Zeke said at the bonfire is making the rounds at the station. I got some odd looks when I came in."

Rappaport rubbed his hand down his face. "Jonas, you know how this goes. You know how gossip flies. I'll step on it when I get the chance. I'll try to remind these men they wouldn't want their personal history put up on a screen or an assignment board. But gossip is gossip. It will die down . . . eventually."

Daisy wondered if *eventually* was one month, two months, six months? If Jonas and Zeke were around each other in the same town, would it die down at all?

Detective Rappaport laid his hands on the table and pushed himself to his feet. "I have paperwork on top of paperwork to fill out. And I have to check with the chief first and see if he needs backup at urgent care with Cooper. I'm sure you two can find your way out."

He opened the door and left it open.

Jonas drove Daisy home in his SUV. She assured him that she could find someone to take her to pick up her car the next day.

They were silent as he drove. When they reached her house and pulled up the driveway, they both sighed. There were cars there and lights on in the house.

"I see your aunt's car . . . and Tessa's," Jonas said.

"My parents' car. And maybe Gavin's." Daisy sighed. "The garage apartment is dark too," Daisy noted. "That means Vi and Foster and the baby are over at my house."

"Are you up for this?" Jonas asked.

"I have to be."

After they went inside, all of Daisy's family came around, hugging her with tears in their eyes, saying how happy they were that she was all right, that nothing had happened to her. Even Gavin was there with

Ben and Emily. He'd wanted to make sure she was unhurt and safe.

Daisy simply wanted to go to bed, but she felt the love and care these people were giving her, and she couldn't just desert the group. Her mom, her aunt, and Tessa had set out refreshments. They'd made iced tea, sandwiches, coleslaw, and fixed a tray of snickerdoodles and chocolate chip cookies. Daisy tried to get around to talk with everyone. Jonas, however, didn't stay by her side. He must have felt she had enough support and didn't need him too. He seemed to be on the fringes. She was worried about what he was dealing with and how it was going to affect them. When she could, Daisy took Sammy in her arms. Smelling that baby shampoo, having his warm infant body against hers, she felt as if her soul was filling up again.

At one point when Daisy was standing in the kitchen rocking Sammy, her mom came to her and gave them both a huge hug. "I'm not going to say anything about what happened today," her mom said. "I know you were only trying to help. But plans we make get scrambled, and other things happen. Maybe that's the way it's supposed to be so we learn lessons."

Her mother's attitude seemed different since they'd talked about her postpartum depression. She hoped they could continue to talk. She might as well tell her mother about the gossip Jonas was battling. She'd hear it sooner or later. "Mom, when Jonas and I went to the bonfire . . ."

Her mom waved her hand up and down. "You don't have to say it. I heard about it. They'll never know who the father is, will they?"

Daisy shook her head. "No, and that's tearing up Jonas inside."

"You know, Christmas is coming," her mom said. "There's always hope for Christmas miracles."

Daisy could only believe her mother was right.

Shortly after her talk with her mother, Gavin and his family left along with her mom and dad. They saw that Daisy was tired. Next, Aunt Iris and Tessa took their leave with big hugs and the support that Daisy depended upon. Daisy and Vi had a short talk about what had happened, then Daisy shooed Vi and Foster back to their apartment. Finally, Jonas and Jazzi were the only ones left.

Jazzi took a look at the two of them. "I'm going upstairs with the cats." She gave her mother a wink.

Jonas lifted Daisy's chin. "Take a bubble bath, get some rest, try to block out everything that happened today."

"I don't want to block out running into your arms. I finally felt safe. I didn't even feel that safe with Detective Rappaport."

Looking conflicted, Jonas's brows drew together as he said, "Daisy, this thing with Zeke . . . I need to sort it out. Can you bear with me?"

She didn't move her gaze from his. "Maybe we have to practice going through thick and thin."

After a moment, he nodded. "Maybe we do. But I think in the next week or so, like Zeke, I'm going to take a trip."

Her heart sank. "Where?"

"I think to Flagstaff, Arizona. I can drive north to the Grand Canyon or south to Sedona. I need to think and I need some of those good vibes out there while I'm doing it."

The trip sounded reflective and positive. "You'll be back for Christmas?"

Jonas smiled tenderly at her. "I'll definitely be back for Christmas. I wouldn't miss Sammy's first Christmas."

Daisy didn't want Jonas to miss any part of her family life, but she did have to give him time. If she did, maybe they'd have the rest of their lives to celebrate many more Christmases.

ORIGINAL RECIPES

Apple Gingerbread

1 cup sour cream (I use Daisy Pure and
   Natural)
¾ cup dark brown sugar
⅓ cup dark Karo syrup
¼ cup water
2 eggs
2 teaspoons baking powder
1 teaspoon baking soda
⅛ teaspoon salt
2 teaspoons ground cinnamon
2 teaspoons ground ginger
2½ cups flour
2 cups diced apples

Grease and flour two 8-inch cake pans (unless they are nonstick).

Preheat oven to 350 degrees.

In mixer, beat sour cream, brown sugar, and Karo syrup. Add water. Beat in eggs, baking powder, baking soda, salt, cinnamon, and ginger. Mix in flour little by little until batter is smooth. Stir in apples and pour evenly into both cake pans.

Bake for 20 to 25 minutes until a toothpick poked into the center of each cake comes out clean. Serve with a dollop of clotted or whipped cream.

Beef and Lentil Soup

1½ pounds stewing cubes
3 tablespoons high heat sunflower oil
¾ cup onion plus ½ cup
2 14 oz. cans diced tomatoes
1 qt. culinary beef broth
1 cup water
½ teaspoon salt
¼ teaspoon pepper
1 clove garlic, grated
¾ cup lentils
¼ cup wild rice
1 cup sliced carrots
1 cup sliced celery

Brown stewing cubes in sunflower oil. Add ¾ cup onions and sauté about 2 minutes. Stir in diced tomatoes, beef broth, water, salt, pepper, and garlic. Bring to a boil, then turn to simmer for ½ hour. Add lentils and wild rice, bring to a boil, and simmer for another ½ hour. Add carrots, celery, and the remainder of onion. Bring to a boil and simmer for another ½ hour. Serve piping hot with crusty bread. This recipe will serve 6.

Fall Fruit Salad

2 apples cut in small chunks (I use 2 different
  kinds for color and flavor—perhaps Granny
  Smith and Ginger Gold)
1 firm Anjou pear, cut in small chunks
1 cup green grapes, washed and drained
1 cup chopped celery
½ cup chopped pecans
1 cup Yoplait peach yogurt (original)
1 tablespoon mayonnaise
1 tablespoon lemon juice

Mix fruit, celery, and pecans in a large bowl. In a separate bowl, whisk together yogurt, mayonnaise, and lemon juice. Pour the yogurt mixture over the fruit and nut mixture and stir well. Chill at least an hour before serving.

Connect with Us

Visit us online at
KensingtonBooks.com
to read more from your favorite authors, see books
by series, view reading group guides, and more.

Join us on social media

for sneak peeks, chances to win books and prize packs,
and to share your thoughts with other readers.

**facebook.com/kensingtonpublishing
twitter.com/kensingtonbooks**

Tell us what you think!

To share your thoughts, submit a review,
or sign up for our eNewsletters, please visit:
KensingtonBooks.com/TellUs.